WHITE DEATH

BY CHRISTINE MORGAN

Cover Design © 2018 by Matthew Revert

http://cargocollective.com/matthewrevertdesign

ISBN-13: 978-1-947522-09-1

ISBN-10: 1-947522-09-4

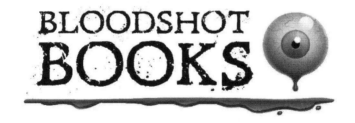

READ UNTIL YOU BLEED!

ALSO BY CHRISTINE MORGAN

NOVELS

Murder Girls

Scoot

Spermjackers from Hell

The Horned Ones: Cornucopia

COLLECTIONS

The Raven's Table: Viking Stories

This one's for Dad

WHITE DEATH

Christine Morgan

PART ONE:

WANAGEESKA

THE HUNTER

A deep, thick, silent whiteness covered the forest. It muffled sound. It hid the contours of the land, so that an innocent-seeming step could bring his foot down on a rock, or into a hole, or send it cracking through the ice of some buried pool.

A misstep or a fall could break a bone. He might be unable to get back, and it would be a long time before anyone reached him ... if anyone came at all.

He'd die out here.

Pierre LeCharles knew what that kind of dying would be like.

Slow. Slow, and cold.

Even in his heavy furs, even with his masses of hair and full beard, he would begin to shiver. His muscles would turn dull, numb and leaden. His mind would play tricks on him, as if the frigid air itself was somehow making him drunk.

He'd spoken with people rescued from the brink of freezing. People who'd gotten lost or injured in deep winter, lost in the woods or mountains, even in their own fields when the land was seized by the grip of a terrible blizzard.

He'd listened to their accounts of the moods and madness that came over them, how they had grown irritable with their companions, how their very thoughts seemed to turn thick and syrupy. Some were afflicted with dreamlike visions of loved ones or angels, cozy hearths and hot food. Some claimed to have felt apart from their own bodies as if mind and soul had already divided from the flesh.

He'd heard how just when it seemed they could feel no colder, when the shivering had stopped, they were suffused with a wonderful glowing warmth... a warmth that quickly became heat... as if they were about to catch fire.

He'd witnessed for himself the grim aftereffects. Skin rubbed away raw where ice had caked on it. Eyelids sealed shut by a rime of tears. Frostbite... fingers and toes, hands and feet, noses and ears turned to purple-grey blocks of icy flesh... inky blisters that seeped with fluid... skin sloughing off in loose crinkled flaps and sheets... amputations.

He'd seen the bodies of some who had not been rescued. The way some had, toward the end, torn open their clothes... perhaps mind-tricked into thinking themselves stifling from an unbearable heat. Limbs might be frozen stiff into whatever contorted poses in which the unfortunate victims had died, so that they had to be thawed before they could be wedged into coffins.

The frontier was unforgiving. If it wasn't the droughts, it was the blizzards. If it wasn't the blizzards, it was the grass-hoppers. If it wasn't the grasshoppers, it was the Indians. Or wildfires. Or disease.

So many people did not realize those harsh truths until too late. They came bringing all their worldly possessions, their wives and livestock and children. They spent every penny they had on passage West, believing the tales the railroad companies told about the bounty and prosperity of the wide prairies, following the feverish rumor-scent of gold or silver.

It was insanity to be out here unprepared.

Sometimes, even the most prepared could still fall prey to that insanity.

Take himself, for instance.

Here he was, miles from the safety of his snug sod-and-log house, where the thick walls would keep out the cold. Miles from a fire where hot stew simmered and flat bread baked on the bricks. Miles from the jugs of beer, cider and whiskey for which he'd traded bales of lush pelts.

Miles from Two-Bird.

Insanity.

She was sick. Possibly dying. She could be gone by the time he got back. Never to smile at him again, or touch his bearded cheek, or raise her dark eyes so lovingly to his.

Two-Bird. His beautiful Two-Bird.

The thought of losing her wrenched at his gut as if he'd swallowed a barbed hook.

He'd been married twice before, long ago when he was young and foolish. Once to a spiteful shrew who'd driven him out of the house threatening to bash his brains out with a skillet for drinking on the Lord's Day, and once to a fat lazy creature who warmed their bed with a blacksmith while he was off trapping. He'd sworn off women after that... until he met Two-Bird.

Or won her, as the case may be.

Won her in a poker game at a saloon in Deadwood. The same saloon, some said, where Wild Bill had met his end several years earlier... LeCharles didn't know if that was true or not, but the same aces-and-eights that had been so unlucky for Hickok were lucky enough for him, winning him sixty dollars and an Indian girl.

Two-Bird. Sixteen at the time, but so slim and girlish she seemed even younger. Quiet and demure in her fringed doeskin tunic and moccasins... glossy black braids hanging to either side of her sweet face... a beaded leather headband with feathers by her temples... nothing like the large meaty women he usually preferred.

He certainly hadn't anticipated falling in love with her. Now he flinched at the thought of life without her. Tiny, graceful Two-Bird. That fear chilled him more than the bite of the wind, a chill from within, a chill no amount of furs or exertion could ward off.

He could have tried to make it to the nearest settlement, find a doctor. But Two-Bird's father had no patience for what he called "white man's medicine," and it was because of the old man that LeCharles was out here in the mountains instead of home with Two-Bird.

Hezekiah Runninghorse, a small wiry man with pale coppery skin, coarse black hair, and bright blue eyes, claimed to be the son of a traveling preacher and a Dakota medicine-woman. Or the son of a Sioux shaman and a schoolmarm. Or of a Gold Rush prospector and a Cheyenne war-chief's daughter. Or of the trickster Coyote and a San Francisco whore. Or the heir and only child of a wealthy Bostonian couple, but abducted and raised by the Cherokee before being called to Jesus.

Whether he was any or none of those, LeCharles had no idea. What Runninghorse *was* was a lunatic. Also a gambler, a fast talker, and possibly a liar and a thief. He'd been run out of more towns than LeCharles had even been to, shot at more times than the target in a Wild West show, and owed money to people from here to the Mississippi.

But he was clever. He spoke many languages and he knew many things. Some said he could do magic.

He was also Two-Bird's father, and despite everything else — despite it being Runninghorse's fault she'd ended up at stake in a card game in the first place — she loved the old man.

She wanted so little, was happy with the most humble surroundings and the smallest kindnesses, and gave so much in return. LeCharles couldn't refuse her. So, he endured Runninghorse, who came visiting unannounced and stayed for weeks or months at a time, eating well and drinking better, borrowing money with shining promises of repayment once some scheme or another panned out.

Two-Bird had been sick for days already when Runninghorse arrived in the lull between one snowstorm and another. Unannounced as usual, and with a furtive air about him that suggested he was on the run from more than the weather.

LeCharles hadn't cared. He'd been nearly frantic with worry by then, not wanting to leave Two-Bird alone, not daring to take her with him, and not willing to just sit and do nothing while she either got well or got worse. He was ready to take any chance, listen to any scrap of wisdom no matter how insane it might seem.

Runninghorse had many scraps of wisdom, and tried them all. He brewed up evil-smelling concoctions for Two-Bird, he prayed over her and read from the battered Bible he carried, he shook feathered sticks and chanted, he painted signs and arcane symbols on her, he puffed from a ceremonial pipe and blew clouds of smoke in her face.

Then he told LeCharles that Two-Bird had no ordinary sickness. It was a spell, a curse, an evil spirit.

"It is," he said, "the *wanageeska.*"

WINTER SPIRIT

"**C**an you make it go away?" LeCharles had asked, holding Two-Bird's hand as she dozed and twitched and coughed and rolled her head fitfully from side to side. Though her brow glistened with clammy sweat, her hand was icy, and she shivered beneath many furs and blankets.

"The *wanageeska* is a powerful spirit," Runninghorse said. In preparation for his efforts, he'd streaked black and yellow marks on his face and donned a bearskin cloak dangling with rabbit bones, eagle feathers, animal claws and beads. He also wore his best felted top hat and a fancy waistcoat with a watch chain, though the watch itself was long since gambled away. "It comes only with the worst winters. Like last year, the Winter of Blue Snow, do you remember?"

LeCharles nodded. As if he, or anyone who'd lived through it, could forget? The winter of '86 and '87 had been a bad one, despite the pretty-sounding name. Cattle that hadn't died of the cold – often with their heads frozen to the ground encased in suffocating clumps of the ice that had formed from the vapor of their breath as they tried to graze – bled to death slicing their legs and muzzles on crusts of ice covering the prairie grass. When the spring thaws came, the flooding waters ran choked thick with their carcasses.

"Or the winter of seven years ago," Runninghorse went on. "The Snow Winter, that one was. My wife died then. My pretty Laughing Moon." He gazed with sad affection at Two-Bird, who had lapsed into sleep. "We had so little food. I went for supplies but another storm came and I could not return for several days. When I did, I found she had given most of her share to our daughter, so that she starved, but Two-Bird lived."

So that, LeCharles thought but didn't say, five years later he could lose her in a poker game. He said instead, "And the ... the *wanageeska*?"

"Dwells high in the mountains where the world is always frozen. Only when the snow is very deep and the wind is very cold can the *wanageeska* come down to hunt. Otherwise the sun would blind it, and the heat would make it melt away to nothing."

"But what is it?" LeCharles had demanded.

"A white shadow that moves with silence, that watches with pale eyes, that howls with the voice of the blizzard."

"You mean it's a... a beast? A bear, a mountain lion, a wolf?"

Runninghorse scowled. "A spirit, I told you. If you hear its howl or look in its eyes, you risk falling under its spell. That is what happened to Two-Bird. She will grow sicker and sicker, weaker and weaker. Then a madness will take her and she will run out into the snow, where the *wanageeska* will find her, and devour her."

And the only way to break the spirit's hold, he had gone on to tell LeCharles, was to confront the *wanageeska* ... face to face, without looking in its eyes or hearing its howl... and pluck out a tuft of its hair while speaking the name of the afflicted person.

So, now here he was, climbing higher into the mountains, searching for tracks or any sign of a beast he wasn't sure existed outside of the crazed mind of the old half-breed.

But this was for Two-Bird, that Runninghorse wouldn't weave a rug of lies when her life was at stake. Runninghorse wouldn't send him out here to die for no reason. Runninghorse seemed to like him well enough, for Two-Bird's sake if not LeCharles' own. It was ridiculous to think that the old man would send him off on an empty fool's errand to die in the wilderness.

But it was cold, and getting colder. The air was still, a strangeness in itself after days of the wind whistling down from the north and whirling in snowy eddies above the valley.

A white shadow... a pale-eyed spirit.

LeCharles had been a fur-trapper since he was fourteen, working his way steadily westward across the country to stay ahead of encroaching civilization with its noise, crowds and ugliness. He reckoned that he'd trapped, skinned, cured and sold every kind of fur-bearing creature from Quebec to Montana. But he'd never seen this snowy spirit-beast of Runninghorse's.

"It may change its shape," Runninghorse had told him, "for I knew a woman who called it the Ghost Wolf, but one man told me had a mane like a lion, and another man claimed it could skate on the river ice like an otter. It also may fly, for I have heard it leaves its kills high up in trees where even a bear cannot climb. And one man told me that his grandfather was killed by a *wanageeska* that had taken the shape of a beautiful maiden with skin and hair the color of snow."

Another time, he would have dismissed it as legend, myth or superstition. Like the thunderbird, or the shaggy man-apes of the coastal forests, or the great serpents that were said to live in certain dark lakes.

For Two-Bird, though...

For her, he would listen to Runninghorse. He would try to find the *wanageeska*, if it existed, and if it did he would rip a fistful of hairs from its cold white pelt.

It was better than doing nothing. Better than sitting beside Two-Bird, helpless, only able to watch her die.

He was well up into the high country now, beyond the furthest of his traplines and the shelters he'd built from branches and hides. The sod-and-log house had never seemed so distant. Around him he saw sparse trees with boughs bent low by the weight of their snowy burdens, the humps of covered bushes and boulders, rocks jutting up cold and grey and edged with glittering icicle knives.

LeCharles paused to stamp his booted feet and brush snow from his shoulders. He had brought dried venison and gnawed at a strip of it, surveying his surroundings.

"Bring back the hair," Runninghorse had finished, "and place it over her heart, and the *wanageeska* will depart from Two-Bird. But you must be quick. The hair of the *wanageeska* is spun from snow, and, like snow, it will melt."

THE HUNTED

eCharles finished the strip of venison and looked up at a sky the color of wet cotton, the clouds only slightly darker than the snowflakes. He scanned the treetops, not expecting to see anything more interesting than an abandoned eagle's nest, and blinked when his gaze happened across something else... something that, from here, almost could have been an animal carcass lodged in the fork of a dead lightning-split tree.

A swig from his flask sent whiskey chasing the venison down his gullet, and warmed him from the inside out in a ruddy flush. He shook himself and set off in the direction of the dead tree.

As he drew nearer, he saw that it was indeed a carcass... a wolf... grey and black pelt caked with snow... body mangled and torn open... legs jutting like sticks... head bent back and throat ripped out... frozen stiff. Trails of iced blood streaked the tree bark. More had dripped to the ground, and frozen there in dollops and spatters like a sprinkling of rubies in the snow.

Most predators, LeCharles knew, might kill other predators in disputes over territory, mates or prey. They did not often kill each other for food. The flesh of meat-eaters was not tasty, and usually the meal of last resort.

From what he could see of the wolf when he was right beneath the tree, it appeared to have been partially eaten. Chunks of meat were missing, exposing bare bone. The pelt was shredded — waste of a perfectly good pelt, he could have gotten a decent sum for a wolfskin like that.

The tail, he noticed, was untouched. A fine tail. A real plush banner of a tail. He could climb up there and cut it off...

He set his rifle aside, leaning it against a rock. The tree wasn't very tall, the wolf carcass no more than nine or ten feet above his head. He could reach it without much effort.

And then, at least, he would have something to show for this long, futile search for a beast that likely came from nowhere but that mad old halfbreed's imagina—

All at once, LeCharles found his skin crawling. His scalp tightened, and the hairs on his arms and the nape of his neck were trying to stand on end. His mouth was a dryness of the aftertaste of whiskey and venison.

He'd heard nothing to alert him... seen nothing... smelled nothing.

Yet his skin crawled and his hair rose.

His hand had already been straying toward his knife, thinking about that wolf tail free for the taking, so he gripped the antler hilt and drew the blade as quietly as he could.

Quiet or not, the scrape of steel leaving leather sounded loud as a shovel scraping rock, and LeCharles winced.

He turned in a slow circle, breath locked in his lungs so as not to send up steamy wisps that might interfere with his vision.

Whiteness. Whiteness broken only by those rearing grey icicle-edged rock faces, dark branches, and the occasional vivid burst of evergreen where the weight of the snow had slid loose. He could see his own tracks, scuffed by the drag of his coat.

Nothing else.

No movement but the irregular falling of the fat white flakes.

LeCharles relaxed, but only a little, and did not return the knife to its sheath.

A jostling shift... what might have been a rustle if not for the heavy muffling snow, the kind of rustle an animal might make while slipping through the underbrush. A tremor shuddered through a cluster of boughs. Piled whiteness fell with a soft thump, and more sifted down as the boughs rebounded, quivering.

And from beneath those boughs, staring back at him, a pair of pale, pale eyes.

Beast eyes, but like no beast eyes he had ever seen.

Spirit eyes? The eyes of the *wanageeska*?

The old half-breed lunatic had been right?

If he was right about that, then he might also have been right about Two-Bird, which meant LeCharles had to pluck some hairs from the pelt of this creature. Spirit or not, he had to try.

He started toward it.

The pale eyes narrowed.

Slit nostrils in a greyish-white nose flared.

Large tufted ears flattened back.

The rest of it was hidden against snow and shadow, but LeCharles had an impression of a long body, low-slung and hunched. He had an impression of white fur and tensed, muscular strength. Larger than a wolf, larger than the dead wolf in the dead tree, but not by much.

"Come on, then," he said, and saw it twitch at his voice.

He realized he was looking the *wanageeska* in the eye... which, according to Runninghorse, meant he would be stricken with the same illness as Two-Bird. He also realized, too late to do him any good, that he'd left his gun leaning against a rock when he should have retrieved it.

If bullets could even touch a spirit-creature at all, that was...

"Come on!" This time he spoke with challenge and command, though his skin had resumed crawling and his guts felt knotted with fear.

He held the knife in his right hand, out and away from his body. His left, he shook free of the fur mitten, letting the mitten swing by its cord and leaving his fingers exposed to the bitterly cold air.

The *wanageeska* lifted its head and opened its mouth. It made a noise that was not a snarl, not a howl, not a screech and not a hiss... but somehow all of those combined. A horrible noise, a noise that made LeCharles' bladder cramp.

Horrible, but what was more horrible was the teeth.

Teeth? Fangs? Tusks?

Sharp ivory against a mouth-lining of so faint a pink it was almost colorless, a mouth like a beartrap.

He saw it crouch, hindquarters bunching to leap.

"Come on, you white devil," LeCharles said, through his own teeth that were gritted so hard they ached.

It leaped. Blurred whiteness lunging at him, and he flung up his knife arm to ward it off. He took the force of the *wanageeska*'s lunge on his forearm and was driven back, staggering, flailing his free arm for balance as he floundered through the snow.

The vicious beartrap mouth clashed shut inches from his face. He could smell its breath, damp and dank, like a chilly root cellar stocked with raw meat.

LeCharles went over backward, landing hard. It was atop him, the full weight of it, and its weight was cold. Cold as if carved from living ice. He braced his forearm against its throat and shoved up with all his might. The knife was in his fist, angled so that the point was more danger to him than to the beast.

Claws snagged the shoulders and chest of his coat. The *wanageeska* yowled-shrieked-roared again, blasting its foul breath at him. He felt a pinprick in his upper arm as one claw pierced the many layers of his garments.

The fingers of his left hand were already numbing, but he groped and clutched and yanked. This time the creature's cry was of surprise – and, he hoped, pain – as his fist came away bristling with thick white hairs.

"Two-Bird!" LeCharles yelled, remembering Running-horse's instructions. And since he himself had also looked into those eyes and heard that howl, he ripped out a second fistful. "Pierre LeCharles!"

It hurled its body to the side, claws hooked deep in his clothes so that he was dragged halfway over in a clumsy roll. Somehow he knew it meant to go for his throat, rip it out in a shower of blood and flesh. He hunched and tucked. The teeth-fangs-tusks plunged into his shoulder with terrible icy agony. It was LeCharles' turn to shriek, and even under the din of his own shrieking and the *wanageeska*'s triumphant growl, he heard teeth grind and grate against bone. A hot, shocking wetness gushed down his chest and back.

His left arm spasmed and flopped into the snow, his fist still closed on the prize he'd ripped from the beast's pelt but the arm limp and senseless. He lashed out wildly with the knife in his right, the tip just catching a large triangular ear and splitting it. Pinkish blood sprayed a fine mist that froze in the air and fell as tiny granules.

LeCharles heaved with his legs, driving the beast up and off with his boots in its underbelly. It tumbled over his head, its breath coughing out with a stunned huff from the impact. It lay there, dazed.

If it bled, if it could be hurt, then...

His left arm was still a flopping deadweight, but LeCharles barely noticed. He rolled to his knees and threw himself at the *wanageeska* before it could recover. The knife slashed, missed, slashed, cut, slashed, cut again. More blood flowed.

A paw swung and claws shredded his right mitten, scored the back of his hand. He slashed the blade across the paw, across fleshy grey-white pads. The beast yipped. It was backing away, trying to retreat, the big shaggy head swinging around in search of escape. Red rosettes spotted its pelt.

Somehow on his feet now, covered with snow and soaked with blood, LeCharles advanced. He shook with adrenaline, with rage and determination.

"Come on," he said to the beast. His voice was a raspy croak. "Come on, damn you, and let's finish this!"

Pale eyes gleamed at him through the thickly falling snow, and with a low dreadful cry, the *wanageeska* came.

SO COLD

The fire blazed and snapped. Shadows jumped against the earth-and-log walls. The jugs and sacks and stores of canned goods on the plank shelves seemed to twitch and move. Sparks whirled up like dancing fireflies. Sizzling sap in the dry wood gave off its sweet scent to mingle with the smoke. She could see the bright flames, the orange coals glowing in their bed of ashes. They had never built a fire so large in their little stone-ringed hearth. A week's worth of wood, a bonfire.

And still, Two-Bird was so very, very cold!

She knew it must be giving off great heat, but she could not feel it.

Sweat ran on her father's face, smearing the intricate designs he'd painted there into black and yellow smears. He had stripped off his hat and cloak, then his prized fancy waistcoat, and finally his shirt. He moved about the room barefoot and bare-chested, wearing only cotton drawers held with a drawstring at his skinny waist and hiked up to his bony knees.

The trouble was not the fire. The trouble was within Two-Bird herself.

Her lower lip was sore, throbbing where she held it pinched to keep her teeth from rattling together like beans in a gourd. For a while she'd held a piece of leather in her jaws, but that made her feel the panic of a wild mare caught and bridled.

Every blanket they had covered her from toes to chin. Wolf pelts and bearskins and the entire fleecy hide of a big mountain sheep were piled atop the blankets. She lay on a plump bed ticking stuffed with hay and dried clover, supported on a wooden bedframe. She wore layers of wool and flannel.

And for all of that, she shivered as though she lay naked on a barren peak of rock, exposed to the wind and snow.

So cold!

Her father went to the window, opening the shutter just a sliver and sticking his head close to the gap, seeking relief from the sweltering heat and stuffy, smoky air. He looked like he longed to wrench the door open and rush out into the winter night. It reminded her of stories he'd told her of sweat lodges, where the men would sit for hours in the fragrant steam, then go outside and hurl themselves into snowdrifts.

After a few moments with his head in the window gap, he returned the shutter to its proper place and came over to the bedside. He bent over her, his braids swinging, and smiled when he saw that she was awake. It was a crooked, tobacco-yellow smile that did not dispel the worry in his familiar sky-magic-blue eyes.

"Thirsty?" he asked.

Two-Bird managed a slight shake of her head.

"Hungry?"

This time the head-shake was more emphatic. She shifted her gaze toward the door, held it for a meaningful pause, and returned it to her father with eyebrows raised questioningly.

"Your man's not back yet, little bird." He patted in the vicinity of her shoulder, though she could barely feel the pressure of the touch through all the furs. "He will be. Soon, I'm sure. Soon."

She drew her brows together, glanced at the door and the window.

"Well, yes, it's gone dark... but I'm sure he's on his way. Nearly here. Just you wait. He's a good man, your Pierre LeCharles. I knew that from the first time I set eyes on him. I knew that he was a man who would take care of my precious daughter, do right by her. He'll be back soon and he'll have brought you something special."

Pierre always brought her something special when he went to town or to a trading post. Always. Even if the trapping had been poor and he could barely afford the basic staples of flour, coffee, bacon and molasses. Even if it meant going short on his own tobacco and whiskey. A ribbon, a handkerchief, a peppermint stick or bit of horehound candy, a tin cup, a sprig of flowers... something. He liked to surprise her, make her smile, see her delight as she accepted each small gift.

This was different.

He had not gone to any town or trading post. The bales of pelts were still stacked against the far wall, and the mule's harness hung on its peg.

Two-Bird waited, looking at her father with steady expectation.

Father sighed. "You look very like your mother when you do that. Did I ever tell you the story of how we met?"

She lowered one eyelid halfway and slanted the other eyebrow. It was one of her favorite stories, and of course he knew that. He was hoping to divert and distract her, but she was not about to be diverted or distracted.

He tried to pretend he had not seen her expression, settling onto a bench and leaning it back so that his knobby spine rested against the table edge and his prominent nose pointed at the low ceiling. "I was preaching the Good Word of the Lord then, going from place to place with not much more than a pony cart and one black suit to my name. This was just after the end of the War Between the States—"

Two-Bird rolled her eyes and exhaled impatiently through her nose.

"You've heard that one before?" he asked.

She nodded. She could have said it along with him word-for-word if she'd been able to speak. The little Indian girl found wandering alone on the prairie, sole survivor of a massacre... the traveling circus that had taken her in and given her a home and raised her as part of the show... See Princess Laughing Moon, the Genuine Indian Maiden!... and finally how Hezekiah Runninghorse had seen her, fallen in love with her, and persuaded her to run away with him.

"I suppose you have." He let the bench tip forward again so that all of its legs rested on the dirt floor. He sighed again. He mopped his face with a calico kerchief, further smudging the designs.

Two-Bird hugged herself under the blankets. She rubbed her hands together. The coughing seemed to have eased for the moment, but the inside of her chest felt like a rough hollow cave that had been scooped from frozen stony soil.

"Still cold," he said. "The fire's as high and hot as it will go. Won't you try and drink some broth? It might warm you."

It wouldn't, she knew. The cold was too powerful. But he seemed to have no better ideas, and neither did she, so she gave another nod. He helped her sit up. She raised her knees and leaned forward against them, pulling the fleecy hide around her shoulders and partway over her head.

The pot had been swung off of the fire to keep it from boiling away to nothing, but was still evidently hot, because when Father poked a finger into it to test its temperature, he yanked it back with a yelp. He ladled broth into a bowl, fetched a spoon, brought it to her bedside. It amused her to see him fussing like a hen.

The broth was rich and clear, smelling of wild fowl and small game, herbs and marrow and onions. She remembered Pierre skinning some rabbits he'd snared... when had that been? Before her father arrived? After? How long had she been ill?

Between sips of broth, she tried to rub more life into her cold hands, then signaled to her father in the silent language they had invented when Two-Bird was barely more than a baby.

"As I said, I'm sure he'll be back soon," Father replied.

Two-Bird clutched at his arm, imploring.

He dropped his head and shut his eyes for what seemed a very long time, then met her gaze again. "He went to find the *wanageeska*, and get hairs from its pelt to break its freezing hold on you. I told him. I sent him."

The *wanageeska* ... she had only the vaguest memories of the stories. A winter spirit that howled with the blizzard and bit like the coldest wind, a great white beast that sent the storms raging out of the north. The *wanageeska* would kill and devour animals not safely secured against the weather, and freeze solid any people foolish enough to be caught out in it.

She had a far stronger memory of her mother telling her father not to frighten her with such tales. That had been the winter of the deep snows, snows that had come before the harvest and lasted until spring. The winter they'd run out of firewood and had to burn twists of hay... endless hours of twisting hay until their hands bled. The winter Laughing Moon had died.

The chills swarmed over her, stronger than ever, turning the warm pool of broth to a block of ice in her belly. She pushed the half-empty bowl away and burrowed back into the furs and blankets. Her eyelids squeezed shut as if she could squeeze the memories from her mind.

"He will come back," Father said.

But she could hear his uncertainty. It made her want to scream at him, which of course she could not do. Just as she had not been able to scream at him when he finally returned with bundles of supplies to find his wife dead and their daughter nearly starved.

Now he had sent her man, her good man, out into the snow to hunt a spirit.

Tears gathered behind her closed lids and even the tears were cold. Her chest tightened. Her breath felt like a harsh north wind across bleak ground. Sitting up for only the short time it had taken to drink half a bowl of broth left her exhausted, bone-weary and despairing.

"It was the only way," he said. "LeCharles is a fine trapper, a fine hunter, the best I've ever known. If anyone can find the *wanageeska*, it is him. He may have had to go far into the mountains, that's all. He must have realized he would not make it back before nightfall and made for one of his shelters. You know he has them scattered all through these woods. I'm sure he is in one of them now."

He touched her shoulder, but she rolled away from him and hid her face. A cough scratched its way up her throat.

"I'm sure he is," Father insisted, sounding anxious. "Now the snowstorm has let up, the wind has stopped, tomorrow we may even see the sun in a clear sky. I'd bet my watchchain that before we've had our morning coffee, he'll—"

A massive weight crashed against the door.

HEALING MAGIC

The wood groaned under the force of the blow. Bits of sod shook loose and fell from the walls and roof.

Two-Bird gasped, and it tore at her throat like shards of ice. She tried to sit up again but it was a weak effort, and she fell back, shivering.

Father sprang to his feet, an absurd scrawny figure in his hiked-up cotton drawstring drawers, with his face a dirty smutch of ochre and charcoal and his braids untidy. But he grabbed up his Colt, which had been lying on the table beside a jug of beer and a loaf of bread. He leveled it at the door.

There was a thump and a scrape, a dragging. A moan.

A voice.

"Two-Bird..."

She did sit up then, eyes wide, a hand flying out. Her father rushed to the door, heaved aside the latch-bar, tugged it open. The flames leaped as frosty air swept in around the tottering, stumbling figure of her man.

He made it three steps in before collapsing to his knees, then to his face. His furs and buckskins were caked with snow, stiff with ice.

Her father blurted exclamations in several languages as he gaped at the man on the floor. Then he snatched for his wits the way an eagle would snatch for a fish in the river, and wrestled the door closed again.

Two-Bird could barely hold herself upright. The world seemed to be going white around the edges, as if riming over the way a pond's smooth surface did during the first hard freeze. Her head spun with the strangest sensation of falling, falling from a great height toward a vast whirling blankness.

Pierre moaned again. He pushed himself onto his forearms and elbows. Through the fringe of fur on his hood and the tangled skeins of his own hair — normally the color of ripe wheat, it and his beard were so snow-whitened that he looked like an old man — he swept his gaze around the room until he found her.

One hand was curled into a tight fist, the flesh looking unnaturally blue-grey in the firelight. A torn bit of cord dangled where his mitten should have attached. The other fur mitten had been ripped open, showing the back of his hand, showing vicious gashes lumpy with clotted blood. More blood covered him, the dark stains becoming visible as snow melted from his garments. His knife sheath was empty, his rifle was gone.

She moved to throw back the blankets and Father gestured her to stay. All she could do was watch as her father helped Pierre up, helped him onto a chair, got him out of his heavy clothes. They were sodden with water and blood.

"Here," Pierre said. He nodded at the hand still clenched in a fist. Several long white hairs stuck out from it, almost like fine pale porcupine quills.

Father made as if to touch one, then hesitated. "The… the *wanageeska*?"

"Found it… pulled its fur." A ghastly frozen smile crossed Pierre's face, twisting it, making him hardly resemble the handsome man she knew and loved, the man who was so kind and gentle toward her, the man who held her snug against his big strong body in the dark of the night. "It didn't much care for that."

"You fought the *wanageeska*?" Father asked in a hushed whisper.

"Had to." His other hand, the mittened one with the gashes, indicated his left shoulder. "Bit me." He looked over at Two-Bird again. He was horribly pale, horribly haggard, but his brown eyes were filled with nothing but love and concern for her.

"Open your hand," Father said.

"Can't." He grimaced. "Think it's the... the frostbite. You'll have to pry the fingers apart."

Her father also grimaced, and Two-Bird knew that he was imagining what she was, the brittle crackle of those fingers bending, perhaps even snapping gruesomely off like icicles from a branch.

None did snap off... but the brittle crackle was even worse than she had imagined. She wanted to look away as her father collected the tufts of white fur and put them carefully aside, far from the fire. But she didn't look away. Pierre was her man, he had done this for her sake, and if she couldn't help him, the least she could do was not look away.

"It is frostbite, yes," Father said. "We'll need to—"

"Cure Two-Bird first," Pierre said. "I'm..." He bared his teeth in the ghastly frozen smile again, perhaps meant to be reassuring. "... fine. Cure Two-Bird. Before the fur melts."

Somberly, his mouth tucked into a line, Father found the tufts of fur he'd set aside. He approached the bedside, where Two-Bird still lay unable to sit up. She lifted one weak hand to touch the fur.

White. Thick. Soft. Not fox, not rabbit, not anything she'd ever felt before. Luxuriant. A fine city lady would pay much money for a cape made from such fur.

"This," Father said, holding it before her eyes, "will make you well again, little bird. This will make you well."

He folded back the blankets, opened and loosened the front of her layers of clothing, and placed a handful of white fur against her skin, above her heart. He added a few strands to the amulet he'd put around her neck earlier. The amulet was beaded doeskin on a leather thong, and already held an acorn, a crow's feather, a hare's foot, a lucky silver dollar and various other objects.

"Keep these here," he told her, putting clothes and blankets back as they'd been and then patting her on the chest. "As they melt, so will the power of the *wanageeska* melt from you. The ones in the amulet will make it so its magic can never reach you again. Do you understand, little bird?"

She nodded, coughed, shivered, and indicated that he should go to Pierre, he had to help her Pierre.

FROST-BITTEN

"**S**he'll be better soon?" Pierre asked, the words slurred. Two-Bird watched with half-dazed eyes as her father fetched a pail of snow from outside and rubbed it on Pierre's cold frostbit-grey flesh. She saw Pierre arch his head back when sensation began to return, saw him grit his teeth so that cords stood out in his neck.

"Ah, God," he said, holding his arm deathly still as if to move it at all caused unbearable pain. "Itches... burns... like sticking my hand in a patch of fire-nettles... ah, God!"

He was down to his drawers, the firelight gleaming gold on his own dense pelt of chest hair... where it was not matted and sticky with blood. She could see all too well the brutal wounds in his shoulder. The flesh was gored, torn, mauled. As he warmed, the blood began to thaw and trickle afresh, like the waters of a creek in spring when the ice went out.

Pierre glanced at the trickling blood, but almost with indifference before returning his attention to the greyish lump that was his left hand. His right gripped a brown clay jug of whiskey, and he brought it to his lips for a deep swig.

"Thought I wouldn't make it back," he said when the shudders had passed. "Thought I'd die out there. In the cold... and when it got dark... but I couldn't give up. Just... just kept... walking. The snow stopped. No stars, but the moon... bright and pale through the clouds... bright enough to make my way."

"You did well," Father said. "I've done what I can for the hand. We wait and see. In the meanwhile, let me look at your shoulder."

"Mmph," Pierre said around the mouth of the jug. He leaned his head to the right, which almost sent him off the chair.

Her father muttered and clucked as he wiped off blood with a wet cloth so he could examine the wounds. Pierre flinched a time or two as Father pressed and poked, and grunted once when Father did something that made a wet sound and a surge of blood, but he did not cry out. He drank the whiskey and, when not looking at the jug, smiled a tight, pained smile at her.

Even from here, where she lay no longer able to hold her head up enough to see well, the wounds looked bad. Deep. Ugly. She had thought he was not moving his arm because it pained his frostbitten hand, but now she wondered if his arm was still able to move at all. It seemed to hang there at his side like a dead thing.

"Bit you," Father said in a musing way.

"Mm-hmm." Pierre swayed a little and braced his good elbow on the table's edge. "Claws couldn't get through, eksh-eksh-except on the mitten an' a little bit on t'other shoulder. Teef shure did though." He glanced at Two-Bird, and she thought his eyes were going bleary from the drink. "Big teef. Biggesht teef I ever shaw."

"Hsssssh." Her father let a breath out through his own teeth. "I'm going to have to sew these holes."

Pierre blinked owlishly after Father as Father rummaged for a needle and thread. "You're gonna what?"

Father found the nice sewing kit that Pierre had given Two-Bird, one of those gifts he brought, something special from town. It was a small tin box stamped around the sides and on the top with images of locomotives and railroad workers. Inside were a packet of needles, a thimble, six wooden spools of thread in different colors, pins, buttons, other odds-and-ends.

"Sew those holes," Father repeated. "It's going to hurt." He set the sewing kit on the plank table and took the jug.

"I'm drinking that."

"You can have the rest. I need to—"

He tipped the jug, and whiskey gurgled out in a brown flood over Pierre's shoulder. Pierre bellowed. His good fist slammed down on the table hard enough to make it jump, spilling a bowl of broth. Then he seized the jug back and drained it, throat working as he gulped and gulped.

Two-Bird stared with wide-eyed accusation at her father, but he only grinned at her and shrugged. He picked through the needles to find one he liked, threaded it, jabbed the tip at his callused thumb, inspected the thimble as if he had no idea what it was for, and hummed a tune she remembered him humming as he smoked his pipe in the evenings by the fire. It was his waiting-for-something tune.

Finally Pierre slumped sideways, his right arm stretched out along the table, his head cradled on it. He sent another smile in her direction, this one lopsided and silly. "You're the besht... besht shing ever hap'n to me..." he said.

His eyes closed, his mouth drooped open, and he started to snore.

"Took him long enough," Father said, and went to work.

She saw Pierre twitch once or twice as the needle punched through his skin with the thread hissing after it like a snake with a strange thin tail. Whenever he did twitch, Father sprang nimbly away, as if he expected Pierre would rouse with a furious roar and swat his head from his neck, like an enraged bear disturbed from its winter slumber.

But at last the worst holes were sewn shut, the bleeding had slowed, and Father was able to wrap long strips of cloth around Pierre's upper body to serve as a bandage. He cleaned up the rest of the blood, then shook him.

"Hnn?"

"It's done. Let's get you to the bed, and you can sleep."

With Pierre only half-wakeful and reeling on his feet, and Father so short and scrawny by comparison, it was a wonder they were able to walk together across the small room without further injury. Father led Pierre around to the other side of the bed, next to the mound of furs and blankets covering Two-Bird.

The bed creaked as Pierre sank onto it, yawning hugely. He rolled his head to the side and gave Two-Bird a look that said he was trying to figure out which of the several hazy images of her was her, but he adored them all anyway.

She was still cold, but somehow not as cold as she'd felt before. That hollow scooped-from-frozen-stony-soil ache still came with each breath, but she didn't have to cough. And though she was weak as a baby rabbit and trembling like a new fawn, she was able to stroke her fingertips along Pierre's cheek.

"Thanksh," Pierre said to her father. "You're crayshee, Heh... Hezhee... Runninghorse, but you're all right."

"You're not so bad yourself, LeCharles," Father said, chuckling. "It isn't every man who could face the *wanageeska* and escape with his life."

"Din't," he said.

"What was that?"

"Din't esh... eshcape. Killed it. Shtabbed it through the ribsh. Shtopped itsh... shtopped itsh damn heart."

With that, he closed his eyes and began snoring again.

Father stood very still and silent for a moment, then shifted his gaze to Two-Bird. A pallor crept into his light copper skin. "Did he just say... did he say he killed the *wanageeska*?"

SUN DOGS

Hezekiah Runninghorse heaved a sigh of relief as the night ended.

At least — thank Holy God and Blessed Christ, thank the Great Spirit — at least the wood had lasted. At least the snow had stopped and the wind had fallen.

He rose from the bench where he'd sat through the long dark hours watching over Two-Bird and LeCharles.

His daughter slept peacefully, the fur of the *wanageeska* curled in her grasp. It had not melted away to nothing after all. Runninghorse marveled at that, but did not question. She seemed better. That was what mattered.

LeCharles might not prove so lucky. Runninghorse doubted there was enough whiskey in the house to make the big man drunk enough for amputation, if such an operation proved necessary. He doubted there was enough whiskey in the entire territory.

And if it should come to that, would he be able to take up the woodaxe and lay the big man's arm across a block and bring the blade down with a solid swing? Would he be able to stanch the bleeding? Would LeCharles survive?

What then? A man couldn't be much of a trapper if he had only one hand. How would LeCharles make his living? How would he care for Two-Bird? What about their children, if and when?

There was also his shoulder to consider. Runninghorse had cleaned the wound, sewed it, mixed a salve of tallow and herbs against infection. For any normal animal bite, that might be enough.

But this was no normal animal bite. This was the bite of the *wanageeska*.

"Killed it," LeCharles had said.

Killed the *wanageeska*?

Stabbed it through the ribs with a hunting knife?

Even if such a thing was possible, it couldn't be good.

Runninghorse dressed in buckskin breeches and a wool shirt, stuffed his feet into boots and his hands into mittens, and pulled on his hat and coat. He took the leather sling Two-Bird used to carry wood from the woodpile.

Thin white light fell on his face as he opened the door. The sky was like a bowl of frozen milk, the still and silent air so cold that Runninghorse's breath prickled icily in his nostrils. The rising sun was a pale ice-flare that seemed to give off no heat.

But what chilled him more than the frigid air was what he saw around the sun... a fine line like a halo of silver, and twin bright spots, wavering and fluid as dollops of mercury. They followed the sun as it climbed, ringing it, making it a pupil of white in a pale, pale eye.

Sun-dogs, some people called them, and Runninghorse remembered the first time he had seen the phenomenon. Out in the Dakota prairie, it had been, and him not much younger than Two-Bird was now.

A bitter cold coming.

Coming?

A more bitter cold than this?

That time so long ago, he and the other youngsters had been marveling and exclaiming at the unusual sight, while the adults of the tribe made preparations with grim purpose... and by the next day they'd been huddled together in the tipis with fires ablaze as the wind whooped and screamed. Runninghorse had scoffed no more.

Sun-dogs in the milky sky. A bitter cold coming.

They would need wood. Much more wood.

He filled the sling and hurried back to the house. LeCharles and Two-Bird slept on. He carried more wood. And more. Between trips, he paused to rest his aching muscles and look over the supplies. He fed the mule, which snorted at him but did not give him a kick. If the storm got too bad, they might have to bring the animal into the house with them, as much to save its life as to save their own by sharing its body heat.

Once a stout supply of firewood had been lugged in and stacked by the hearth. Runninghorse drank more coffee and ate a chunk of bread, then took the woodaxe and ventured out again.

His aim now was not firewood, but fresh-cut boughs of white spruce, which would help to ward off malevolent—

His foot struck what felt like a buried mossy log. He did not go headlong in the snow, but he did drop the axe atop whatever he'd tripped on. When he bent to retrieve it, what he saw was not moss-coated bark but... bloodstained white fur.

He crouched, and used the axe handle to sweep away snow until he had uncovered the carcass.

Fur so white as to be next to invisible against the snow. Thick, lush fur. Frozen blood on its side, on its head, all over its muzzle. Mouth open. Grey tongue protruding. The great teeth curving from the jaws. The pale eyes half-lidded, glassy, vacant.

LeCharles hadn't been lying, and he hadn't been wrong.

Here was the proof. Right here, stiff and dead.

A shiver worked its way through Runninghorse. He did not think it was because of the temperature.

His daughter's man had indeed killed the *wanageeska*.

Fought it, stabbed it, killed it. And then, wounded though he was, his trapper's instincts had taken over. No man who earned his money from pelts could have walked away from a prize such as this, so he'd brought it home. Draped over his shoulder at first, perhaps. Later, dragging it by the scruff or the tail or one rigid leg. He'd gotten it this far before his strength or his determination gave out.

Runninghorse looked over his shoulder at the eastern sky. The sun was higher, the halo fainter, the sun-dogs less bright but still there. Like an eye fixed upon him. A pale eye, the eye of a spirit.

An angry spirit.

He jumped up from his crouch and hastily swept at the snow again, as if by hiding the carcass he could hide the crime. He had to struggle against a very strong urge to hide the axe, fling it away from him or bury it, though it wasn't even the weapon that had ended this *wanageeska*'s life and he wasn't even the man who'd done it.

Fragments of stories raced through his mind, everything he had ever heard about angered spirits, vengeful spirits, retribution, justice and punishment. This was not a matter of offending one such as Coyote, who could sometimes be placated or flattered enough to overlook an insult or theft. Runninghorse was sure he remembered a tale of one Indian brave who'd seduced Coyote's favorite woman from under the trickster god's very nose... and Coyote had been so impressed by his sly boldness that he'd rewarded the brave instead.

But... placating the *wanageeska*?

No stories about that occurred to him. The best he could come up with was to be glad LeCharles had only killed it, that he hadn't gotten around to skinning it yet, curing its pelt, and turning it into a coat.

Somehow, he didn't think it would help much. Not against the *wanageeska*, fierce snow-spirit and wind-spirit, bringer of blizzards.

The pale eye was still rising in the east. Fainter, but... yes, still there. Still fixed upon him.

A high breeze gusted past, whirling up flurries of snow, whistling thinly between the trees. Runninghorse ducked — as if that would do him any good at all — and imagined for a moment he heard the hiss of a promise in that icy breath of air. A promise that if he thought it was cold now, he'd seen nothing yet... in a while, and not a very great while either, he would be praying for a cold like this instead of the sheer frozen wrath that was about to be unleashed.

He turned from that merciless eye, turned toward the house. He'd gotten no more than three paces when he was gripped with the unmistakable sense of being stalked.

Snow fell from disturbed branches.

There was a blurriness near Runninghorse, a vast movement, something so white as to be next to invisible against the snow. Looming huge and near. He heard and felt its cold breath. He could smell it like frost in the night air.

But its shape was an indistinct ripple. His eyes were unable to focus on it, their very orbs straining and aching from trying to see.

"*Wanageeska*," Runninghorse said.

He had the woodaxe in his hand, but its haft felt stupidly small and useless. He let it fall. It thumped into the snow and disappeared. He held out his mittened hands, open and empty. Harmless. Defenseless.

It was in front of him.

Suddenly, he could see it. Clear as could be. The blurriness and rippling were just... gone. Gone, and there was the creature. Far bigger than the other.

If he hadn't already dropped the axe, he would have then. The strength ran from his body like water from a sieve. His knees buckled and his legs folded. He collapsed into the snow. He could only lie there, staring up.

The *wanageeska* lowered its huge head, then cocked it slightly to one side, contemplating Runninghorse the way a barn cat might contemplate a cornered mouse. The pale eyes swam with cold fire. The long curved teeth glistened. The slit nostrils flared in its pallid greyish nose, sniffing him, then snorting out twin streamers of frosty white vapor. He couldn't see past it but he heard the slow, anticipatory swish of its tail.

WEATHER TURNING

A gunshot cracked the air. In the snowy silence it was loud as a thunderclap, louder than a cannon blast.

Fur puffed on the *wanageeska*'s side. Blood appeared in a startling blotch. The head, which had been inching nearer to Runninghorse, snapped up. A fierce shrieking yowl burst from the jaws. It swiped — claws like scythe blades whickering — but missed.

Then it whirled-sprang-bounded, kicking up snowstorms with its big paws. It crashed away through the trees and was gone.

Gasping, Runninghorse hitched himself up on an elbow and looked toward the house. Two-Bird stood there, wrapped in bearskins and blankets, holding in both small hands the Colt revolver he'd left on the table. Smoke spiraled lazily from the barrel.

He got up, discovered he'd pissed himself, decided he didn't care.

From inside came LeCharles' voice, muddled from whiskey and sleep. "What the... what? Two-Bird? What's going on?"

Runninghorse grabbed up the woodaxe. He rushed to Two-Bird, turned her around, ushered her back inside, then slammed and latched the door.

She looked shaken, thin and tired. But she no longer looked ill, and she no longer shivered. She tossed the gun back on the table and patted at Runninghorse as if to make sure he was unhurt.

LeCharles struggled to sit, bedclothes piled in his lap, bandages swathing his shoulder and chest. His eyes were red as a weasel's. "What happened?" he asked.

"The *wanageeska*," Runninghorse said. He put the axe beside the gun.

"I killed it."

"Another."

"What?! How many of these damned damnable things are there?"

"I'm all right, little bird," Runninghorse assured his daughter, who was continuing to pat at him.

"I heard a shot," LeCharles said.

"Two-Bird shot at it."

She nodded, pointed at the Colt, interlaced her fingers with the pointers extended, and mimicked gunfire.

"You're feeling better? Already?" LeCharles asked. "It worked? The... the spell or... medicine... whatever it was? She's well now?"

Two-Bird hurried around the table and perched on the edge of the bed. She stroked his beard. He smiled at her. She returned the smile.

"Yes, but the *wanageeska*—"

"It's dead too? This other one?"

"No," Runninghorse said. "But she drove it off, scared it away. For now."

"For now?" echoed LeCharles. "What do you mean, for now?"

The same sentiment showed in Two-Bird's worry-creased brow.

The wetness at his crotch had gone from liquid-hot to ice-cold and now to a clammy unpleasantness. "The *wanageeska*... the second *wanageeska*... it must have followed you back here. Or followed the scent of the one you brought with you."

LeCharles' eyes muddied, then cleared. "Ah... I did bring it? The carcass? All the way to the house?"

"You wanted its pelt."

"Of course I wanted its pelt. There was a wolf... had a fine tail, but..." He pinched the bridge of his nose with the thumb and forefinger of his good hand. "Hard to remember exactly. I couldn't get at it. And the white pelt... you saw it... you touched the fur... it'll be worth a fortune."

"Don't you understand what you've done?" Runninghorse got into dry britches and a dry shirt.

"Saved Two-Bird's life, by what you're telling me."

"You've angered the *wanageeska*. You killed one of them. You dragged its body through the snow like any other dead animal... so that you could skin it... turn its pelt into... a... a coat or something. When the second one came to avenge the crime, it didn't get vengeance. It got shot at."

They both looked at him, expressions ranging from incredulity to indignation.

"Would you rather Two-Bird let it eat you?" LeCharles finally asked.

"But now we've only angered it further! We've offended the *wanageeska*. If their wrath was terrible before, it'll be doubly as terrible now!"

"What wrath? What's it going to do? We're in here, I have other guns. If it shows itself, I'll have more fur to sell." He glanced at his left hand, which was partially hidden in the blankets, flinched, and glanced away. "Which would be just as well... my trapping days might be over and done with."

Two-Bird uncovered his hand, and she also flinched. The skin had gone a darkish purple-grey, and begun to blister. A white-man doctor might have already been going for his bone saw or hatchet. The gangrene, a horror that had become all too well known since the War, would soon be setting in. Nothing to do but have the hand off.

"There's no use arguing about it now," LeCharles said at last. "What's done is done and all that."

"Yes," Runninghorse said. "But the *wanageeska*—"

"Just what is it you think will happen?"

He found his tobacco pouch. "I don't know. The beast may return, or there may be a blizzard. Or both."

"We've weathered blizzards before."

"Not the likes of this."

The day passed in a dry and crackling cold that made Runninghorse feel as if the skin was going to shatter right off his face.

The sun-dogs vanished as the sun continued its climb through that watered-milk sky. It shed enough light to turn all the world white, making a snow-glare so strong that he daubed smudges of ash on his cheekbones to keep from being blinded when he went out again to chop wood.

By noon, the woodpile was high. The mule was fed and watered. The guns were loaded and set at the ready, within easy reach. Two-Bird made cornmeal cakes fried in bacon grease.

The wind did not rise in a war-whoop. New snow did not fall. The *wanageeska* did not rip the sod roof from the house and snatch them up in its vicious teeth.

They ate. They drank cider. The men smoked. Two-Bird, freed from her affliction, was not yet fully recovered, and fell asleep beside LeCharles with her head resting on his arm. He managed to move her to the bed without waking her, then sat by the fire stirring it with a poker.

Runninghorse was keenly aware of the other man watching him. Waiting. Waiting not for anything to happen, but for him to give up and acknowledge that nothing was going to happen.

"How is your hand?" he asked.

LeCharles shrugged. "Like a chunk of half-dead meat at the end of my arm." He drained the dregs of his cider, yawned. His gaze shifted to the shuttered window and then to Runninghorse. "It doesn't seem the weather's turned."

"It will."

He grunted. "We should get some sleep."

Runninghorse settled into his blankets, but lay wakeful. His ears wanted to twitch at every slight strange noise. More often than not, it was only the mule in its shed on the other side of the wall.

At some point, he must have fallen asleep, because the next thing he knew, he was abruptly wide awake.

Something had changed in the night.

LeCharles had stopped snoring. But that wasn't it.

A soft breeze made a low, almost musical sound in the chimney-pipe, the way a man might blow across the neck of a clay jug.

Runninghorse got to his feet and padded quietly to the window. He placed his palm near the edge, near a crack, where a thin cold draft should have been issuing in.

There was a draft... but it was... well, not warm, not exactly... but certainly not as frigid as it should have been. Quite a bit warmer than it should have been. It smelled damp.

Now that he was up, he heard something else in addition to the hollow jug-blowing music of the breeze on the chimney. He heard a steady, gentle dripping.

He opened the door and looked out. The sky was still dark, the snow seeming to glimmer with its own inner light. It was January. He was sure of that... not which day down to the exact date, but he knew well enough that it was January.

This felt more like the pre-dawn of a mild April morning.

A trick. A lie.

A storm would come. A blizzard, a fierceness of wind and snow greater than anything they'd experienced. It would come with winter's full, icy wrath.

PART TWO:

FAR ENOUGH

UNSEASONABLE

William Thorpe stood with his hands folded behind his back, listening to his wife weep downstairs, looking out the window at what was to have become his legacy.

The window had real glass panes and real muslin curtains. It was in a real house, a frame house with floorboards, brick chimneys, good wooden walls. With fine furniture and a well-stocked pantry.

No more log cabins or humble soddies for the Thorpes. No more thick earthen walls to be infested with mice, snakes and insects. No more swept floors of packed dirt. No more smoky, iron stoves with crooked chimney-pipes that poked up through the sod like an old man's arthritic finger.

He had done this for them, done well by them.

His wife, his family, his neighbors.

And the thanks he got?

Thorpe frowned.

He had a forbidding frown. Even in what ghostly reflection he could see of himself, he knew it was so. A stern and forbidding frown in a face of hard planes, lines and edges. His hair was thick but prematurely grey. His eyes were also hard, chips of flint.

A man had to be stern, hard and forbidding in this part of the country. The weak and soft could not survive, could not endure. Could not succeed.

Who had led them all this way? Who had organized the long journey by train, the longer journey by wagon? Who had financed much of it? Who had led them on and on across the vast expanse of the Dakotas in search of land that wasn't already claimed and settled? Who had brought them here into the foothills of the Rockies, where they could farm and raise cattle and pluck gold from the very creek beds?

Some had given up and gone back East. Others had chosen to stop in the little towns that had sprouted here and there on the prairie, taking what undesirable scraps of acreage as were left rather than press on.

The weak and the soft.

Oh, they had been full of ambitious talk and pioneer spirit when they first set out! This great nation, this land of bounty and opportunity! Where a man could prove himself by the strength of his back, the sweat of his brow and the tenacity of his resolve!

How quickly they changed their tunes once faced with true challenge and obstacle. How quickly they turned tail and fled for the safety and comforts of the cities or railtowns.

Not William Thorpe.

He would show them all. He would raise up a town of his own here, in this small corner of the world. A real town. A town of note.

Hadn't he already worked his fingers to the bone to do so? Hadn't he spent every penny he could afford, and more? Hadn't he suffered and sacrificed? Hadn't he lost his own youngest son, his cherished Little Will, to a fever and wet cough last year?

This would, by God, be a real town. His town.

Someday. Someday soon, and sooner yet once gold was found. Gold, or even silver, silver would do, the mountains were riddled with it. Even copper, for that matter, or iron ore. He wasn't choosy. A single rich strike was all it would take. Only a matter of time.

And then… oh, and then! Miners and prospectors would flock here by the hundreds. By the thousands! Merchants would follow, and preachers, and whores, and gamblers. The railroad would come. The telegraph wires would come. The soldiers at Fort Winston would bring their payroll here instead of squandering it in Juniper.

Thorpe's forbidding frown almost – almost – curved into a tight smile at the thought. He could see that burgeoning boomtown rising before his eyes, storefronts and livery stables, saloons, a hotel or two, stagecoaches and buggies, board sidewalks, electric lights...

Then the happy vision faded and he once more saw only the view as it truly was. The churned lane of frozen mudpuddles and slush was no Main Street, and the road leading off toward Juniper was only a road in the barest sense of the word. Two narrow ruts with a hump down the middle... dust-cloud dry and brittle brown grass half the year, mud or snow-covered mud-ice the other half.

Dean Hadden's split-log trading post was the closest they had to a general store. The foundation had been set for Reverend Erlich's church but full construction wouldn't begin until spring. The newest structure was the tidy one-room schoolhouse.

Only a few other families had followed Thorpe's example and built proper houses and split-rail fences so far. Most of the rest, too poor or too stuck in their old-country ways, contented themselves with barbed wire, rambling rock walls from their cleared fields, log cabins, dugouts, or soddies.

Thorpe's frown deepened. He was not about to admit that thick log or earthen walls and small window-holes shuttered with planks or leather might be more practical.

There were more important things than practicality.

Pride, for instance.

He thought of his oldest boys, sons from his first marriage, two of whom hadn't even cared to come with him on this journey West. One would sooner stay foreman in a factory, to work for some other man, rather than seize and shape his own fate. The second would not leave his sweetheart, and she would not leave her parents, and so the foolish lovestruck boy stayed.

Thorpe's frown deepened toward a scowl.

Downstairs, his wife wept on. She had been at it since she awoke. Not a single gushing spate of sobs, but this steady, monotonous, eternal trickle... like a bucket with a slow leak.

Nothing physical ailed her, Josephine insisted. She was not sick, she was unhurt, she was not pregnant again. She did not know why she felt compelled to weep today, but weep she did, and she could not stop. Maybe it was the change in the weather.

His hands, still folded behind his straight back, clenched into fists.

It was enough to drive a Christian man to drink. Or at least to drive a man out of her presence before he lost his temper... or his mind.

Josephine had been sixteen and pretty when he married her. She'd been a good wife for the most part, a good stepmother to the boys and a good mother to their half-siblings who'd come along in due course... she'd borne up bravely under the hardships of their journey, and through Little Will's untimely death.

She did not even know that her husband hated her, let alone suspect why.

But he did.

Oh, how he hated her.

He had hated her since the day they settled here.

Since the day she defied him and made him a laughingstock. Made a mockery of his dream.

"This is far enough!" she had said that day all those years ago. "No more, do you hear me, William Thorpe? This, right here, is far enough!"

Annie Hadden had backed her, and all of the other pioneer women agreed, in their unity presenting such a fiercely steadfast front that the men dared not argue. The communal wifely foot had been put down, and put down hard.

Far enough.

When he'd wanted to press on, seek a pass through the mountains, perhaps make for Oregon...

No.

That spot, there and then, was far enough.

And so, the wagons stopped their journey westward.

This was far enough, they said.

It became a joke, and then it became habit, and before William Thorpe realized what was happening, it became ingrained. The settlement, his future town... which he had hoped to name after himself... was referred to then and would be forever after as Far Enough.

The temperature must have climbed forty degrees overnight, going from bitter sub-zero winter chill to a balmier mildness more suited to early spring.

The sun was a tarnished coin lost in a hazy whiteness of sky. Meltwater dripped from the icicles.

A January thaw, Thorpe's hired man called it, and said they could look forward to several days of pleasant weather. Perhaps even a week or more.

People who had been cooped up indoors through the recent long cold spell were out and about, tending to their animals and seeing to the chores that had gone neglected while they'd hunkered down against the storms. A few men readied horses, wagons and sleds to make the trek to Juniper for supplies. Children who had not been allowed out in weeks headed for the schoolhouse, laughing and swinging their lunch-pails and clutching their readers, some of them coatless and hatless in the thinly warm morning light.

William Thorpe, still gazing from his window, did not frown at the people out forking hay for their cattle or hauling firewood. They were good stout hard-working folk, tireless and grateful, uncomplaining.

Nor did he frown at the children, for after all, had he not been the one to pay for the building of the schoolhouse, and arranged for the hiring of the teacher? Having a school and a teacher was a gift, a privilege, yet one more debt for which his neighbors were beholden to him.

He did frown at the men readying for their trek. Thirty miles through the snow... thirty miles to purchase supplies when they should have had a store here instead of just Dean Hadden's trading post... thirty miles to get the last of the grain milled into flour when they should have had a mill here...

From the sitting room came the voices of his daughters as they tried in vain to comfort their mother's ongoing, undefined misery. Josephine seemed unable to reply, except with more weeping... which had the baby whimpering as well.

He went downstairs to put an end to this nonsense.

The older boys, Thorpe saw as he reached the door, were doing their best to ignore this shameful display of emotion. Samuel, the eldest at nearly sixteen, was unmoved by his stepmother's tears. Elias, not quite ten, sought to mimic Samuel's stoicism... he idolized his older half-brother. But clearly, her distress was upsetting the younger boys, sickly Peter and young James.

They all glanced up when he came in, with something akin to hopeful desperation in their eyes. He was their father. He would take care of whatever needed taking care of. He could do anything. If he could bring them out here, build a house, keep food on the table and shoes on their feet, he could get Mother to stop crying, couldn't he?

"School," he said, jerking his chin sharply in the direction of the door.

The children stared at him. Cora's little mouth fell open but she didn't make a peep. Peter, who enjoyed school despite his perpetual sniffles and cough, slid at once from the bench where he'd been sitting. James, who didn't enjoy school, scuffed his foot on the floor and stuck out his lip. Samuel heaved an exasperated sigh and rolled his eyes – he was too old for school, that sigh and eyeroll said. Elias imitated him.

"But, Father—" Mary began, then quickly hushed herself and looked startled by her own temerity.

Thorpe raised his eyebrows at her.

"William," said Josephine, her voice weak and watery. "I... I don't think they should go to school today. Not today."

"Nonsense," he said. "It's a fine fair day. They should go while they can and not waste the good weather."

"I..." She hitched in a breath. "I have... I have the most dreadful feeling that something awful is going to happen."

"Nonsense," he said again. "It's a fit of the nerves, that's all."

"Please, William. Please, let me keep them home."

"And how would that look? I didn't build a schoolhouse and hire a teacher all the way from Chesterton so that my own children would sit about and not learn their letters."

"I know my letters," Peter piped up.

"It's the most dreadful feeling," Josephine repeated, cradling Grace on her lap. "I'd feel so much better if they stayed."

"Samuel will stay," Thorpe said. Before this pronouncement could bring too wide a grin to his oldest son's face, he added, "He has chores do before this warm spell ends and the next snow comes."

"I can work," said Elias. "I can help."

"You," Thorpe said, fixing him with a stern look, "will go to school, and you will behave, or I'll take my belt to your backside."

He swept the stern look across all of them for good measure, to let it be known that he would brook no more discussion on the topic. Then he turned on his heel and strode from the room.

THE SCENT

enry Greeley thought it was the recent confinement that had his dogs so unsettled, just him and them alone in the cabin for days and days on end.

He thought getting them out of doors a while would soothe their mood, despite the weather.

So far, it wasn't soothing them much.

If anything, they were feistier than ever. Snarling at each other, sometimes nipping. Snarling at him, even, though not one of them dared go so far as to take a nip at their master.

He loved his dogs, but there were some things he just wouldn't tolerate.

A command in a stern voice was enough to settle them some, but they still weren't as he had expected they'd be. Instead of running around in the snow, rolling, leaping, chasing up whatever birds or small critters there were to chase up, all five dogs stuck close to Henry. Crowding him sometimes, crowding so close that their furry sides bumped against his legs, and if he tried to turn direction, he risked tumbling over one or another of them.

They stared off at nothing in particular, with their lips all skinned back from their teeth, hackles rising. Chief, the big one, kept a low rumbling going deep in his throat and chest. Queenie had her ears pricked up and held her lean black body stiff, ready to point at a moment's notice ... point at what, Henry had no idea. The girls, Buttons and Bows, were half-grown now, not pups anymore, but both kept whining and whimpering up at Henry as if wanting him to carry them in his arms.

Only Nugget, the oldest of the pack – greying around the muzzle now, and half-deaf – didn't seem overly excitable. Ol'

Nugget just plodded along with his head down and his tail dragging.

Hadn't liked being kept in, didn't like being took out.

Henry took them out all the same. They all needed a breath of fresh air and to stretch their legs. He reckoned it would also be good of him to look in on his neighbors, see how they were getting on in the winter.

And, on a more practical side, Henry had grown mighty weary of his own larder of canned goods, and even wearier of his own cooking. Oatmeal and pork-and-beans was filling, but dull. He hungered for hot baked bread, or chicken stew with dumplings, or a nice pie. Dropping by to look in on his neighbors could well mean being invited to stay for a meal.

If such an invitation wasn't immediately in the offering, well, he'd also brought along a sack of the whimsical little spoons, whistles, critters, dolls and toys he carved from knurled wood. They made for good trading.

The Adamses were his nearest neighbors, some two miles if he followed the creek, half a mile less if he cut through the woods. There was a widowed Adams sister-in-law who'd lost her husband a couple years back; she was a shapely thing with a snub nose and big brown eyes; she even liked the dogs—

"Heh," Henry snorted. "Think a man would learn his lesson."

Chief looked up at him, then resumed staring at the surrounding whiteness with that rumble deep in his chest. Buttons whined again, squatted, made a yellow patch, and pranced around it kicking snow with funny high-legged steps.

Once, and not so long ago, Henry'd had a woman. He'd made a good bit of money at a silver strike in California, enough to keep him and his dogs in comfort, but he'd somehow got the idea that a wife would make everything perfect. So he'd started reading those newspapers where lonely ladies placed ads, and he'd written to the ones that caught his fancy, chose the one that seemed to suit him best, and arranged to purchase her a railroad ticket out to meet him.

It had gone well enough at first... but Aggie hadn't much cared for the dogs. Didn't want them sleeping in the house at all, let alone on the bed. Said they ate too much, and they smelled, and there was no way on earth she would even consider having a baby with those 'vicious animals' around.

Oh, they'd had some fearsome arguments, Henry and Aggie. But he'd thought she would come around. She'd get used to the dogs eventually. See how useful they were, how loyal, how friendly. She would come to love them.

So he'd thought.

Right up until the day he'd come home from working in the mines to find Aggie gone. Along with his best horse, his best rifle, all the clothes he'd bought for her, and the strongbox where he'd had close to a thousand dollars saved up.

A hard-earned lesson indeed.

Queenie stiffened, then tipped back her head and bayed. Buttons tried to imitate her mama, while Bows cringed against Henry's boot. Chief's rumbling grew louder, like the rolling thunder of a stampede approaching from far off. Even ol' Nugget picked up his head.

"Now, girl," Henry said. He moved to pat Queenie and she whipped around toward him fast. Damn near went for his hand but caught herself. By her look, she was as shocked as Henry.

They were in the woods, Henry having decided to cut through because the snow wasn't so deep under the tree cover, and a half-mile shorter to walk meant the sooner he'd be in the Adams kitchen, sitting down to a nice plate of stew and dumplings. The shadows made everything a murky grey color, like a blind eye speckled with brown clots of dead leaves and dark veins of bare branches.

Again, Queenie bayed. This time Henry didn't try to pat her. She had given him an abject apologetic grovel to be sure, but he wasn't about to take the chance. Once bitten twice shy was wisdom enough, but better wisdom was not to be bitten in the first place.

Then Queenie bolted, and Chief with her. Both of them barking up a ruckus as if they'd caught the scent of a bear.

Nugget uttered a wheezy. "Whoof!" and went lumbering after them. Buttons and Bows pranced in place, wild with indecision.

"Chief!" Henry called. "Queenie! Come! Come here, you!"

A bone-freezing howl was his answer.

"Hell-blast-damnation," Henry swore. His rifle was on his back, slung there with a leather strap, and he unslung it now to bring it around into his hands. He'd never, never heard any of his dogs make a noise like that.

"Follow," he ordered the girls, and they fell in obediently enough, as if glad to be told what to do.

He found the other dogs at the base of a big oak. Queenie was up on her hind legs with her paws on the trunk and her long nose angled skyward, still howling fit to freeze his bones. Chief was digging at the snow some yards away, flinging it in all directions along with clods of dirt, leaves and bitter-black rotten acorns. Nugget snuffled around in a slow circle, and now he was rumbling too.

"The devil is the matter with—" Henry began, his gaze following Queenie's.

His words broke off clean when he saw what she was howling at. Something tattered and wooly and crusted with blood. The carcass of a sheep. A gutted, mauled, throat-torn-out sheep. Great chunks of meat were missing. It looked half-eaten.

The Adamses kept sheep. Henry knew that they did; hadn't he been over to help with the shearing the past few springtimes? Hadn't he given them one of Queenie's pups to be a herd dog in exchange for a warm wool blanket and two pairs of good socks three years ago?

Nugget shuffled over to Chief and raked his paws at the snow and earth. Henry told the girls to stay, and went to see what they were digging at. Muddy snow and the soft mulchy shards of acorns. And a buried heap of what looked to be animal droppings.

Chief had no sooner uncovered and sniffed at these than he went purely mad, leaping and barking, attacking the ground, fur bristling, spit flying from his jaws. He hunkered and sprayed what seemed a gallon of steaming piss onto the droppings, flailed furiously at the dirt and snow, hunkered again to leave his own brown pile, kicked more dirt and snow, leaped around some more, bayed, howled, barked.

"Chief!" yelled Henry.

The big dog paid him no attention. All five of them were barking now, running in to piss on the disturbed spot, digging and kicking. Queenie jumped straight up as if she meant to snatch the sheep carcass out of the branches and give it the same treatment.

Henry backed up, heart hammering in his chest. He held his gun but not in any meaningful way – what was he going to do, shoot his own dogs? Even if they came at him in a murderous pack, he couldn't shoot his own dogs!

At the height of his frenzy, Chief ran headfirst into the oak tree. It made a sound like a mallet striking a wedge. He tottered diagonally a couple steps, shaking his head, then fell over with a thump.

SCHOOLMARM

Emma Curtis was a big, solid girl ... broad across the hips and shoulders... almost as tall and strong as a man... healthy as an ox... and, as her parents had always said, plain as a slice of unbuttered bread.

She was also nineteen, unmarried and unlikely ever to be. Not that Emma was in any hurry to have a husband and household of her own. She liked children well enough. But she liked them best when she could send them home to their mothers at the end of the day.

Being a teacher suited her. She had her schoolhouse, her slates and pencils, her books. She had room and board in a nearby farmhouse. And she had twenty dollars a month.

Twenty dollars a month was hardly a fortune, but it kept her clothed and shod, it let her send a pittance home to her kin in Chesterton, and it gave her a meager savings for whatever her future might hold.

In the surprisingly mild morning, Emma left for the schoolhouse without her heavy coat and boots. She wore a short wool cape around her shoulders instead, pinned her long brown braids up under a bonnet rather than a fur hood, and decided that her leather shoes would be good enough for the short walk across the fields.

Her lodging was with the Rennekes, whose house was a soddie huddled low between two rises, and for the past several days everyone had stayed indoors as the wind whooped and the snow fell. The only times any of them had ventured out at all was when snow clogged the soddie's chimney-hole and someone had to brave the cold to clear it before they all smothered, or when they ran out of fuel for the fire, or to check on the precious livestock.

With Johann Renneke needed to help his father and uncle with chores, only Kirstie accompanied Emma that day. The girl was, under protest but at her grandmother's insistence, bundled into her thickest winter clothes before she was allowed to leave the house. Emma herself thought it was unnecessary – she'd seen spring thaws before, growing up in Chesterton. But she was not about to stick her nose in on family matters, least of all when Mrs. Renneke and her mother-in-law were already butting heads.

The school sat in a scoop of meadow cradled between the juncture of two creeks, creeks that rushed and burbled whitewater in the spring but were frozen solid now. People called the place Thorpe's Meadow, and the creeks Thorpe Creek and West Thorpe Creek.

It was, they said, where the Thorpe Party had first made camp when they came to the valley some years back, and where the pioneer wives had decreed that they had gone far enough, this giving the settlement its name.

Emma could hardly be sure, but she rather thought that Mr. Thorpe didn't much care for that name. If he'd had his way, she reckoned, the town itself would have been called Thorpe, like the creek and the meadow and the valley itself.

She walked with Kirstie – who fussed with her coat and hood and mittens at every step – to the plank bridge that crossed the frozen creek.

Though the sun was hidden behind a pearly veil of mist that turned the whole sky white, the air was clear and Emma could see bustling activity at every farm and building. Everyone seemed to be industrious but in a good humor, all glad to be out and about instead of huddled by the fire waiting to see which would run out first, the food or the woodpile or the bad weather.

A few other children were making for the school, bright young voices calling back and forth, lunch-pails in hand.

The boys came hooting and hollering and throwing mushy snowballs. Most of them didn't see much use in school, excepting that it sometimes got them out of their chores, and for that reason alone they were glad enough to go. The ones that were good students often found themselves the butts of jokes or pranks by their less scholarly classmates.

The girls tended to be quieter and more mannerly, though some of them seemed to regard their lessons as a waste of time – what need would they have of history and geography when they would be married soon enough? – and big plain Emma herself with the sort of pitying scorn better reserved for the terminally ill.

It was, she realized, going to be an even emptier classroom than usual that day, despite the nice turn of weather. Emma supposed that many of her pupils would be, like Johann, hard at work at home. Not a single one of the Kradenmeyers had turned up, though they also did live furthest from the schoolhouse and were said to be reclusive even among frontier folk.

Emma fell busy as soon as she arrived. There was snow to be swept from the steps, a fire to be lit and kindled in the woodstove that sat in the center aisle between the rows of pewlike desks, winter over-clothes to be collected from the children and hung up in the coatroom where the smell of wet wool and leather wouldn't be such a bother.

Some of her students had their own duties, with Maggie Jordan responsible for making sure all of the slates were wiped clean in preparation for the day's lessons, and husky seventeen-year-old Amos Trotter seeing that the woodbox was filled.

The students chattered as they put their things away, and Emma let them while she unlatched and opened the shutters over the tall narrow windows that ran the length of the classroom's east and west walls to let in the thin white daylight.

"Our mother wanted to keep us home," she heard Cora Thorpe telling her seatmate, Minnie Granger.

"My grandfather did, too," Ben Adams said. "He said there were sun-dogs chasing the sun yesterday, and the Indians told him that sun-dogs only chase the sun when a bad, bad cold is coming."

"What do Indians know?" sneered one of the Wood twins. Emma could never tell them apart. No one could, aside from their own mother, and they knew it and made the most possible mischief of it.

"It's true!" Ben insisted.

"They're just stupid savages," the other Wood twin said. "Does your grandfather believe in the White Beast, too?"

"She was crying and crying," Cora went on, though her sister Mary tried to shush her. "But Father said we had to go."

"Except for Sam," Elias Thorpe added, and kicked the seat in front of him. "Sam got to stay."

"Sam's older," Peter said.

"Not older than Amos."

Amos looked around from the woodbox. "Me and Pa took care of the cows already," he said. "Pa's helping the neighbors, so Ma said I should come to school."

Emma moved to the front of her room and rapped her stick on the desk to get their attention, so that class could begin.

GOD'S COUNTRY

"**E**verything's so fresh after a snow, so clean and pretty," Ruby Erlich said, drawing a deep breath of the brisk, mild air.

Edgar smiled at her, thinking that she was, too. Fresh and clean and pretty as could be, his dear wife.

Thirty years of marriage hadn't changed that, not a whit. Her eyes were still the brightest of blues. Her cheeks, framed in the fur trim of her hood, glowed a rosy-pink flush, as did the tip of her nose. If her hair was more silver than gold these days, if her bright blue eyes had crinkles at the corners, what of it?

They walked on through the snow, gloved hands linked.

Their daily strolls were what they missed most during the depths of winter. Every season was God's gift and glory, but He must have been in a crotchety mood when He decided to make one of them a spun-sugar beauty of crystal and lace but too cold for His children to enjoy it to the fullest.

And out here? Out here in what truly was God's own country? The great wilderness, un-grimed by soot and smoke and coal dust?

He did not regret bringing them here.

Oh, to be sure, if folks the like of William Thorpe had his way, Far Enough would eventually become the same as those other places... crowded, noisy, people living crammed up against neighbors whose names they mightn't even know, neighbors who were strangers.

The day could come when doors had to be locked, when the town needed its own sheriff just to keep the good peace, when they'd have dens of sinful temptation, a jail, even a gallows tree on the hill up by the humble graveyard. Yes, that day could come, would come sooner rather than later if that rumor about a saloon this summer panned out … but as far as the right honorable Reverend Edgar Erlich was concerned, all that could take its sweet time. He was not eager to have to rail against vice and temptation from the pulpit. He'd just as soon praise the Lord, raise up his flock, not scold them.

His church, when it was finished, would be for welcome, for comfort and praise, not condemnation. Until then, he found himself quite content to lead his sermons outside in the open air, weather permitting. Something about standing head-bowed beneath God's vast and blameless Montana skies had a way of awing and humbling even the most wicked of souls.

They'd traveled west from St. Louis last year. Edgar and Ruby were perhaps old for it, but not too old, praise the Lord, and both of them still hale, healthy and hearty. A snug little cabin or cottage, a fruit tree or two, a vegetable garden, some hens and a rooster, and Ruby's beloved goats would be all they needed.

Childless themselves – God's will, but still sometimes to their sorrow – they'd taken in and raised Edgar's niece when Randall Erlich struck off to prospect in Alaska. Not once had dear Claire given them cause to regret it. She couldn't have been a better daughter if she'd been their own.

It amazed him sometimes to think how she'd be a grown woman soon, set to find a nice young man and settle down. Nearby, he surely hoped.

For now, she was their help, a dutiful girl, smart as anything. Before Thorpe announced his intention to hire a schoolteacher from over Chesterton way, Edgar had suggested to Claire she consider taking on the teaching of the town's children herself, but she had modestly demurred.

Ice crunched beneath their boots as he and Ruby followed their usual route along the treelined hillslopes overlooking the valley's farmlands and fields. The turn in the temperature had melted the top layer of snow, but the hard-packed layers underneath that had frozen it to a crust. Boughs glittered with icicles, and bushes sparkled as if scattered with seed pearls.

True, their route did take them around behind the graveyard hill on its way into the woods, but even the graveyard looked clean and pretty, graves blanketed in white, crosses crowned with it. The decrepit barbwire fence, sagging in places and missing completely in others, was a delicate frosty latticework on the far side of Thorpe Creek.

The creek itself, wider here than it was down toward the school, was iced at the edges but flowing free at the middle.

"Just look at the water gurgling between the snow-covered rocks," Edgar said. "And the way the branches hang down, almost touching."

Ruby squeezed his hand. "Shh, I hear something," she whispered. "An animal, poor thing, such a hardship this weather must be on them."

She did love the wildlife, all of God's creatures, even the ones that might be called nuisances by some. The birds, squirrels and mice never went hungry by their house for the millet she scattered in the yard each morning and the corncobs she hung. A jackrabbit in their garden or a deer nibbling at the fruit trees might make Edgar grumble, but the sight alone never failed to cheer Ruby's entire day.

They paused there, listening to the chuckling of the creek.

"A clump of loose snow sliding from a branch," Edgar said.

"Shh! There! Look, through the trees, do you see it?"

At first, he couldn't make out what he was pointing at, seeing only a vague whiteness in the cool greyish shadows. Then the whiteness almost resolved itself into a shape... then he lost it again.

"Where? What is it? A deer?"

"Can't tell." Ruby took a step in that direction. "Bigger, I think."

"An elk?"

"It looks white, whatever it is. Are there white elk?"

"I suppose there must be."

She took another step, tugging his gloved hand in hers.

"Ruby, you'll scare it."

"I'm not going to scare it. I just want a better l—"

Where it seemed nothing had been, something suddenly was. Something large and white. Something with pale eyes fixed on them.

Ruby and Edgar went perfectly still.

"Oh my God," he murmured.

"Edgar... what is it?"

Those eyes... they were so pale... so cold. The rest of its shape seemed blurred, indistinct, blending into the background. But those eyes!

"I don't know," he said, still keeping his voice so low as to be almost inaudible. "Back up, Ruby, nice and slow."

Now he tugged at her gloved hand, at the same time easing himself forward so his body was between hers and the unfamiliar animal. His mind continued to not want to make sense of its outlines, its shape. Some hazy quality about it made it impossible to clearly discern.

He had an impression of powerful muscles bunching and flexing beneath thick, sleek white fur. Of a long lush tail sweep-twitching side to side in ominous, grand motions. Triangular ears, tufted with fur, pricked up and alert.

And of those pale, pale eyes never wavering.

Edgar heard someone muttering the Lord's Prayer and realized it was himself.

Another slow, backward step brought their heels to the ice-choked edge of Thorpe Creek.

Ruby screamed on the inhale as the creature advanced, a thin teakettle whistle that sounded throat-clenchingly painful.

"Run!" Edgar yelled, spinning her by the shoulders of her warm woolen coat. "Across the creek! Go!"

She made an ungainly leap, arms waving in pinwheels. The sole of one boot found, then lost, purchase on the flattish surface of a low boulder. Her foot skidded from under her. She cried out as she bellyflopped onto the far shore.

Edgar's leap was even less successful. His foot came down with a colossal shin-deep splash that sent freezing water all the way up to his thigh. He plunged wildly through the creek, and reached Ruby by the time she started to push herself up.

He grabbed her under the arm, but overbalanced and they both went sprawling again. His kneecap struck a rock with what felt like bone-cracking force.

The frosty barbed wire fence poking up from the snow at the edge of the graveyard looked very far away.

And ridiculously flimsy.

SUPPLY RUN

On a day like today, only the top half of the mile marker posts along the road to Juniper rose above the heaped snow. Another couple storms, Cyrus Freedman thought, and they would've been buried entire.

Those posts, Cyrus Freedman knew, were William Thorpe's doing, like most everything else around here. Folks guessed that, in his mind, the rich man saw them as marking where the telegraph poles would one day be, rising high and stringing their wires over the prairie and into the hills to Far Enough.

Thorpe also saw to it that a road crew went out each spring, in between duties of planting and plowing. Cyrus was no stranger to the road crews. They spread layers of pebbles and gravel, or laid down rows of corduroy logs, wherever the ruts were in most danger of becoming pits, ditches or mires.

Seemed unnecessary, but Thorpe paid well, so Cyrus didn't care.

Work was work, and pay was pay.

It was better than the sweaty back-breaking labor of putting down railroad track, and he hadn't had to toil alongside any heathen Chinee.

It was much better than how it'd been for his daddy, and his daddy's daddy, and his daddy's daddy's daddy. No plantations here in Montana. No chains, no whips, no slave shacks where a man could be sold away from his family at any time.

Sissa was old enough to remember their momma crying when she heard the news of how President Lincoln was shot, but Cyrus had been born after the War, in Kansas where the Freedmans had settled. All he knew of it was from the stories.

But the stories, they were enough to convince him. Whenever he might start in to thinking he had it bad, he only needed to remember those stories.

His uncles had showed him the scars on their backs. His grandfather wore an eye patch, one eye having put out by a hot poker as a lesson to him for seeing a white woman's breasts, by accident, through a window. One of his momma's sisters had died bearing the child of a white man's rape. Another had hanged herself after her husband was beaten to death for trying to run away.

Ahead, Rutger's team stamped and snorted and tossed their heads. The men were in similar good spirits, telling jokes, laughing, passing a jug from hand to hand. Rutger's younger boy had brought a banjo, and plucked out tunes as he jounced along on the wooden seat.

It had been a long stretch of time since any of them had been out on a fine day. Did a man hard, being cooped up indoors, unable to see to his fields or his flocks, unable to do anything but sit and be underfoot. Tempers got fearsome short at times like that. The sweetest of wives would turn to nagging, the best-behaved of children would become little monsters, and the most even-tempered man in the world might find himself ready to bloody someone's nose or black someone's eye.

Cyrus had seen that happening already. He had come west with Sissa and her husband, to help on their pig farm. Sissa and Aaron Burdock had nine youngsters already – two more had died young – and another on the way. They were good people, fine people, his family. He loved them to the ends of the earth.

But holy God Almighty, if he'd had to stay in that farmhouse one more day...

He stretched in the saddle and ran a hand through his crop of wiry curls. Felt good to be bare-headed, to have his coat off and his shirt buttons partway undone. The breeze was mild and moist-smelling, wafting over the snow like a promise of springtime to come.

Felt good to be on this road again. If someone needed a message taken to Juniper, or if there was an emergency that called for a doctor or medicines beyond the skills of Doc Marlowe, then Cyrus Freedman was the one to send. He had a good horse—

"Best horse in the territory," he said aloud, and slapped Lucifer on the side of the neck. The stallion nickered and flicked his ears.

—he was trustworthy, and there was a pretty red-headed lady in Juniper who was always as happy to see him as he was glad to go.

On a day such as this, he would have been on his way to Juniper whether anyone else had been planning the trip or not. First fine day after weeks of it being colder than a whore's icebox? He couldn't have been on his way early enough.

Several of the households had run short of supplies during the cold spell. Some grain hadn't yet been milled into flour, and without flour, the women couldn't make bread.

Rutger's wife Anna was one of those who held the firm conviction that her children would surely starve without proper bread. She had, last Christmas-time, gotten into a fistfight with a neighbor whose argument was that boiled grain was just as good. To this day, Anna Rutger and Bess Granger were not on speaking terms.

"They hiss like cats and just about spit on each other if they pass in the street," Sissa had told Cyrus.

Sissa wasn't the only woman who'd taken to grinding scorched barley or breadcrumbs and using that to make a drink that she called coffee, though as far as Aaron and Cyrus were concerned, it resembled coffee only in the color of the resulting hot brew. There wasn't a can of fruit or tomatoes left to be had, let alone fine sugar.

At first light, Rutger had sent his older boy around to announce his intentions, and by the time the big Swede was ready to set out, he'd been visited with so many requests that he'd had to scribble them down on a scrap of brown paper.

He'd also soon found himself the head of this modest parade, leading them through the snow toward the bend at the end of the valley.

John Arlen was second in line, driving his oxen. His young wife hadn't wanted to stay home alone with the children – or, being known as a jealous thing, she hadn't been eager to see handsome John go off on his own – so she sat with her husband while their two little ones rode in the back.

The Howe brothers had a small mule-pulled dray, gliding on sled runners in the path the wagons were breaking. George and Virgil were built short and broad, with bulbous noses that resembled the potatoes they farmed. They had no livestock and there was nothing to be done for potato fields under all that snow, so they were more than up for a change of scenery.

Franklin Wood, astride a dapple-grey horse called Gunpowder that was almost Lucifer's equal, grinned over at Cyrus and passed him the jug. "Supplies, is it? That why you're going all the way to Juniper?"

"Need coffee," Cyrus said. "And some other things. Sissa told me a list, made me memorize it." He took a pull – it was applejack whiskey, heady and strong.

"Bet she didn't put no green-eyed redhead on that list."

"Well... that, I already got memorized." He returned the grin and the jug, and added a wink.

"Pretty lady, that one."

"Sissa?"

"Here, now, I wouldn't go saying that about your sister."

"Only because Aaron would gut you and feed you to the pigs."

"That he might. But no, I meant your redhead in Juniper. You plan to introduce me to some of her friends this time around?"

Cyrus eyed him. "Ain't you got a girl? Ain't you getting married?"

"Not until summer." Franklin gestured at the snowy expanse spread out around them, broken only by the jut of another of Thorpe's mileposts and a single tree standing gnarled on a hilltop. "Summer's a long way off. And so's my girl. She's in New York, won't be here for months."

The tree looked peculiar, and Cyrus couldn't immediately figure out why. It was just a dark silhouette against a sky that was pearl-colored, just a leafy tree fluttering in the wind...

Then he realized that while there was the moist and mild breeze, there really wasn't much of a wind. After that, he realized any leaves on that tree would have turned color and fallen off long ago.

He peered at it. "Take a look there," he said. "Tree's full to bursting with birds... all of 'em just... perched there."

"Where else you expect birds to perch?"

"Seems odd, that's all. And take a listen... all those birds, but they're stone quiet, every single one."

Franklin was uninterested in the birds. "I recall there was this one friend of hers, dark hair worn all in ringlets, blue dress—"

Lucifer chose that moment to act up to his name, baring his teeth and snapping at Franklin's horse. The dapple-grey pranced sideways, the sudden movement almost tipping Franklin out of the saddle. He swore but recovered.

"Here, now," Cyrus scolded, thumping Lucifer.

The breeze made a sudden shift, brisk and cold from their left. From the north. A new noise grew in the previously quiet air, rushing and gathering, like the sound of an oncoming speeding train.

Cyrus looked north. So did Franklin, and Lars, and John Arlen and George Howe.

Only there was no north anymore.

A MAN'S BUSINESS

They turned out in droves that morning to buy up whatever he had left on the shelves. Which, to their disappointment, proved to be not much.

Dean Hadden reckoned that Will Thorpe would have something to say about that. Something along the lines of how, hadn't he been urging Dean to turn the old trading post into a proper general store? All last spring and summer when he'd been working to help his boy Dan get the cabin ready for Stella and the little one, couldn't and shouldn't he have been putting some of that time, money, and honest labor into fixing up his own place?

Well, but if he had, Dean would have had plenty to say right back. Thorpe wanted everyone to be as all-fired and hell-for-leather rarin' to go about the town's prospects as he himself was. It galled the man something awful that his neighbors didn't share his burning desire to put Far Enough on the map.

Of course, the way Thorpe also looked like he'd just sunk his teeth into a lemon whenever he heard that name always did make Dean smirk a little behind his hand.

In truth, when they'd first settled here, he'd full well intended it to be something more. He'd made the trek West as a man not yet past his prime, and the change was to have been a new start for them. For him and Annie, and their boy. Their Dan. Their only child.

Lord knew, they'd wanted more. And Lord knew it hadn't been for lack of trying. But a body could only take so many miscarriages and stillbirths, so many tiny coffins laid to rest in the churchyard, before having to own up and admit what wasn't meant to be.

Annie had been sorrowful to leave their babies behind, but she'd agreed how much more sorrowful it would be to stay, haunted by those memories. It would be better for Dan, too, she agreed. He'd been a lonesome kid, with her having a tendency to fuss over him and fret every little thing; this had been an opportunity for changing those ways as well.

The trading post had been fine when they settled here, adequate for their neighbors' needs and those of whatever travelers happened to pass through – fur-trappers like that LeCharles fellow, prospectors bound for rumors of gold strikes, even peaceful Indians now and again. Their room above it wasn't much but it'd do for a while, until they were ready to build themselves a good frame house.

Except that his Annie fell sick and died of the same wet cough that carried off Thorpe's youngest and so many others that first winter. After that, much of the heart had gone out of Dean Hadden. He didn't see the need of building a new house just for himself and Dan to rattle around with like the last two beans in a can, especially when Dan had already made his plans to join the Army.

So, it may have been a burr under Thorpe's saddle, but the place did for Dean all right. He'd given his order-list to Lars Rutger when the big Swede was preparing to set out, and money to cover even what inflated cost there might be, assuming folks in Juniper had been as hard-hit by the past few months as folks in Far Enough.

He doubted Lars would be able to lay in the entire order, the canned goods being downright optimistic, but anything would help. As it was, his neighbors had about picked him clean. He was glad he'd had the foresight to tuck away a jug of maple syrup and a cake of lye soap to take out on his next visit to Stella and the little one.

Which…

Dean glanced at the sky. The day before had been a peculiar one, those sun-dogs or whatever Jonas Adams would call them, but clearly the old-timer's prediction of a storm had been wrong.

Bart Jordan ambled over from his place the next plot of land over. Just as Dean heard regularly from Will Thorpe about the merits of a real general store, so did Bart often find himself on the receiving end of a lecture as to how his catch-all smithy and stable would better them all if he turned it into a decent livery.

"They leave you your drawers?" Bart asked.

"Barely," Dean said, giving a tug at his belt and grinning. "I'd offer you some coffee, but—"

"Yeah, well, the way that's been scarce as hen's teeth, Lars Rutger will be lucky they don't mob and overturn his wagon when he gets back."

"Best I can offer instead is a cup of brown water with what might be tea in it."

"Thanks but I'll pass," Bart said with a chuckle.

They talked business for a moment, and weather for another, watching the bustle of activity. Then Dean briskly smacked his palms together.

"Doubt anybody more will come around," he said, "but, mind keeping half an eye on things while I go on out to see how Stella and the little one are holding up?"

"Don't mind at all. Poor girl; she thought you were joshing her about the winters."

"That she did."

Bart scratched at his beard and said, musingly, "Fine-looking woman, though."

After an uncomfortable cough, Dean asked, "Would May like to hear you saying that?"

"Only observing. Dan's one lucky fellow."

"How are May and the girls, by the by?"

"I'll tell you, this warm spell came just in time. Sarah's at that age where she thinks she knows everything and ought to be treated like an adult. It was a genuine relief to shoo them out the door to school this morning. May can use the reprieve. She's been plum tired out, what with the next one on the way."

"Give her my best."·

"I will indeed." Bart touched his hat brim.

Dean touched his hat brim back to Bart, put on his wool coat, fetched the bag of goods he'd laid by, and struck off down the slushy mud-frozen lane in the direction that would bring him to Dan and Stella's property.

Would that he could have better changed the subject. Yes, and to be sure, Stella was a fine-looking woman. This was a fact that Dean had been aware of since the moment Dan first introduced them, and a fact he'd become increasingly aware of during the long months of his son's absence.

Perhaps too aware of. More aware of than he ought to be, than was proper.

A fine-looking woman.

Soft, somehow, though. Delicate. Not the best suited for the hardships of the frontier, or at least she hadn't been made to dig in and find her strength yet, the way Annie had.

Could be this winter would do it.

A good thing.

Also something of a shame.

He didn't mind at all helping to look after her and the little one. She fretted how she was making extra work for him, and he told her that it was the least family could do, but the plain truth of it was that he welcomed the feeling of being needed. Of having someone rely on him, depend on him. Someone soft and delicate, like Stella was. Made him feel good. Made him feel young again, more like a man.

Not that he would ever, in any manner, let her think she was indebted to him, or take advantage. No matter how fine-looking, how pretty, how helpless and grateful.

No matter how lonesome she might be, what with Dan away at Fort Winston—

She was his boy's wife, for God's sake! Mother of his first and so-far only grandchild!

He had no business doing more than the most cursory observation of her full lips and rosy cheeks, certainly no business noticing the sway of her backside or the press of her ample bosom against his chest when she gave him an affectionate farewell embrace—

No. No business in the slightest.

Dean shook his head, set his hat more squarely upon it, tucked his scarf closer around his neck, and trudged on through the snow.

ICED WINE

Hannah Trotter saw them off, her husband and their son, with a good hearty breakfast in their bellies. She did up the dishes and set to her chores, then decided to indulge herself by brewing another pot of sassafras tea and taking her Bible out on the porch to read in this glorious mild weather.

The sky was a shining brightness. The blanketed snow sparkled as if strewn with diamonds. Icicles hung down like crystal chimes from the eaves and branches, and along the garden fence.

After a quiet while, she closed the Good Book and folded her hands atop it. Her thoughts went – as they often did – to the children.

To Amos, such a dutiful boy, so hard working and respectful. Not even a boy anymore, not truly. She only hoped that he would stay with them once he found the right girl. They had the land, Lord knew. Land aplenty. The house had room to spare, or they could build another.

Amos wouldn't leave them.

He wouldn't leave them the way Jane had done. Wicked girl, run away with a snake oil salesman and a married man at that ... run away to live in sinfulness.

Every night before she lay down to sleep, Hannah prayed that Jane would see the error of her ways. She'd repent and come home. They'd forgive her, of course. Welcome her with open arms. The prodigal daughter.

Paul might harbor some anger toward the girl. But, he'd had his own fallings and failings in the past, which he'd put all behind him. He should know as well as anybody how easy it could be to go astray, and what a hard but worthy struggle it was to find the right course again.

She thought of little Charlotte next, with a sad pang. Little Charlotte, who slept in the arms of the angels now. Too goodly for this world and so God had brought her to His Heaven.

Movement in the thicket drew her attention. A clump of snow slid loose with a wet thump as something passed among the trees.

Large movement.

Paul, come home from the Grangers' place already?

Amos, back from school? Had the schoolmarm not gotten enough pupils shown up to bother?

Some neighbor paying a call?

Reverend Erlich's house, the building of which the Trotters and several neighbors had helped with, wasn't far from here. He and his wife were like as to stop in if they'd gone for one of their rambling walks. She was glad she'd put on that second pot of coffee after all. A nice plate of those oatmeal jumble cookies –

Could be they'd have their niece with them, as well. Claire, her name was. Pretty thing, industrious and sweet-natured, if a bit too book-learned for Hannah's tastes. Niece of a reverend would be a fine match for Amos...

But, no. As she glimpsed it again, Hannah decided it was animal movement there in the bushes. Approaching the yard.

One of their cows? That'd make little sense; Paul and Amos had driven them from the barn down to the south pasture, where they might find some grazing among the overgrown hay-grass and scrub brush.

Bear?

Wolf?

Before her nerves could whip themselves into a frenzy, a deer came into view.

A pretty brown doe, stepping gracefully between the tree trunks... she could see the keen flick of its ears, the alert posture, the gentleness of its large brown eyes.

Suddenly the deer's head twitched in alarm. Beneath the sleek hide, its muscles bunched.

It gathered its hindlegs, bounded, kicked up a flurry, and was brought down in a flailing tangle by something huge, something white and indistinct.

The doe screamed.

Hannah had never known deer could scream, hadn't known they could make any sounds at all, had never really thought about it before.

But, yes... there was no denying it... that was a scream.

As blood gouted in a crimson torrent, Hannah Trotter also screamed.

She saw the doe torn to pieces.

Scraps of meat and hide.

Blood squirting up into the trees, staining the crystal-chime icicles red.

Blood gushing across the snow, so hot it steamed, melting in and then freezing into patches and blotches like spills of iced wine.

Blood spattering onto a pelt of white fur, so white, white as the snow, whiter than the snow.

Thick ivory-looking claws sprouting from enormous splayed paws.

Teeth.

Knife and razor teeth, fearsome enough.

The fangs...

Vicious downcurves, sickles extending well below the bottom jaw.

Clutching her Bible to her bosom, Hannah knew she was looking at the very image of evil. A snow-demon, an ice-devil, a malicious winter spirit the likes of which the Godless Injuns spoke of.

Its head – roundish, shaggy, with a ruff of fur almost leonine but the alert triangular ears of a wolf – swung up and around to regard her.

Its muzzle was drenched in blood.

When its mouth gaped to yowl at her, blood ran in trickling streams from those sickle-fangs.

"Gone with you, devil!" she cried, bolting up from her rocker with such force it tipped over to make a loud clatter on the porch planks.

The eyes, pale and gleaming, narrowed in malevolence.

A terror pierced into her such that she thought she would drop dead on the spot. Only the Bible gripped tight in her hands seemed real now, seemed solid, her anchor of faith to this world.

It crouched, hunkered low as if to spring. Its tail swept in a menacing arc.

"Gone with you!" she repeated. She raised the Bible high.

It advanced with slow, cautious strides.

Hannah swallowed. She edged backward, holding out the Bible in one hand, groping behind herself for the door with the other. When she found it, she whirled, flung it open, darted inside and slammed it shut again.

The porch creaked.

The ice-devil snuffled at the door. Its breath, cold, stinking of blood and dead meat, wafted through every crack.

Its claws scraped with a slow, hideous sound over the wood.

It couldn't get in. She'd shut the door, bolted it, dragged the heavy oak table halfway across the room with a strength ten times greater than her own.

The walls were sturdy. The planks were thick.

The windows...

Only the one in the front room had glass panes, an extravagance she hadn't needed but Paul insisted upon. Even if the glass broke, the opening was surely too small for a beast that size to squeeze itself through.

It couldn't get in. Couldn't, wouldn't.

She was safe in here.

Safe... for now.

She had wood, and food, and God.

But her husband and her boy were still out there somewhere.

PART THREE:

THE BLIZZARD

LEADING EDGE

Where north had been, land rolling away toward mountains and foothills, there was only a churning curtain of darkness and white blotting out everything else, erasing the ground as it came.

"Cyrus?" Franklin Wood asked. "Cy, what is it? Avalanche?"

"Snowstorm, I think."

"That's no snowstorm!"

It was the source of the rushing train-roar, the source of the blast of cold wind. Pale tendrils of lightning flickered at its leading edge, the kind of weird unnatural all-directions dance that the old-timers called St. Elmo's Fire.

A roiling cloud bank. A storm front, sweeping southeast at terrible speed. A blizzard, but like no blizzard Cyrus Freedman had ever seen before.

And they were directly in its path.

"D'you hear it?" hollered George Howe. "God A'Mighty!"

His brother was fighting the reins, their mule having suddenly taken it to mind to go into a fit of bucking, lunging and kicking. It was a fight the Howes lost. A strap broke, the mule bolted half-loose, the sled careened around in a crazy half-circle and tipped over. George and Virgil went pitched headfirst into a mound of snow at the side of the road. The mule took off at a dead run, the sled breaking into a tangle of boards, runners and harness bouncing behind it.

"We've got to turn back," Franklin said, raising his voice to a shout. "Lars! We have to turn back!"

"Can't!" Lars replied, also at a shout. His plowhorses weren't in a panic like the Howes' mule, but even from here Cyrus could see their wild eyes rolling in their tossing heads.

Lucifer was high-stepping but otherwise calm. Gunpowder reared up of a sudden and damn near sent Franklin spilling backwards out of the saddle.

"It's coming too fast," Cyrus said. "No way we can turn these wagons before we're overtook."

"Well, we can't make it to Juniper in that!" Franklin was not so much riding as he was hanging on for dear life, Gunpowder rearing again with hooves lashing at the air.

The Rutger boy stood up on the wagon seat beside his father, gaping pop-eyed at the approaching curtain of white-dark-lightning. He was thirteen or so, but slim and blond and pretty as a girl, and Cyrus had heard tell how most times he didn't even go to school because the other boys tended to make fun of him for it. "I think I see a twister!" he cried – he even had a girl's sweet voice, unlucky for him. "A snow-twister!"

That couldn't be... but sure enough, when Cyrus squinted, he saw thin funnel-shapes spinning down through the raging clouds.

"It's between us and Juniper," he said to Franklin, though he doubted Franklin was listening. "Juniper may as well be gone off the face of the earth."

Virgil Howe came up sputtering, with a busted nose and the palms of his hands abraded just about down to the bone from his tussle with the mule's reins. He went to help George, who'd lain there dazed where he'd fallen.

"Have to find shelter!" Lars Rutger shouted. "We'll freeze!"

"There's nowhere!" Cyrus shouted back.

The Arlens' oxen let out great gusty snorts, set their feet, lowered their heads, and would not budge no matter how John Arlen whipped at them.

Gunpowder had finally quit rearing, and Franklin reached across to clutch at Cyrus' arm. "We can make it if we ride like blue hell," he said, this time not in a shout, this time in a low voice that only carried across the two feet of space between them. "Fast horses and no wagons, we can outrace that storm!"

Cyrus stared at him. "We can't all—"

"No, we can't all. But we can."

To the north, there was hardly any sky left at all. The top of that monstrous front was what Cyrus imagined some great wave would be like, a wave towering all the way up to heaven and bearing down like it was going to crash over them with devastating force. It stretched east and west as far as he could see. The very air shuddered in its awful roar, and it seemed all the breathable portions of that air had already been sucked away.

"Franklin!" John Arlen called. "Cyrus! You two can make it, you can ride for it, you can beat the front! Take Bella and the children with you!"

"John, no!" his wife wailed. Both the children were crying, terrified.

"You have to, Bella!"

"Go on," George Howe said. He still looked dazed, cradling one arm, his face as white as the rest of the world. But he spoke firmly. "John's right."

Virgil nodded, and wiped at his bleeding nose. It was squashed into yet a new lumpy potato shape, and gushing at a pretty respectable flow. "Get Missus Arlen and the kids out of here. Don't fret about us."

"We can carry them," Franklin said. "They're light enough."

"What about my boy?" Lars Rutger asked. "He's light... can you carry him as well?"

"Da—"

"Hush, Stefan."

"We'll try," Cyrus said. "But hurry!"

Quick as they could, they got Bella Arlen up behind Franklin and Stefan Rutger up behind Cyrus. Each man then took one of the little Arlens in front of him. The children had stopped crying, but only, Cyrus thought, because they were now too terrified to cry.

"Tell your mother I'll be home soon," Lars Rutger said to his son. "And tell your brother he's man of the house until I am."

John Arlen had thrown a blanket from the back of his cart over one child and his own coat over the other. He smiled at his wife and squeezed her hand. She sobbed.

"Now go!" Virgil slapped Gunpowder on the rump, which made the dapple-grey rear up again, almost dumping all three of its passengers, and causing Bella Arlen to scream.

"H-yah!" Cyrus gave Lucifer a kick. He had the reins bunched in one hand, the other arm tucked around the little Arlen. The Rutger boy proved strong for such a slim lad; he had such a hold on Cyrus that a blacksmith couldn't have pried him loose.

Lucifer surged forward in a burst of powerful speed. His shrill whinny drew a reply from Gunpowder, and then both horses were thundering back the way they had come. Dish-sized clots of ice and mud flew up from their racing hooves. Cyrus felt as he always did the terrific thrill of running Lucifer at an all-out gallop, but he'd never felt it quite like this before. Not with certain death bearing down on him.

The rush and roar of the storm was joined by the rapid thudding of hoofbeats and the wind of their passage hissing in his ears. Ahead was innocent-looking winter land and the distant – the dismayingly distant – wisps of smoke from chimneys in Thorpe Valley. The smoke rose against the sky like dark threads unraveled on white cloth.

Cyrus risked a look back and wished he hadn't.

Already, the seething white curtain had closed on the spot where the wagons had come to a halt. He could see small dark specks of shapes against it... and then he couldn't. They'd been engulfed.

He heard Bella Arlen scream and knew she'd been looking back as well. But then he felt Stefan Rutger pounding on his back, heard the boy shouting in his ear, saw his arm jabbing at something off to the right.

"There! There! Those saplings, see them? The Goss place is just over the rise!"

The Goss place? Cyrus knew no one by that name, but there was indeed what could have been a line of saplings visible above the snowy rise. Or a line of spindly sticks poking up in a crooked row. He'd seen similar lines of trees before, planted as windbreaks by homesteaders, and felt a flicker of hope.

Cyrus called the news over to Franklin, whose expression was set somewhere between grimness and devil-may-care. Though it meant leaving the track the wagons and larger animals had broken, it was a chance at shelter. And at the rate the wall of icy wind came roaring toward them…

Lucifer and Gunpowder veered from the track at their riders' urging. Their pace slowed as they had to force their way through deep drifts, and Cyrus was breathless with the fear that one of Lucifer's hooves would come down in a hole, breaking his leg like a dry twig and sending them all crashing to the ground.

But they crested the rise without incident, and saw the Goss place.

What was left of the Goss place, anyway. A shack, an old homesteader shack, lopsided and just about falling in on itself, huddled abandoned in the snow. It couldn't have been more than ten feet on a side, the walls of stick and sod, the roof askew.

"There's no one here!" Cyrus said.

"No, they gave up on it, went back East. It's shelter, though!"

Shelter.

The front bore down, and if anything it was gaining in speed and strength as it swept into the narrowing gap of the valley. Cyrus swore he could see snow on the ground being whisked upward into the maw of the storm. An ominous white darkness – he wouldn't have thought such a thing was possible, but there it was – turned what had been mid-morning into a premature dusk.

"Hurry!" Franklin shouted.

Cyrus dismounted in a clumsy half-slide, holding the little Arlen to his chest. He floundered through the snow toward the shack. The door had fallen partway in, wedging in the opening at an angle with snow piled atop its slant and a gap underneath. He pushed the little Arlen through the gap into the shack, seized the other little Arlen from Franklin and did the same, then turned to him and Stefan.

"Help me with this!" He grabbed the door.

Together, the three of them were able to dump off the snow and wrestle it aside enough to clear the doorway.

"In!" Cyrus told Stefan, giving him a shove. "Lead the horses!"

"Cy, it's coming!" Franklin caught his shoulder so hard it hurt.

The horses had a squeeze of it getting through, and with all of them inside it would be so crowded they'd barely have room to draw a breath, but Cyrus wasn't about to leave Lucifer out to face the blizzard, and he knew that Franklin felt the same about Gunpowder. And, he realized somewhere in the back of his mind, they'd be glad of the generous body heat of the two big animals.

"Where's Missus Arlen?" Stefan asked from inside. "They want their mother!"

"What?" Cyrus peered past and around horses, seeing the two small children with their arms around each other and their tearful eyes wide.

"She..." Franklin whirled and cursed. "Bella! Bella Arlen! Come back!"

Cyrus saw her about five yards from the shack, impossible to miss with her green dress and yellow shawl vivid against that white-dark ominous roiling mass. She stood facing away from them, facing the storm, with her arms down at her sides, as if simply waiting for it to snatch her up.

"John!" she called. Her bonnet had blown off and hung by its ribbons against the back of her dress. Her hair streamed, witchlike, in the rising wind. "John!"

"Shitfire and save matches!" Cyrus cried.

"Get inside!" Franklin broke into a run. "Stay with them, I'll fetch her!"

Then the blizzard was upon them.

THE OTHER SCHOOLMARM

Mumma-Dadda didn't let them go to regular school.

Mumma-Dadda said they wouldn't be welcome, that the white folks wouldn't want them in school with white-folks' children. Mr. Kradenmeyer from the next place over, for instance, who didn't even want his kids so much as playing with the little nigrah neighbors.

Mumma-Dadda said Mr. Thorpe wouldn't take too kindly to them sitting in the schoolhouse he paid to build, neither, and listening to the teacher he paid to hire.

Tessa Burdock wasn't sure she believed it – and Reverend Erlich preached otherwise – but she would never dare argue back to Mumma-Dadda.

So they just made their own school.

There was a wood-lot ravine at the back of their property, with steep rocky sides and overhanging trees and a skinny waterfall spilling into a skinny creek. It was a good place to bring the pigs to snuffle around for nuts and mushrooms on fattening fall days... a good place to splash in the creek and enjoy the shade when summer's heat came on... and just a good place to play whenever their chores were done.

In winter, of course, the waterfall was like sugar-candy and the creek was a ribbon of ice... but the trees kept most of the snow from falling all the way to the bottom, so the ground stayed bare and loamy, deep with dead leaves and pine needles.

Two springs ago, they'd discovered that an opening behind a boulder led into a shallow cave, big enough for them all to fit comfortably. The walls were dirt rather than stone, the ceiling was crisscrossed with tree roots and sometimes dropped loose a wriggling worm or two, and it got muddy in rainy weather... but none of that stopped the Burdock kids from claiming it as their own.

The boys had wanted to use it as a secret hideout and a fortress against Injun raids. The other girls wanted to play house, and make-believe they were grown up mommas with husbands and babies of their own.

Tessa, though, stood fast and got her way. It was their very own school. And she was the teacher.

Her brother Lester thought he should be, on account of how he was thirteen, more than a whole year older than Tessa. That was plain silly. Lester was no good with letters and worse with sums.

Besides, it had been Tessa's idea.

They'd dragged in logs and arranged them in rows like real school benches, and made a real teacher's desk by propping an old board across two upended wooden crates. There was a real stool for the teacher to sit on, which Dadda said they could have. They had some flat rocks to be slates, and some burnt-ended sticks for charcoals. They had a kerchief on a stick to be their very own flag. There was a dented old cowbell that Uncle Cyrus had given them, telling Tessa that if she was going to be a schoolmarm, she needed a good bell to call her students.

It all didn't quite take away the disappointment Tessa always felt when she saw the other children walking out to the real schoolhouse in the meadow, but it helped some.

She remained hopeful that one day soon, Mumma-Dadda would change their minds and let them go like everyone else... she looked forward to hanging her coat in the coatroom, bringing the teacher an apple, reciting her lessons, and doing all the things school children got to do.

Maybe she'd even become a teacher for real, when she was older. She'd heard that Miss Emma got twenty whole dollars a month, and nobody gave her guff about not being married or anything. That, Tessa thought, would be a fine life.

Until then, she had her own school, and it'd just have to make do.

That morning, Mumma-Dadda woke them early because of the wondrous warm change in the weather. Everyone had work to do. Dadda and the boys tended the pigs, Mumma and the girls tended the house, and Uncle Cyrus saddled Lucifer to go to town. Hard work, but they'd done it quick, and after, Mumma-Dadda turned them loose until lunchtime.

School! She had been fit to bust with excitement, the first school day in weeks and weeks! Couldn't wait to get back to their lessons!

Except then Lester and the other boys hadn't wanted to have school. Lester and the other boys wanted to have snowball fights, and go sliding on burlap sacks down the hill.

Boys.

But then the littler girls up and announced how they didn't want to have school either!

"We had to stay inside forever already!" Nancy had said, sticking her bottom lip out in that stubborn way she had, the way that made her look exactly like Mumma. "It's stupid to go sit in a dirty-smelly cave after we been inside forever already!"

So, it was only Tessa. She sat on her stool, swinging her feet, looking out at the empty rows of log benches. Looking at her board desk, which had the burnt-stick charcoals all tied up with twine in a neat bundle, and the cowbell sitting on a cracked china plate Mumma had given her.

She'd brought her book, her only book. It was a real school reader; Mary Thorpe had gotten a new one this year and given Tessa her old one. Tessa reckoned that this was proof how the Thorpes couldn't be that against nigrahs, not when Mary would give her a nice school reader and ask nothing in return.

Nice, having a real book. Sometimes, Uncle Cyrus brought back newspapers, magazines and catalogs from Juniper, and that was fine, that was good, but a real book was better. Tessa hoped to have a lot of books when she was a grown-up.

Why, she would have piles more books than Miss Emma, the real schoolteacher. She'd have as many as at Reverend Erlich's house... he had one whole room just for books, which had awestruck Tessa to being jawdropped the time she'd gotten to go along out there with Uncle Cyrus to deliver a letter from Back East.

Yes, she'd have a room like that in her own house someday.

A room with bookshelves halfway to the ceiling...

She only realized she'd drowsed off when she woke with a start and a gasp. That was no way for a teacher to behave, falling asleep at her desk with her head on the open pages of her reader! Thank goodness none of the others had been here to see, or they—

The school-cave had gotten very dark, and there was a horrendous howling-wind noise outside. It sounded like a train going over a trestle and through a tunnel both at the same time.

Tessa blinked into the gloom, wondering how long she'd been sleeping, had she slept the whole day through and it was dusk already? If she hadn't come home for lunchtime like Mumma had said, she'd be in trouble for sure. Dadda might take her over his knee.

Why hadn't anybody come to get her? They knew where she was.

Then she shook off the last foggy cobwebs and realized that it wasn't dusk, it was something else. The air had gone cold, not so cold she could see her breath but much colder than it had been when she first got there.

A snowstorm... a bad one... like the ones she heard the old-timers talk about, the Winter of '80, when Tessa had been too young to remember.

She left her stool and went toward the entrance, finding that she had to walk with care and feel her way in the suffocating chill of darkness. When she looked out past the boulder that partly sheltered the cave mouth. The trees along the sides of the ravine were thrashing this way and that. Snow blew everywhere. Branches creaked, cracked, fell.

"Lester!" Tessa shouted. "Rufus! Isaac! Dadda? Anybody?"

Given that she could hardly even hear herself, she wasn't surprised when she heard no answering shouts.

THE GOAT-SHED

laire Erlich never would have thought the day would come when she'd be tired of reading, but, lo and behold, here that day was.

She must have read every book in the house that winter, it seemed like. Or, at least, every book in English. Uncle Edgar had some written in Latin and French and other exotic languages. Someday, she hoped, she'd be able to read those ones too.

But, for today, she was more than ready for a change.

It felt good to get outside, into fresh air that wasn't so cold it tried to snatch the skin right off her face. It felt good to be busy and industrious, active.

As soon as her aunt and uncle left for their stroll, Claire went to work, wanting to surprise them when they returned.

There were the goats to be herded into the pen so she could muck out their shed, a fresh hay bale to be broken down and spread on the floor. Later, the mangers piled with alfalfa, she would set to the milking. There was the house to be opened to rid it of stale stuffiness, mattresses to be hauled onto the porch for an airing, clothes to be washed and hung on the line. There was kindling to chop and firewood to stack.

Hard work, lots of chores, but Claire did not begrudge a one.

She did not begrudge anything about coming here from St. Louis, had no misgivings except for a vague worry that her parents, if they went looking or sent letters, would not know where to find her.

This possibility, however, she knew was remote.

Her mother, Carrie, had left them when Claire was still a little girl, claiming that she had never been meant for a homebody's life. She'd been meant for New York, the stage, the theater! She'd send them programs and playbills, and once she was famous, she'd send for her daughter. Claire would have the fanciest dresses, go to all the best parties, and maybe become an actress or singer herself!

A few programs and playbills had indeed arrived, and did indeed list the name 'Cariella Early' among the credits... in the chorus, or as 'Third Chambermaid' or 'Woman on Train.' The letters became briefer, and terser... further and fewer between... until the last one had arrived some seven years ago now.

They had married young, Randall and Carrie, Claire knew. Married young and had a baby right away. "You came along about two months premature," Aunt Ruby once told Claire, with a slight, knowing smile. "Many first babies to young couples married in haste are born premature."

Randall Erlich did his best, but eventually decided he hadn't been meant for a homebody life either. Or for the life of a laborer in the brickworks, long backbreaking hours at miserable wages. Turning his daughter over to the care of his brother and sister-in-law, he'd announced his intention to make for the Yukon. He'd strike it rich there, panning or mining for gold.

He, too, had written regularly to start with. He'd even sent a tiny gold nugget, so small Claire could fit it on the moon of her pinkie fingernail, as proof that wealth and fortune were on the near horizon.

Then his letters also slowed, grew shorter and more sporadic, and finally stopped.

She often wondered what had become of them, and if they even remembered that they had a daughter. Did they have other families now? Had Cariella Early, after being the darling of New York, married a European prince? Had gold-rich

Randall Erlich settled down in the Yukon with some plump, cheery Eskimo woman?

Or, as her imagination suggested in darker moments, had they met more unfortunate, morbid fates?

Claire shivered from her grim turn of thought.

She finished pinning the wash to the clothesline, then noticed that the goat pen was empty, just snow pocked with cloven hoofprints and littered with droppings. The goats, who'd frisked so eagerly to be let out of the shed, had now all gone back inside. She heard their familiar bleating as they jostled for position.

Another shiver struck her and this time she realized it had nothing to do with her thoughts, grim or otherwise. A distinct chill replaced the balmy change to which they'd awakened. The air went somehow glassy, crystalline and brittle.

To the north, a great hollow hissing sound grew louder and louder. The treetops shook, shedding hailstorms of ice. A turbulent black wall of clouds loomed into the sky. Lightning, the strangest lightning Claire had ever seen, flickered and flashed. Fine, stinging, spitting granules of snow pelted down. Her skin prickled as it seemed every hair tried to stand on end.

Abandoning the wash-basket, she ran for the house and began slamming shut all the doors and windows she'd propped open to air the place out. She hadn't had time to chop kindling but the hearth and stove were still hot, she could build up the fire—

Aunt Ruby and Uncle Edgar weren't home yet.

Dread filled her with cold as if she'd swallowed a pile of snow.

They were spry for their age, but...

What should she do?

Wait?

Go after them?

She knew where their strolls usually took them, but could she find them?

The blizzard struck, engulfing their little homestead in freezing white wind and shadow. The walls shook. The windowpanes frosted over into blank eyes. Claire lit a candle, put the kettle on the stove, and hung a cook-pot on the iron hook by the re-stoked fire.

This storm was worse, and by far, than any they'd had all winter.

And they were out somewhere in it, Uncle Edgar and Aunt Ruby.

Just a walk, their daily stroll, not leaving her the way her parents had, but still they were gone.

They would come home. They had to.

Uncle Edgar would tell her to wait, and pray, and have faith.

She brought his Bible from their bedroom and set it by his chair.

Wait, and pray, and have faith, yes.

Also look after matters until they got back. She'd have hot coffee brewed, and soup ready...

In the shed, the goats began bleating again, but with none of their usual familiar quality. They bleated in agitation, thudding and bumping against the wall where the shed butted up against the house. Imperious matriarch Nonna's distinctive blatting rose above the others, indignant.

Claire remembered the outer door between the shed and the yard, which still stood open. The goats had known, had sensed the storm and gone inside, but not even Nonna was clever enough to shut the door.

She was, however, clever enough to complain about it. In high queenly dudgeon, as Aunt Ruby would have said.

A side-door connected the shed to the kitchen, which let Claire see to the goats' feeding and milking even in the worst weather. She went through, smelling clean hay, alfalfa, and milk.

Why, the silly things just could not make up their minds!

Despite the shrieking blizzard, a logjam of goats clogged the shed door, pushing and shoving and milling about. Those nearer the back were trying to get out, while those at the front found the bitter cold not to their liking after all and tried to reverse their course.

"Oh, you ninnies," Claire said, with a gentle chiding affection. Setting the candle on the high shelf with the milking pails, she waded into their midst. She nudged them aside until she reached the opening.

The bitter cold was not to her liking, either. She'd gone to her chores in a simple gingham-cloth dress, the sleeves of which she'd unbuttoned and rolled to the elbows as exertions warmed her body. She hadn't even bothered with a bonnet, let alone coat or gloves.

Daisy, one of Nonna's daughters, sweet-tempered but if anything far from clever, resisted Claire's urgings, even though the ice was already forming clumps on her hairy hide. She squalled and protested until Claire finally had to pick the goat up in her arms, grunting from the effort. Daisy, kicking and struggling, acting more terrified than anything else as Claire lugged her into the shed.

"You're icing over!" Claire told her, feeling like she was icing over herself, her breath freezing on her lips, her eyes painfully watering. Her teeth chattered like dozens of woodpeckers at work in her head.

She groped for the latch-handle, hauled the door shut, and her numbed hand stuck to it so that when she pulled away, it was with a tugging sensation that left some of her skin behind.

The goats crowded around her, their sturdy round bodies welcomingly warm. They were still skittish, of course, long-pupiled eyes rolling, nostrils flared. She hugged and patted them, murmuring comforting nonsense.

Gabriel, the biggest billy, did not join the herd but stood squarely a ways apart from them. His posture was stiff, legs braced and horned head lowered. Nonna stamped and snorted beside him, clearly still in that state of high dudgeon. Their attention seemed fixed on the shed's far corner.

Something... was there.

In the hay. Something... furry, and white.

FREEZING TEARS

Hilde Renneke cooked when she felt uneasy.

She had been uneasy all morning, uneasy since waking with a start well before dawn in the narrow cot that was her bed.

As a result of her uneasiness, there was a beef-and-potato pie baking in the Dutch oven, a bowl of dried apple slices soaking in sugar-water to be made into a cobbler, and fresh biscuits ready beside the last pot of strawberry preserves. The interior of the sod house was so warm as to be almost uncomfortable, and filled with tantalizing aromas.

Oh, how she wished the rest of the family would come in!

But her sons — dutiful Klaus and poor simpleminded Jorgen — and her grandson were out in the hayfield and cowbarn, bringing cartloads of fodder back for the cattle. Her daughter-in-law Johanna had taken advantage of the warm spell to go over to the Rutgers' farm with a full butter crock, hoping to trade for some eggs. Her granddaughter had gone off to school with the teacher who boarded with them.

So, Hilde was alone.

The soddie was small to start with, and when all seven of them were in it, always seemed even smaller.

Now, with just her, it felt too large, and too empty.

She wished they'd come back inside.

She wished they'd stayed inside to begin with. She'd asked them to. She'd told them of the uneasiness with which she'd awakened, and that it was not a good day to venture outside. There was an unlucky feeling in the air.

Everyone else thought she was being superstitious. She was in her sixties – exactly how far, she wouldn't say because she knew Johanna would give her that look. The one she couldn't stand. The sort of pitying look reserved only for the helplessly feeble.

It had been difficult, going from running her own house to answering to Johanna. They butted heads from time to time, as any two women will. Such as this morning, when Kirstie hadn't wanted to put on her winter garments before going to school. Johanna would have let her go as was, but Hilde had insisted.

And Johanna had given Klaus that look. The ever-so-slight upward roll of the eyes and ever-so-slight shake of the head, the one that said, "Klaus, your mother is a doddering old fool."

Hilde loved her daughter-in-law, and she was grateful to Klaus and Johanna for taking her and Jorgen in after Heinrich had died. But that look...

When the sound began, it first made her think of the Atlantic crossing all those years ago, the endless violent crashing of waves on the steamship's hull. The flames in the stove gave a startled leap, then guttered madly.

Moments later, the entire soddie bucked as if shaken by a tremor. Bits of soil fell in a gritty patter from the ceiling. A huge invisible fist thudded against the plank door.

There was a small window dug into the north wall, covered by hide stretched over a wooden frame, and it was blown inward by the buffeting force of wind and snow. Icy granules struck Hilde in the face, stinging like a handful of thrown broken glass.

She gasped, eyes watering in the sudden freezing gust. Grabbing up her shawl, she slung it partway around her body and held the rest out over her arm, shielding her head as she made her way to the window. She picked up the hide-covered frame and fought to wedge it back into place. It was like trying to cram a stopper into a gushing pump-spigot, but finally Hilde got the window blocked and used lengths of firewood propped as braces.

In just that short a time, her face felt numbed and frost-scoured. The bib of her apron was so dusted with white that she looked like she'd spilled the flour. She was breathing in ragged gulps, and trembling.

Klaus and Jorgen. Johann. Out in the hayfield... or in the barn?

"*Bitte, Gott,*" Hilde said, crossing her frail hands over her chest. "Please God, they were in the barn when it hit. Let my sons and grandson be safe."

And Johanna? Could she have reached the Grangers' house already? It was a goodly way, almost a mile, and she was lugging that heavy butter crock. Had she seen the approaching storm in time to take shelter? Had she tried to turn back?

She went to the door. It was well-made, the planks fitted so that there were barely any gaps between them, and what gaps there were had already caked over with snow and ice. The crosswise wind pummeled it with glancing blows like stones skipped over a pond.

Hilde wrapped her shawl even tighter and opened the door. Snow swirled in, fine as sand. Her gingham skirt whipped and flapped against her legs. She looked out and could only see a furious world of white.

There should have been a clothesline strung between trees just ten or twelve paces from the door. Johanna had hung out some washing before leaving for the Rutgers' place, but Hilde could not make a single piece of clothing, not even the bold color of Klaus' red flannel shirt. Either the wind had already swept everything halfway to Nebraska, or the sideways-blowing sheets of snow were too thick to let her eyes reach even that far.

"Klaus!" she called at the top of her voice. "Jorgen! Johann!"

The wind seemed to sweep her words halfway to Nebraska as well, before they'd more than finished leaving her lips.

"Klaus!"

She was freezing, all the warmth snatched from her body, all the heat from her morning's cooking already snatched from the house. Blinking at tears that wanted to freeze on her cheeks and eyelids, Hilde had to retreat and struggle the door closed.

They had to have gone to the barn. If they had been out in the fields...

Hilde wiped her face with the edge of her shawl and steeled herself. She had crossed the Atlantic with her husband and sons, she had endured the hardships of the prairie on their first hardscrabble farm... droughts, grasshoppers, wildfires, and blizzards that must have been as bad as this. She hadn't fallen apart when two of her boys had died — one from illness aboard the steamship, the other years later in a place called Gettysburg — or when Heinrich had fallen from that ladder and broken his neck.

The fire was almost out. She stoked it until it was blazing, and held her icy hands as near to the flames as she could without roasting her own skin. She put on hot water for coffee and tea. They would need something warm to drink when they came back. And dry clothes... she hurried to lay out dry clothes. The activity helped calm her, but all too soon she was done and did not know what else to do.

What seemed like forever passed, and nothing changed but the hoot and howl and whistle of the dreadful wind.

Klaus was a sensible man. He would have gotten them to the barn in time. Unless he'd been too worried about the cows. He could be stubborn that way. Without the cows, the Rennekes would have no milk, no butter and cheese, no excess to sell or trade to their neighbors. The cows were their livelihood.

More important than his own safety? Hilde feared Klaus might think so. More important than his own son? When he only had two surviving children left to him?

That made her think of Kirstie, at the schoolhouse. Emma would have to keep the children there. Emma might be plain but she was far from stupid, and she'd know that they couldn't dare go out in weather such as this.

The door thudded again, but it was not the wind, it was an irregular thumping kick, as of a man's boot. Hilde ran to open it.

Another whirling torrent of wind and snow came in, but in the middle of it was a lumbering figure. Head-to-foot white, a walking snowman unlike the stick-armed, coal-eyed ones the children sometimes liked to make.

"Jorgen!" Hilde cried.

"Mutti?" He had Johann up a-back, the boy clinging with arms around Jorgen's neck and Jorgen's coat unbuttoned so it would go around them both.

Hilde glanced from them to the open door. "Klaus... where's Klaus?"

He shook his head, shedding snow from his hair. Hilde looked at the open door again, and though she hated to do it, pushed it closed. They would all freeze in here like hams in an icehouse if she didn't, she knew. Then she turned her attention to Jorgen and Johann, brushing off the snow.

Jorgen had lost his hat. His face was chalk-white with a grey-blue tinge around his lips and at the tip of his nose. His eyes...

She almost fainted from the horror of realizing that his eyes were frozen shut, the lids sealed together by a glaze of mingled ice and tears.

Johann, whose face had been sheltered against his uncle's broad back, was pale with a hectic flush in each cheek and teeth that would not stop chattering. Hilde freed them from the coat and helped Johann down. He stood, staring at her as if unsure who she was or where he was.

"What happened?" she asked. "Ach, Jorgen, your poor eyes!" He reached up as if to prod at them with his fingertips and Hilde stopped his hands. "No, no. Don't touch them. Sit here by the fire, turn your face toward the fire. Let the heat do it but you do not touch. Mind your Mutti, Jorgen Renneke."

He nodded, and let himself be led and sat and turned toward the fire. The snow on him was melting, dripping to the floor, making puddles.

"F-f-f-f-f-f," Johann said. "Father!" he blurted out. "Father's still outside."

"He didn't come with you?"

"Th-th-the c-c-c-cows."

Slowly, piece by piece, she got the story from them. They had been in the field, letting the cows paw with their hooves and push their muzzles into the snow to get at the grass underneath while the two men and Johann uncovered the white humps of haystacks. They'd forked hay into the cart, which did not roll so well in the deep snow but Jorgen pulled it like an ox just the same.

Then they'd felt a change in the air. Klaus looked to the north, shouted and pointed, and they all saw the roiling cloud wall bearing down on the valley. They'd moved fast but with purpose, herding the cows back toward the barn, and were almost there when the storm overtook them.

Klaus had ordered Jorgen to take Johann up on his back, under his coat, and make for the house. He would, he said, secure the cows and follow after. They hadn't gone more than six steps when they realized they couldn't see the house, or the barn, or any other landmarks to guide their way.

"Uncle Jorgen told me to cover my head," Johann said, his teeth having ceased their chattering and a more natural color beginning to return to his face. "He just put his head down and walked, Oma."

Again, Jorgen nodded. The melting ice dribbled from his eyelids, trickling like tears. He fidgeted, but minded her and did not touch. "Couldn't see," he said. "Couldn't see nothing. Couldn't hear nothing. Just kept walking until I was home."

"Father should be back by now," Johann said.

Hilde brought him more tea, and a heaping serving of the beef-and-potato pie. Her smile felt threadbare. "He must've decided to stay in the barn with the cows."

"What about Mother? And Kirstie? And Miss Emma?"

Her smile frayed a little more. "I don't know, *liebling*. I don't know."

SHRIEKINGS

Lettie had been supposed to be fetching a can of apricots for Mrs. Thorpe, but Sam had followed her into the pantry to steal a few kisses.

She'd resisted, but not very hard.

Kisses led, as they always did, to more.

Sam Thorpe was some years younger than her, and in her head she knew he would marry some well-off man's daughter, a shopkeeper or a lawyer mayhap. But in the deep corner of her heart where she kept her most secret secrets, she let herself treasure the fancy that he might, just might, might possibly...

They went at it quiet-like, or as quiet-like as they could be. With Lettie bent over the apple-barrel, her skirt and petticoat halfway over her head, and Sam behind her, holding her by the hips. He'd been panting hard and trying not to moan too loud, and she'd been wiggling her bottom and gasping how good he was and how much she loved him...

Then, the storm. Almost, it seemed, blowing the house clean off its foundation. Howling screeching wind, snow and ice like pellets of birdshot against the walls and glass windows. The milk-water sunlight blotted out, dimming the rooms as if everything had been wrapped in layers of cotton. Freezing drafts whirled through every gap and cranny.

And Mrs. Thorpe started in shrieking. She had been in a state all morning, crying and not wanting the children to go to school, but Mr. Thorpe had laid down the law and so off they had gone, all but Sam and Baby Grace.

Lettie and Sam went running out of the pantry, tucking and straightening and buttoning their clothes on the way through the kitchen. By the time she and Sam reached the sitting room door, his father had Mrs. Thorpe by both wrists, holding her back when she would have pelted straight out into the blizzard.

"You sent them to school!" she screamed at him. "You sent them, I wanted them to stay, I told you I had a bad feeling but you sent them out there!"

"Don't you raise your voice to me!" Mr. Thorpe shoved her at her chair, shoved her into it so she sat down hard with a cough as the breath was knocked out of her.

Breathless she might have been, but she bounced back up from that chair and sucked in a lungful, then let it out so loud it nearly cracked the window-glass. "They'll die!"

And, sakes alive, she went for Mr. Thorpe's face with her fingernails!

Lettie was astounded, absolutely thunderstruck. She couldn't have budged if she'd been told to, which she wasn't, as it wasn't her place to interfere in family quarrels.

Mr. Thorpe cuffed his wife backhand across the mouth. She flew at the chair she'd just sprung up out of, collided with it, and both she and the chair crashed to the floor. A little table tipped over as well, breaking a vase and a teacup, spilling tea onto one of Mrs. Thorpe's ladies' magazines.

"Father!" Sam took a step, then stopped as if he didn't know any more what to do than Lettie did.

His father ignored him regardless. His gaze was fixed sharp on his wife, as she heaved and gasped and sobbed and struggled to right herself.

"How many times must you defy me?" Mr. Thorpe asked, almost too soft to hear. She had scratched his cheek, not badly, no more than a shaving nick, but enough to draw blood. "How many times must you contradict me, and make me look the fool?"

"The children!" sobbed Mrs. Thorpe. "At the schoolhouse, they're at the schoolhouse, they'll never get home in this!"

"Be silent!"

"I knew this would happen!"

"I said be silent, woman."

"They'll be fine," Sam said, taking another step, squaring his shoulders and mustering himself up all brave. "They'll know to stay indoors. Peter's smart as a whip, and Emma's—"

"Shut your mouth, Samuel William Thorpe, or I will shut it for you," his father said.

"But, Father—" he began.

This time, it was Sam he struck, and no mere backhand cuff. Mr. Thorpe hauled off and punched his son, mashing the lips that Lettie had only a little while ago been lavishing with kisses. Sam slammed into the wall, knocking an unlit lamp from a shelf so it broke on the floor.

His name jumped to the tip of her tongue but Lettie held it, afraid of Mr. Thorpe's wrath. Sometimes he acted as though she was not there at all, and she hoped with all her might this would prove to be one of those times.

Groaning, looking addled, Sam slid down the wall until he was sitting with his back propped against it and his legs splayed out.

"I will not be lectured by a boy, even if he is my own son," Mr. Thorpe said. "I will not be defied and made a fool of by any woman, least of all my own wife! Never forget who's the man of this house! Never! I won't allow it!"

"We—" Mrs. Thorpe said from the floor. She had managed to hitch herself up on one elbow, her ruffled skirt bunched and petticoats rumpled around her knees, stockings showing and one shoe fallen off.

"What did I just say?" Two long strides took him across the room. He dropped to a knee, swatted away the arm that Mrs. Thorpe raised to defend herself, and reached for her neck.

She had such a slender, white, graceful neck, Mrs. Thorpe did. She always wore a dainty frill of lace at her collar, or a cameo on a satin band, or for the most special occasions a string of pearls. Hers was a proper lady's throat, suitable for dabbing just a bit of fine perfume below each ear.

Mr. Thorpe's hands latched around that fine slender throat and squeezed. His thumbs dug into the soft white flesh.

Mrs. Thorpe made a dreadful choked sound. Her eyes were huge and her whole face turned the color of a ripe strawberry. She clawed at his hands, gouging them, drawing more blood, but he would not let go.

"Father, no!" Sam, still reeling from hitting the wall, crawled over to them. He pulled at his father's sleeve, then at his wrist, trying to break that strangling hold. "Lettie, help me!"

Lettie, still in the doorway, couldn't move. Sam was calling to her, calling for help, but she couldn't move. All she could do was stand and stare at the mess, and try to make sense of what she was seeing when no sense would come.

She remembered hoping that she'd be allowed to look at the magazine when Mrs. Thorpe was done; though Lettie had never been very good at reading, she did so love to see all the pictures of what was new and fashionable in New York and San Francisco. Now it was all soaked with tea, and she'd have to dry and smooth the pages but they'd still be spotted and stained.

Mr. Thorpe let go with one hand long enough to clout Sam aside. Sam's head struck hard against the corner edge of a wooden chest. There was a solid thud like a hog being felled with a sledgehammer, and Sam grunted and went limp.

"Sam!" This time, his name did burst from Lettie, in a squeak that could barely be heard above the battering of wind and ice.

Mrs. Thorpe's heels — one stocking-clad, one shod — rattled on the floorboards as her husband resumed throttling her two-handed. She was beyond strawberry-colored now; she was purple as a plum and her eyes had rolled up. Her fingernails scrabbled more weakly, then stopped and her arms drooped away to lay at her sides with her tender palms upturned and helpless.

Mr. Thorpe crouched over her with his grip clamped tight and his hard-edged face twisted into a sneer-mask of pure hatred. Although he was not a powerfully-built man, his arms had bunched so that the seams of his shirt were straining fit to split.

Then he let go of his wife with a violent shoving-away gesture. She collapsed rag-doll and unmoving. His breathing was harsh, ragged. Hers was... not at all.

He turned his head to look at Sam, sprawled unconscious beside the chest. He turned his head the other way until his gaze found Lettie.

Lettie felt her galloping heart miss a beat. All she saw in Mr. Thorpe's eyes was murder. He had killed his wife, he might have killed his son... a hired girl was nothing compared to that. Especially when she had seen him do it.

"Come here," he said.

Her head made a quick little side-to-side shake as if of its own accord.

"I said come here, girl." He rose to his feet.

She stepped back and was in the doorway.

"Lettie," he said, turning her own name into a warning.

Another step and she was in the hall.

"Don't make it worse for yourself," Mr. Thorpe said.

She spun and ran for the front door.

He shouted after her with mingled rage and incredulous laughter. "Where do you think you're going? It's a blizzard out there, you stupid sow!"

Lettie yanked and the door flew open, blown inward on a gale of sheeting, blinding snow. She couldn't see more than half a foot, couldn't feel anything but a cold so intense it sucked all the warmth straight out of her body. Swarms of ice like frozen rock salt pelted her skin.

But Mr. Thorpe was right behind her, so Lettie closed her eyes, crossed her arms in front of her face, and ran.

SNOW DOGS

So close... they had been so close when Henry felt the shift in the wind.

If not for the gruesome discovery the dogs had made, he wouldn't have been nearly that close when the storm struck. Seeing that gutted half-eaten carcass wedged high in the fork of that branch, and witnessing his dogs' reaction to the scent they'd caught, convinced Henry to hasten his steps. Whatever had done that wasn't any animal he wanted to meet.

As he'd moved, he'd wondered... what had done it? Not a bear, for certain. Not a wolf, either. No bobcat was big enough or strong enough to drag a dead sheep up a tree.

He'd been damn near running, or as near to running as was possible in the deep snow, by the time he emerged from the woods and saw what was coming at him from the north. That roiling whiteness, shot through with crackles of cold lightning, and snow sheeting up from the ground like a wave.

The Adams place had been only another quarter-mile or so ahead. The big rambling farmhouse... the long low sheepfold and outbuildings... a line of washing hung out to dry... people rushing about, herding the sheep toward cover, slamming shutters they must have opened to take in the pleasant morning.

He ran. Yelling and waving his arms. Looking like a fool, no doubt. His knapsack of wooden carvings jounced on his back, the top coming unlaced and scattering horses, trains, dolls, spoons and eagles into the snow.

The dogs, barking, barking as they ran.

The farmhouse in front of them.

So close.

He almost made it.

Maybe he would have made it, if not for Nugget and the girls. The old dog and the half-grown pups couldn't keep up with Queenie and Chief, for all that Chief was still addled from charging headlong into the tree trunk. For that matter, they couldn't keep up with Henry. They were exhausted.

Henry couldn't leave them. He slowed, and when slowing didn't do the trick, he picked up Buttons in one arm and Bows in the other. They were small enough to be carried but too heavy for him to carry them far, and he wasn't sure how long he would be able to go on.

"Come on, boy," he'd said to Nugget. "Come on!"

And Nugget, lumbering, wheezing, looking as if he was going to collapse at any time... struggling through the snow... floundering in it... stumbling... trying to get on his feet again.

Henry went back for him, lugging the girls in his arms. He didn't know what he would do when he reached Nugget, but that hardly seemed important. He couldn't leave his good old dog. Couldn't leave the poor youngsters. Who'd brought them out here, if not Henry Greeley?

The white roar filled the world, swallowed them up.

Snow so fine-ground it was like sand dashed against Henry's skin, into his eyes. It froze his mouth and nose with each attempt at a breath. He could feel Buttons and Bows shivering against him, as much from terror as from the temperature. He could feel Nugget against his legs.

He was blinded by snow, deafened by snow, numbed by snow. Every sense he had was stifled, choked with ice.

Somehow, Henry dropped to his knees without falling flat. He hugged the pups and ol' Nugget close to his chest, hunched over them to protect them as best he could from the raging frost-wind. Then he felt the other two press up to either side of him, Chief and Queenie, leaning against him, all five dogs and Henry huddled together.

How long did they stay like that? Henry couldn't guess. Time had lost all meaning in that harsh whirling hell of sleet.

He just put his head down, burying his face in Nugget's fur, and waited for it to be over. One way or another, it'd soon be over.

Then it wasn't over, but it was lessened. The wind and snow eased off.

But instead of relief, Henry had a sudden vivid memory of Aggie and how she would get when she was really set to give him an earful about something – the dogs, more than likely – she'd start off with a bit of hollering, then she'd pause for a deep breath and to ready herself to deliver the real tirade. Gathering strength.

Queenie barked. Chief shoved his muzzle into Henry's armpit and gave an urging push.

Henry straightened up. Snow fell in clumps from the back of his head and neck. It was caked into every crease and fold of his clothes. Ice clung to his hair.

Again, demanding, Queenie barked. She gripped Henry's sleeve in her teeth and tugged, then let go and moved a few feet away and looked at him with undisguised impatience.

Just past her, just visible in this reprieve of clearer air, Henry saw the Adams clothesline. The washing that had been hung out to dry was ice-glazed and frozen stiff as panes of glass.

He let go of the girls, who ran to Queenie and tried to crowd under her the way they'd done when they were tiny furball puppies. It took all the strength Henry had left to burrow his arms under Nugget and get the old dog on his feet.

The weight of the air changed. Again Henry thought of Aggie, and how this was the inhalation before the shouting really commenced.

More snow streamed past, sideways in a slashing gust. Henry hooked one hand into the bunched looseness of fur and skin at the nape of Nugget's neck, and groped out with the other until it found the clothesline.

He shuffled his feet, following the line, following the line to the house, with the dogs crowded around him. The wind rose and rose. There was a terrible moment when he reached the post at the end of the clothesline and had to forge straight on and hope for the best.

His shin cracked against a hard edge and Henry flailed and shouted as he fell over something — a wheelbarrow? — and went headlong into the snow. He lay there, thinking that was it, he was done, he could do no more, he was used up and worn out, he'd just lay here until...

Gripping. Pulling. His body moving.

Chief and Queenie had him by the shoulders of his coat. Their full weight was thrown into the effort. They were dragging him. Dragging his body, inch by painstaking inch. His face plowed up a heap of snow.

He could make out the sounds of shrill barking, of paws and claws scrabbling on wood. He thought he could feel another dog bumping at one of his trailing boots.

Then he heard a man's amazed voice.

"Sweet Jesus our Lord and Savior," it said. "It's Henry Greeley!"

CAUGHT AFIELD

Was she still going in the right direction?

Which direction was she going?

Which direction was the right direction?

Johanna Renneke stumbled onward in whatever direction she was going. So long as she continued to put one foot ahead of the other foot, she was bound to go somewhere, wasn't she?

If that somewhere turned out to be the Rutger house again, fine and well, so be it.

She'd tried to turn about when the blizzard struck, since she had only just left. She'd said goodbye to Anna Rutger and thanked her for the eggs, told her she hoped that Lars and the boys enjoyed the butter, and away she'd gone.

Then, the blizzard.

Johanna had known immediately that she was in trouble. Not just trouble. Deadly danger. Her linsey-woolsey dress, flannel petticoat, calfskin shoes and the crocheted shawl her mother-in-law had made were fine for a regular winter day, but not enough to ward off this chill.

The Rutger house... she should have been there by now. It hadn't been that far. A short walk. If she'd accepted Anna's offer of a second cup of tea, she would have still been sitting in Anna's cheery kitchen when the weather turned. They could have waited it out together, she and Anna. They could have had each other for company in their worry over their families.

Or would she have tried to get home anyway? Would she have told herself the storm wasn't as bad as it seemed, and taken the risk?

She could have asked Hans Rutger, Anna and Lars' strapping twenty-year-old son, to go with her. Hans would have offered. Hans might already be out searching for her. Anna would have sent him.

Would Anna have sent him?

Anna must be worried sick. She'd seen her husband and younger son leave that morning with their wagon and horses, headed for Juniper. There was no way they'd reached the town before the storm struck. It would have overtaken them on the road. If Anna had Lars and young Stefan to be worried about, the last thing she'd want to do would be to send Hans out into this weather as well. Lars and Stefan could be lost to the storm. She wouldn't want to lose Hans when he was all she had left.

But could she keep him indoors if he was determined to find and help Johanna?

What would she have done in Anna's place?

The cold made it hard for her to think. All she knew was that she hadn't reached the Rutger house yet. She hadn't reached her own house. She hadn't reached anything she recognized, she couldn't see, could barely breathe. Her arms were hugged tight around her body, one hand up to hold the edge of her shawl over her face to keep her skin from being scoured off by the ice that seemed ground to powder, like sifted flour, like crushed glass. The egg-basket's handle was tucked in the crook of her elbow, the basket itself thumping against her hip with each step. How cold would it have to be before the eggshells cracked?

Her family...

Dear God, and Kirstie had gone to the schoolhouse with Emma.

What about Johann? With his father and uncle... but where? In the house? In the barn where they would at least be warm and sheltered? Out in the fields? What about the cows? If the cows were left to this freezing fury...

It occurred to her that she was not being so cruelly buffeted by the wind and fine-ground snow. She rubbed at her eyes — they stung with pain, and she realized that the very moisture of her tears was half turned to ice. She blinked until she could see, then looked around.

No Rutger house. No Renneke house. No houses at all. She didn't know where she was. She'd not only gotten turned around, she'd wandered off and now there wasn't a familiar landmark in sight.

More tears, these ones brought on by dismay rather than the cold, flooded her vision. Johanna hitched in a breath, bit her knuckle — her hand was so numb that she could hardly feel the pressure of her teeth on her own flesh — and wiped her eyes with her shawl.

She looked around again, and saw the white-covered hump of a haystack not far off. She was in someone's field... but whose? Which way was the house? If she missed it, she would continue wandering until her legs gave out. She hadn't come to any fences that she could follow...

The wind whooped again. Johanna smothered a sob against her fist. Before she could lose sight of it, she faced the haystack and fixed its position in her mind. Not far. It wasn't far.

The blowing whiteness engulfed her, but Johanna continued on the path she'd tried to fix in her mind. She came to the haystack and almost went weak-kneed with relief. Her stiff-fingered numb hands dug at snow and then at hay, scooping out a hollow in its musty heart.

Soon she had made a hole in the haystack large enough to let her crawl inside. She scraped and patted hay over the opening, then drew herself into a shivering ball.

BLIND PANIC

A man had no business hitting a woman. Just wasn't right. Wasn't done.

She fought him like a wildcat, though. Hissing, spitting and clawing.

He was afraid he might have to hit her, if —

Her knee hiked up between his legs. Hard.

If her aim had been better, the struggle would have ended right then and there. As it was, his inner thigh took the brunt of the blow and he was able to hang onto her.

Barely. Cloth tore. The same vivid green cloth that had let him see her when the wind eased. Just green glimpses in the snow. Moments earlier, in the full sheeting fury of the storm, he could have passed within inches of her and never even noticed. She was a slight thing, not hardy, not sturdy.

"Missus Arlen!" Franklin hollered. "Bella! Stop!"

He'd reached her, hauled up her limp body, seen the ghastly white pallor of her face. He'd shaken her, shouting how he was going to get her to shelter, take her to her little ones, out of the storm, someplace safe. She couldn't go after her husband in this, he told her.

That was when she had gone wildcat on him. The limpness was gone and the bundle of frenzy replaced it. She was a sackful of maddened snakes writhing in his arms. At first he couldn't make out what she was saying, and then when he could...

Well...

He was fairly sure she called him some words he'd never heard a good respectable woman say... words that he would have sworn on a stack of Bibles that a good respectable woman shouldn't even know.

A man had no business hitting a woman, but...

Her fingernail hooked the corner of his eye, an eye already raw from blinking away the scouring granules of snow. Pain sliced. Vision blurred. Wetness — tears? blood? — gushed and then froze. His eyelid, reflexively squeezing shut, stuck that way.

He hit her.

Thud and his fist met her chin. Bella Arlen uttered a startled-sounding grunt and went limp again. He held her in one curled arm, the other hand going up to probe at his eye. All he felt was an icy mess, and his fingers were too numb to learn much of anything helpful.

Lord-have-mercy, had she blinded him?

Franklin lifted her and stumbled around until he thought — hoped — he was facing back the way they'd come. Back toward the falling-apart homesteaders' shack where Cyrus would be with the horses and the kids.

It was just beyond belief. All of it. Beyond belief.

His feet were numb. Snow had worked its way down inside his boots, soaking his wool socks. The chill of slogging through the drifts permeated the leather.

Could it be that not an hour ago, he'd been riding along not a care in the world? That jug of applejack whiskey going from man to man, everyone in fine spirits... Gunpowder prancing beneath him and champing for a good gallop... so glad to be escaping his uncle's farm for the day, and not having to take his troublemaking little cousins with him because they were off to school to be their teacher's problem for a change... some spending money in his pocket...

And then the storm. Filling the sky. Devouring the world.

They'd gotten that gallop, but not at all in the way Franklin had hoped. A life-or-death race to outrun the storm, with the precious cargo of other men's families clinging to their saddlehorns.

If the Rutger boy hadn't pointed out the Goss place, they would have been swamped by the blizzard with no hope of survival. As it was, their chances might be slim.

With Mrs. Arlen going mad the way she'd done...

Well, she and Franklin's chances might be less than slim, now.

He dragged his benumbed feet, squinting with his good eye. Or his less-bad eye, as it might not be frozen shut, but it wasn't seeing so well either. Mrs. Arlen was not heavy, but she pulled at his arm. He supposed that if her clothes were as soaked and frost-caked as his, he must be hauling an extra hundred pounds' worth of ice as well.

The wind, which had briefly stilled as if bracing itself, whistled around him. Snow that had been falling straight in dense fluffy flakes began to whirl.

He couldn't see the Goss place.

It didn't seem he had gone that far in pursuit of Mrs. Arlen. Five or six yards at the most. They should have been to the shack by now. Such as it was. But beggars couldn't be choosers, as the saying went. A shack that was on the verge of falling down was still better than no shack at all.

Franklin remembered the Gosses as a hatchet-nosed man and his beady-eyed wife, both of them the sort to blame anyone and everyone else for their misfortunes. Quick to borrow, slow to lend, and never a friendly word. They'd built a shoddy house, planted some shoddy crops that failed, raised some shoddy cattle that died, and finally moved on for something easier.

Funny to think that his very life might now depend on them.

On second thought, not funny. Not funny at all.

Shivers set in, his own muscles betraying him as they twitched and leaped and jittered under his skin. He tried to control it and couldn't. The shivering didn't rouse Mrs. Arlen, who hung draped over his arm like a rug on a line.

A rug heavier than an anchor, and about as cumbersome. If he dropped her, left her...

Not his wife, after all. John Arlen would have to understand.

Hell, John Arlen might not mind so much being widowed, if the talk about him and those saloon girls was true.

Be a different matter if this was Kate. Kate, he'd carry to the ends of the earth if he had to. Never set her down so long as there was an ounce of strength in his body.

But how would he feel if this was Kate and he was someone else? Would he want that someone else to leave his Kate behind to die in the snow?

This wouldn't be Kate.

Oh God and he had been joshing with Cyrus about that girl in Juniper, the one with the dark ringlets and the blue dress.

Here was his punishment.

He was going to die in this blizzard. He'd be found frozen to death with another man's wife, a woman he'd been entrusted with and failed to save. Kate would learn about it, and what would she think of that?

He staggered and fell to his knees, too plain bone-weary to take another step.

Seemed he could almost hear someone calling out to him.

"Franklin!"

Kate?

Didn't sound much like Kate's voice the way he remembered it.

"Franklin Wood!"

Not Kate. A man. What man?

"Answer me, damn it!"

Cyrus?

He tried to call but a croak was the best he could do. The air he sucked into his nostrils crackled and hurt. Felt as if it was crystallizing in his lungs, making delicate frost patterns.

"Cy..." he wheezed.

"Franklin, where are you? Can you hear me?"

He tried to stand. His snow-laden clothes were too heavy. Hands, feet and face were so numb they might've been carved from cold clay. He tried to crawl toward the voice but couldn't tell which way to go. Couldn't see. Both eyes were blinded now, or the flying white grit was too thick. Didn't matter. He couldn't see. Couldn't call out. Couldn't walk.

Then someone was grabbing him, supporting him, keeping him from folding into the snow. He heard Cyrus' voice — unmistakable this time — shouting directly into his ear.

"Hold on, Franklin, hold on, I got you."

He tried to answer but only another croak came out.

"Stay with me," Cyrus said. His arm was around Franklin, guiding him. "It's not far. Keep moving."

"...shack..." Franklin said.

"Almost there. I had a rope in my saddlebag. Tied it off and came out to find you when the blizzard let up some. We just gotta follow the rope back. Can you make it?"

He nodded his ice-crusted head. Leaning on Cyrus, dead-cold feet plodding, he let himself be led blindly through the snow.

"That was some crazy-brave of you," Cyrus hollered into Franklin's ear. "Shame you couldn't find her."

Only then did Franklin realize that his arms were empty, and Mrs. Arlen was gone.

THE HIRED MAN

Brody O'Connor heaved a sigh.

"Now or never, laddie," he said.

He was not eager to leave the barn. It wasn't solely because the barn was a stout structure, sheltered and warm and companionable, while the pasture he'd have to cross was a blisteringly cold wasteland.

Mr. Thorpe was not going to be pleased by this turn of events.

Which wasn't to say that Mr. Thorpe was ever particularly pleased by much of any turn of events; Brody was well aware that he worked for a man who could find the one wooden nickel in a barrel full of free money. Give William Thorpe a new suit of fine wool tailored to his size, and he'd take exception to the color. Give him an orchard of apples and he'd see only the one that had a worm.

Nothing was ever good enough. Nothing was satisfactory. Every drawback and flaw was disaster heaped upon catastrophe and insult added to injury. The whole world was against Thorpe, fate spat in his pie, nature laughed in his face. If it was not one thing, it was another. And another. And another atop that.

This storm was the latest in that long line of offenses, affronts, indignities and drawbacks cruel fortune had aimed at Mr. William Thorpe.

Brody wondered if it might not even be the proverbial last straw. This might be the end of Thorpe's vision. Another terrible winter, when so many people had only made it through the last one by the skin of their teeth...

Wasn't his worry. He was the hired man. He had a space to sleep in the loft above the barn, he ate well enough, and he received a tolerable decent wage. If the work was hard, and if his boss treated an Irishman with less respect than he gave the nigrah hog-farmers down the way, well, what else was there to expect?

The worst Thorpe could do was fire him, and if that happened, Brody knew he could find hard work and scant respect just about anywhere.

He had just finished mucking out the barn when he saw the northern sky. It was a hectic time getting the livestock all under shelter before the snow began to dump down like someone emptying a flour sack, but he'd made it with bare moments to spare.

Nobody would fault him if he stayed where he was. He'd done his duty. He'd seen to the valuable animals. Thorpe wasn't going to be accusing him of shirking, and demanding Brody pay back the cost of some fool cow that had wandered off in the snow and frozen to death... not this year.

Wasn't like he could do much other work in this blizzard, either. No reason he couldn't go up to the loft where his cot and trunk were, and uncork the jug he'd been saving. A day like this needed a good pull at a jug.

But he reckoned he should go over and check how they were doing at the house, and if he was going to do that, now was the time. There was a lull in the storm's power, maybe an easing-up or maybe a pause while it gathered its strength.

Several days of January thaw, had he said? Running his mouth to Mr. Thorpe, as if he had the slightest idea?

Foolish.

No doubt, he'd be reminded of it henceforth, and in sharp tones.

Still, he could cross on over there and see if they needed him for anything. Not for Thorpe himself, but there was Missus Thorpe to think of. She'd be anxious about the little ones if they hadn't yet come home from school, and somehow Brody doubted she'd find much in the way of sympathy from her husband.

Brody buttoned his coat clear up to his neck, pulled his hat low, and wrapped his scarf around his face until he had covered everything but his eyes. He had a real struggle to get the barn door open — snow had blown into a drift against it that went halfway up — and then out he went with a knobby walking stick in one gloved hand to prod ahead for secure footing. He didn't want to set his foot in a gopher hole and turn his ankle.

He followed the fence, thinking that if the wind did come up again and he found himself snowblind, he'd be able to use it to lead him to safety. Right away he discovered that even with the air stilled, he could hardly see more than ten yards in any direction. The snow hadn't stopped, but it was sifting down steadily.

At what he judged to be about halfway to the house, Brody got the chills all down his spine, and it wasn't from the cold. The very corner of his vision caught something moving through the falling whiteness... something huge... something dangerous... something that moved with a silent graceful speed.

It leaped the fence.

For a heart-freezing instant it was above Brody, an immense pale blur soaring effortlessly over his head and showering him with snow. He felt the muffled thump of its landing reverberate up through his feet and legs. He saw its shaggy head with flattened-back ears swing around to regard him. The frosty exhalation of its breath washed into his face.

"Yahh!" Brody shouted, and whacked at the creature with his walking stick. "Yahh! Yahh! Yaaaah!"

The blows were more like a farmer's wife walloping away at a mouse with her broom than a man in a fight, just a flurry of wild ill-aimed strikes. Most missed completely or glanced off the hard bone or thick fur, but a couple were solid enough hits that the white beast flinched away and snarled.

It swiped at Brody, snagging his coat and ripping long rents in the wool. It swiped again, knocking him against the fence.

The creature's mouth gaped, revealing more teeth than Brody had ever seen.

"Yahh!" he shouted again, with a spurt of intensified terror that gave his arm a surge of strength.

The end of the walking stick clacked against the teeth with an impact that jarred it out of Brody's grasp and left him weaponless. But the creature whipped its head back, screeching, and he saw that one long tooth had broken off, leaving a rough stub.

"Yahh! How do you like that?"

By the way it whirled and bounded from him, vanishing into the snow as the wind once more began to rise into a furious scream, Brody decided the creature hadn't liked that, no, hadn't liked that much at all.

UNPREPARED

They warned her about the snow, about the cold.

And Stella Hadden, fool that she was, had laughed it off.

"I've seen snow before," she'd said. "How bad can it be?"

That had been in the summer, when Dan sent for them to come from Sacramento to be nearer to Fort Winston. A compromise; she'd wanted to take lodging at one of the bunkhouses at the fort, but he'd figured she and Danny would be happier at a place of their own.

It meant a change from citified life, to be sure, but it also meant that his father, Dean, who ran the trading post in Far Enough, would be close on hand to help out. Which was nice and all, if not quite the same.

Both of them had warned her, tried to prepare her for the the harsh realities of Montana winters.

Now she knew. Better than she'd ever wanted to. The first dusting had come mid-September, before the leaves were even off the trees and the crops fully in!

September!

She'd been tired of it by Thanksgiving, and half-to-death sick of it by Christmas. Here it was, January, and...

"Momma!"

She mumbled something in reply that even she herself couldn't quite make out. The bed was a cozy nestle of comfort, missing only a man's strong body to make it perfect and complete. She burrowed down, eyes still shut, the quilt bunched over her shoulder and ear.

"Mommmmmaaaaah!" Danny dragged the word into a whine that went straight through her skull. He tugged at the quilt.

Stella peeled one eyelid open and peered at a small sturdy dark shadow-blotch, a Danny-shaped shadow-blotch against the dull red embers glowing from the woodstove.

Brr.

Cold.

Less cold than before, but still by no means pleasant. Too cold for her liking. Left to her own doings, she would have stayed in bed.

For that matter, left to her own doings, she'd just as soon sleep all winter like a hibernating animal.

Danny, however, was bright eyed and full of beans, excited, delighted, eager to get outside and play.

Days and days of being pent-up in the cabin by snowstorm after snowstorm had worn tiresomely on them both. Soon, Danny had grown fussy, bored with any diversions or amusements she could come up with, and it had taken a toll on her patience.

He'd bounded around the cabin in his nightshirt, chattering, while she blearily clambered out of bed, washed, dressed — she pulled on an old pair of Dan's flannels under her skirt — and stoked the stove.

Grampa would come see them today for sure, Danny said.

Him and Grampa would play outside in the snow, he said.

They'd make a snowman, and throw snowballs, and ride on his sled.

"Nobody's going outside until after breakfast," Stella told him, mixing the batter for flapjacks.

Hopefully, she thought, her father-in-law would pay them a visit. They were down to about the last dregs of the maple syrup... coffee would be welcome, though Dean had told her supplies of that were running scarce all around the valley... if there was any to be had, she knew, he'd bring some.

He was a good man. There for them as often as he could be, making the walk from town whenever weather permitted. It was comforting, knowing she could rely on him. Dan was strong, but his father, his father was steady. A rock.

Danny kept up his chatter the whole time he devoured a stack of flapjacks that would have done credit to a grown man's appetite. Then he ran to get dressed, and commenced an impatient waiting by the door.

Dean could go outside with his grandson to play; the two of them could keep at it until their noses were red and running like a primed pump, only coming in when she called them to the table.

Stella herself could barely stand it long enough to dash to the chicken coop, let alone the outhouse. She'd never been gladder for the ceramic necessary.

But, this was how it was, and this was how it would be. Except for when Dean visited to help with the chores and bring provisions, they might not see another soul until the spring.

"Momma?"

"Yes, Danny?"

"Why don't Grampa live with us?"

"Well, Grampa's got his own place, his room above the store."

"Then why don't we live with him?"

"Because we have this cabin he and your daddy built for us."

Though, in truth, Stella did sometimes ponder those very questions herself. With Dan away at the fort for months on end, it'd be nice to have someone there all the time instead of just when Dean could make the trip.

Or, as long as she was being honest in her own mind, she'd just as soon have other people close by. Nearer neighbors... other women to talk to, share the cooking, have sewing circles... other children for Danny to play with.

"We'll make a houseful of playmates for him soon," Dan had said. "I grew up without any brothers or sisters, and it was lonely."

The prospect of trying to manage an entire houseful of rambunctious youngsters through a long winter such as this was a daunting one, she had to say. However, at the same time, it was strange to think how in another couple of years, Danny would be old enough to start his schooling. He'd go off half the day, and then what would she do?

The damp, drippy morning went on, and when Dean still hadn't arrived, Stella let Danny go with her to collect the eggs. The chicken coop, a low slant-roofed shack against the back wall of the cabin, was filled with a dim, musty, doleful clucking.

"When will he be here?" Danny asked.

"Maybe he's busy at the store," Stella said.

"Can't I play outside by myself?"

"No, Danny."

"Can't you play with me, Momma?"

"It's best if you wait for Grampa."

He sighed like the weight of the world settled on him, and commenced to waiting again.

But Dean still didn't come.

Then the blizzard hit.

From nowhere and with no warning, the blizzard hit. A white-black wall of freezing fury, just crashing over their cabin like an enormous wave. Stella, startled, screamed as if a rat had scurried over her shoe. Danny burst into tears, his own storm, a tempest, a tantrum, brought on partly by fright and partly by frustration.

She did her best to reassure him, letting him cry himself out until he fell into an exhausted slumber. After she tucked him into her bed, she paced fretfully around the room, rubbing her hands together in an effort to warm them.

And she'd thought it was cold before?

This cold... this cold was the worst yet... it wicked all the heat out of the room, up the chimney or through the very log walls... no matter how much more wood she piled into the fireplace and stove. Soon, both were blazing, and Stella still felt cold.

What if Dean had been on his way and got caught in this?

Surely not. He, and others in town, were far more weather-wise than she'd ever be. Half their conversations had to do with it.

She burrowed under the quilts with Danny, draped an arm around him, and drifted off to sleep as the fire crackled, spit and snapped.

THREE SISTERS

Sarah did just have to be stubborn!

Stubborn, and willful, and mule-headed, and ornery. There was a big word for it, too, a fancified word, but Maggie Jordan couldn't bring it to her mind just now.

Lordy but it was too cold even to think!

She couldn't remember having ever been this cold. Not ever!

Cold all over.

Her whole face hurt from it, or at least the parts of her face still had feeling.

Where she wasn't cold, she was numb.

Her feet, near as she knew, might as well have been stuck in blocks of ice. Each step through the snow was a trial of heaviness and lifting.

Shivers wracked her upper half, clattering her teeth together. She knew her hand was still linked with Polly's on account of how she saw her arm stretched out, and their fingers folded around each other, but it was like seeing someone else's arm, hand, and fingers. Beneath the buttoned sleeve-cuff of her blouse, her skin was a horrid kind of bruised-looking pale.

They'd gone to school without their winter clothes that morning. No coats and gloves, no hats and boots. And why not? The day had dawned so wonderful warm and mild compared to the past weeks, almost springtime-warm!

Oh and to get outside! Out of their four-room house where the lot of them had about been climbing the walls after being storm-bound so long... Polly fretful, Ma tired and sickly with the baby on the way, Sarah bossy and...

Contentious, that was the big word!

...bossy and contentious, Pa bored and irritable, and Maggie herself just plum tuckered from trying to keep the peace.

So and off to school they'd gone, the three of them, with Sarah carrying their slates and pencils, Maggie their readers, and Polly the lunch-pail of jelly fold-overs. In their calico skirts and pantaloons, leather shoes, knee-stockings, and muslin blouses, with bonnets tied over their braids.

Polly, only five, didn't care so much for school as she did being able to play with the other children.

Sarah considered herself too grown-up to need schooling. She didn't get along well with Miss Emma, said the teacher thought herself above the rest of them, too smart for her own good. She also said how Miss Emma was a drab heifer who couldn't catch a husband with a bear trap and would be stuck an old maid until the end of her days.

Mean talk from a girl who wasn't very pretty herself, not to mention who had her heart set on handsome Hans Rutger for all he was twenty years old and never given Sarah even a look... but Maggie wasn't about to point out any of that.

On another day, Sarah might have argued to stay home. After all that bickering with Ma, though, Maggie suspected Sarah got it in her head that if she did go, that'd show Ma how much extra work Sarah took on, and how little appreciated she was.

And then, coming home early because of the blizzard, that'd show Ma not only how well Sarah could look after her sisters, but how unable Ma was to manage on her own.

Except they weren't home yet. It seemed to Maggie as if they'd been walking miles and miles. Their house was just a ways east of the schoolhouse; they'd crossed the creek bridge with no troubles... what must have been ages ago, now... why weren't they home yet?

She'd been trudging with her head bent down to keep the worst of the wind-lashed ice out of her face, rarely lifting it further than was needed to see that Polly was still ahead of her. Wincing, squinting, she tried to look around.

Snow. Wild white snow everywhere, as far as her stinging, watering eyes could see. Her tears froze to a glaze on her cheeks. It felt like the jabbing pinpricks of a thousand tiny needles.

What if they were lost?

What if Sarah had gone and gotten them turned the wrong way and they were lost?

It was hardly possible to consider, but what other explanation was there?

Yes, they were walking at a snail's pace, bogged down by the snow caked to their skirts, their feet ice-block numb... just the same... their house... the school's peaked roof within sight from their own porch...

How could they be lost that close?

"Sarah!" Maggie called.

The icy wind snatched the breath, voice and word out of her mouth.

They couldn't keep going like this! Least of all Polly, who'd already fallen over twice so they had to pick her up and set her right again on her legs.

"We have to go back!" Maggie tried again, shouting at the top of her lungs.

Was that an answer?

"Sarah! Sarah, it's too cold, we have to go back!"

Again, she didn't know if Sarah heard, understood, answered or not. Maggie stopped in her tracks and tugged at Polly's arm to get the little girl's attention. Polly stumbled to a weary halt.

The colors of Sarah's calico skirt appeared out of the blowing snow. The three of them huddled together, exhaling on their clasped hands. The air inside them didn't feel much warmer than the air around them.

"What are you doing?" Sarah demanded. Her lips looked blue where they weren't split with tiny cracks that had crusted over in iced blood. "Why'd you stop? We're almost there!"

"Are we?"

"I... we gotta be!"

"Shouldn't we be there by now?"

"It only seems farther."

"Sarah, we're freezing! Maybe if we went back to the school—"

"No! We're going home!"

"We're freezing out here!" Maggie repeated. "We could die!"

"You shut your mouth!"

Polly just stood between them with her head down and a steady shiver quavering her entire body.

"We're lost!"

"We ain't! Come on!"

With that, Sarah began marching again, leaving them no choice but to blunder along in the path she broke through the drifts.

But, after only a few steps, Polly faltered. She went to her knees again, which meant plunging waist-deep in the snow.

"Sarah!" Maggie dropped to her knees as well, hooking her free arm around Polly's waist in an effort to hoist her upright.

Sarah either didn't hear, or ignored Maggie, because she kept going until Polly was half pulled out of Maggie's grasp.

Maggie held on. Taking a deep enough breath to really shout her sister's name was like sucking shards of frozen, broken glass down her throat and into her lungs. "Sarah!"

The pulling ceased. Polly's arm extended into the tattered sheets of wind-whipped ice. It was a doll's arm, sticklike and stiff, as if it didn't belong to Polly at all. The rest of her pressed into Maggie's chest and stomach. She wasn't shivering anymore, but, somehow, Maggie knew that was a bad change.

A sudden great roiling whiteness barreled past. A huge, fast, rushing movement that made Maggie think of trains and avalanches, stampedes, and runaway white horses.

There was a hard yank, almost brutal. Maggie fell full length on top of Polly.

There was a shriek that didn't sound like the wind, and an abrupt slackness nearly as jarring as the yank.

Maggie struggled up, hauling Polly with her. The little girl's arm, still stiffly outstretched, ended in a hand hooked on nothing, fingers snapped and askew, jutting like a bundle of ice-coated twigs.

"Sarah?"

The wind howled.

The blizzard raged.

And Sarah was gone.

MANY MOUTHS

They'd done all they could think of to help the others find their way home in the storm. All they could think of, short of venturing out themselves.

That, Leo Kradenmeyer knew, would do little good, if not be suicidal folly outright.

It'd serve only to get more of them lost out there too.

His wife and their four oldest had gone out that morning, at first light of the mild day, to see if anything could be dug up and salvaged from the snow-covered mess of their fields. Even a handful of grain or some winter-shriveled vegetables would be a help.

The pantry was about bare. It had been burnt-flour soup for most of their meals lately, the ground barley flour scorched in a pan, with water and salt and pepper, and what lard they'd had left.

Wasn't much, wasn't much at all. Leo worried they'd be reduced to boiling tree bark and boot leather next.

Or killing the last of the chickens after all. Only three hens and one scrawny rooster had been spared the autumn slaughter, hardly enough to get the flock going again come springtime. The few eggs the remaining hens laid, small and on an irregular basis as winter-eggs were, couldn't do much to forestall the hunger of an entire family. Without the chickens, though, they'd not need to save back the feed, either... of which there also wasn't much left, but, better than nothing.

Better than some of what they'd already had to do.

The rats, for instance.

At the time, he'd been appalled, and ashamed.

To think it had come to this, when a man couldn't provide for his own... to the point when a rat one of the boys caught in the shed should be greeted with the delight only due a fat Christmas goose!

What he wouldn't give for a rat right now! Even a skinny one, stringy and tough.

Not that he'd say so. Not that he'd admit it, not to his wife, not to any of the children. Certainly and above all else, never to any of their neighbors!

Least of all to the Burdocks.

A man also had his pride.

Sometimes, all a man had was his pride.

His pride, his reputation, and the keeping up of appearances.

It would be a cold day indeed, a cold day in Hell, before the Kradenmeyers went begging. Before they let on just how bad their harvest had been, more corn-weevils than corn it seemed —

— even those, once Berta fried them up with spices so they sizzled and snapped, had been surprisingly tasty —

In the bowels of his heart, he knew that one of the reasons the middle children had clamored to go to school that day was less to do with learning their lessons and more in the hopes of some classmate being generous with the contents of his or her lunch-pail.

He knew it, and he didn't like it, but he also knew it was why he'd agreed to let them go.

No one had said so, of course. No one would.

Kradenmeyers did not beg, and they did not complain. They wouldn't dare whine about being hungry. They never let on how deeply in debt they might be, or how poor.

When the middle children, those from roughly ages eight to thirteen, asked permission to make the long walk to the schoolhouse, they'd even said themselves that since it was such a fine day, they didn't need coats and boots... omitting any mention of how few of them had ones that fit.

And then off they'd gone, leaving their fourteen-year-old sister to help Leo look after the youngest bunch of the brood, while Berta and the older ones went out to the fields.

They had eleven children, he and Berta, two each from their previous marriages and the rest together. The twelfth, they also claimed as their own, pretending Berta had given birth to him instead of acknowledging the shameful truth.

Step-brother and step-sister...

No. No one outside of this house ever need know.

Leo had come West on a tidy inheritance, his bankroll second only to William Thorpe's own. But, while he'd raised a bumper crop of children, the rest of his luck had taken a much more miserly turn.

An accident on the trail left him with a lamed leg. As a result, he'd been unable to see to his farm as well as he would have liked. He hadn't let that stop him building a frame house with glass-paned windows, also second only to Thorpe's. It had three bedrooms – one for him and Berta and whichever cradle-baby was youngest at the time, one for the boys, and one for the girls.

Year after year, the yields came thinner and thinner. Their livestock proved no luckier, beset by injuries and illness. Bit by bit, his savings frittered away, while they did their best to keep up the ruse of prosperity.

Once – only once! – his wife had had the temerity to suggest he approach Thorpe for a loan. Leo would hear nothing of it. Nor would he cotton, pardon the pun, to charity from their nigrah neighbors.

Now, this.

This lying warm spell, this false thaw preceding the worst blizzard of all time...

When the temperature plunged and the wind rose, Leo had realized right away that it was going to be bad.

The middle children, who'd left late for school after some dithering to be sure they'd all be presentable to their teacher, had barely been out of sight over the hill before the cloud-wall rolled in. It came like bales of black wool strung together with silver wire and white thread.

His fine frame house was nearly slapped from its foundation in that first roaring crash of wind and ice. As the toddlers screamed and the babies cried, Leo stood at the door with fourteen-year-old Louisa. They shouted into the blind white teeth of the storm, shouted after the children, shouted for Berta and the others in the fields.

When the wind snatched away their voices like wisps of smoke, they'd taken up the biggest pots and pans from the kitchen, then stood banging on those instead, banging like gongs, like cymbals, thinking that the sound would carry some farther and guide everyone home.

No one appeared.

Snow gusted in past them. It found every crack in the walls to form spidery fringes and cobwebs of frost. Shivering, their teeth chattering, their hands so numb they could no longer feel the pot-handles or the ladles with which they clanged them, Leo and Louisa had to retreat back inside and shut the door.

They set candles next, candles and lamps in every window, so the lights might serve as a beacon, if anyone could see further in that nightmarish whiteness than the tips of their noses. And still, no one appeared.

His wife, his family...

Out there in the blizzard. Out there in the fields, in the long snow-covered furrows where they would have been digging at the hard, cold earth, searching for any overlooked kernels of corn, grains of barley, onions or parsnips. Out there in the hills and gullies between here and the school, wearing the clothes that Berta's skillful needle kept from looking shabby, but without coats and boots, without hats or gloves.

Even indoors, the air soon felt near to freezing. Louisa bundled up the younger children and gathered them close around the stove. Leo fed it full, fed it until it glowed red-hot.

And still, they shivered.

If they were this cold, those outside wouldn't have a chance.

Through all of their hardships, they had not lost anyone yet.

Though it would mean fewer mouths to feed —

The very thought was unbearable.

FOUNDLING

Outside the goat shed, the blizzard continued to whoop and holler.

Inside, the goats continued their agitation, but Claire had been able to get Gabriel and Nonna moved aside enough to let her take a better look at the furry white thing that lay sprawled motionless in the corner.

A better look still didn't tell her for sure what it was. An animal, about the size of a raccoon but no raccoon... not a bobcat or lynx, not with that full brush of a tail... but no fox, either...

Blood matted its pelt in places. A scrap of fur stuck blood-pasted to one of Gabriel's horns. The billy goat, defending his home and his harem, must have attacked the intruder, head-butting, kicking and stomping it into unconsciousness.

Possibly with Nonna's help. Her horns, like those of all their does, had been disbudded to make the milking less dangerous, but she wouldn't let that stop her when she was in a temper. Nothing would get her in a temper faster than a wild animal, a predator, in among them, even when there currently were no kids in the herd.

Claire, holding the short-handled pitchfork she used to muck out the old straw, crept closer. She crouched. She prodded at one outflung, oversized paw. The leg moved with boneless limpness in response.

Such a paw... broad, with pale pads of flesh and those silky-fleecy white tufts of fur...

Not quite like a dog's or wolf's... not quite like a cat's either... like a bear's?

And the color, so white!

Any kind of animal could be born pure white, she knew. It was rare most times, but it did happen. Albino, it was called. She'd read about Indian tribes hunting sacred white bisons, and white stags in folklore, and there'd been an article in the newspaper not too long ago about a famous white bull being auctioned in Texas.

Then there were far north animals, whose pelts were normal color most of the year but grew in thick and white for the winter. Or like the seals and polar bears up past the Yukon, where her father had gone.

This, though, this didn't seem to be any of those.

She prodded it again.

At first, she thought it was dead, then saw its side rising and falling in slow, shallow breaths.

The more she looked at it, the more she became convinced that it was a young one, whatever it was. The proportion of the head to the body, those big clumsy paws, that rounded tummy...

A baby?

A cub, or a pup, or a kit, or what have you?

Separated from its mother, maybe even not weaned yet, lost in the storm and come into the goat shed following the scent of milk? Hungry and desperate, not accustomed to going without its meals, it might even have been lured to try and nurse.

Was that what had Nonna in high dudgeon?

Claire knew how territorial the goats could get. If a kid not their own tried nosing for the udder, that kid was apt to be sorry. Nonna was worst of all about it. She'd knock over her own grandchildren if they got so presumptuous.

Let alone some other creature altogether, some baby predator.

But if this was a baby...

If this was a baby, already the size of a raccoon or bobcat...

How big were the adults?

She stretched out a hand to touch it and found it so cool that, if not for the visible rise and fall of its breathing, she would have been convinced all over again it must be dead.

That coolness was the first impression to cross her mind, and then she felt how lush and soft its fur was. Softer than rabbit, softer than fox, softer than anything she'd touched before. Mrs. Thorpe had a cape with mink trim and Claire was prepared to say this was far softer, far more luxurious.

Gabriel tossed his head, snorting with renewed impatience. He pranced stiff-legged in a way that suggested he'd be rearing back and lunging soon, going to butt with those horns again. Nonna gave Claire a look that said either she better do something herself, or get out of the way.

Run it through with the pitchfork?

It was only a baby.

A baby what, though? A baby something dangerous, she could tell that much just by looking at it. Those big clumsy paws, broad-padded and tufted with fur, had the tips of undoubtedly sharp claws tucked between them. Its greyish muzzle was parted enough to show the suggestion of equally sharp teeth.

And where were its parents? What if they came looking for it?

She hefted the pitchfork, imagining how it would feel punching through the furry hide, scraping on ribs, plunging into that plump little body. She saw the blood from Gabriel's horns red against white and imagined more redness welling up in a horrible scarlet flow from around each of the tines. She imagined the pained, pitiful noises it might make if the jab didn't kill it instantly.

Shuddering with revulsion, Claire put the pitchfork aside and found an empty burlap sack instead. She arranged this on the straw so she could heave the limp body onto it.

That fur, soft as anything, so cool... only when her hands sank into the plush undercoat to get a grip could she detect any sort of living warmth. Wasn't that another reason the coats of northern animals were so prized, because they insulated, and kept the heat so well?

Half-dragging and half-carrying, she lugged the white creature through the connecting door and into the house. Though it still hadn't moved or made a sound, she took care to bind it down with some leather straps, then went back out to soothe the goats.

A few scoops of mixed grain into their mangers quickly had them most of them concerned with nothing else. She patted Gabriel, praising him, and scratched around his horns and ears. Nonna was less eager to forgive. Claire had to bribe and coax her with bits of dried apple until she relented.

Finally, the shed secure, she returned to their visitor. She tied a strip of cloth around its jaws — it did have teeth, and big ones too! — and set to seeing what she could do for it in the way of doctoring.

A wet rag served to clean the blood away. When she parted its fur to examine the wounds, she saw that its skin was a frosty grey hue, darker at the nose and lips and on the callused pads of the fuzzy feet. The wounds themselves were small, some swelling bumps split with cuts already scabbing over. She washed them and dabbed them with ointment.

What in the world would her aunt and uncle would say when they came home to this surprise in their house?

Aunt Ruby loved animals, was unfailingly delighted when birds flocked to the millet she scattered, and squirrels and chipmunks enjoyed the corncobs she hung out. But, for those same reasons, she wouldn't keep cats or a dog... she liked them well enough, when visiting neighbors, just couldn't bring herself to keep them. Her own cats hunting the birds, her own dog chasing the squirrels? There, she had to draw the line.

She picked the loose straw from its pelt, tempted to get a comb or her boar-bristle brush. In this better light, she could see the fine spikiness of the topcoat, as well as faint markings... dapplings in a shadowy pewter-silver... feathery stripings that almost looked blue.

So beautiful, so soft!

And so young, just a baby.

It twitched under the palm of her gently stroking hand. It mewled and squirmed. Its eyes opened. They were not the eyes of a white cat, not bright blue or amber or green. Nor were they the pinkish-red eyes her books said to expect of an albino. They were pale and at the same time somehow shiny, reminding her with a chill of the sky's color yesterday, before the blizzard, when those bright spots flanked the sun.

THE GAMBLE

veryone had always warned that gambling would be the death of him, but this hadn't quite been what Paul Trotter had in mind.

He felt as though he'd been encased in rock from the knees down. He had his arms across his chest and his hands buried in his armpits in an effort to keep them from becoming blocks of ice, but this made his balance even more precarious. His nose and ears had lost all feeling. They could have been sliced off him by some bloodthirsty Injun for all he knew.

It had started off such a glory of a day, too. He'd gotten up, his wife made a nice big breakfast of hashed browns, eggs and fried ham, and then he and Amos had gotten the animals seen to nice and early.

Hannah hadn't objected when Paul said Amos should take himself off to school while he went over to see if he could help out with chores at the Granger place. She was as glad to have them out from underfoot as they were glad to go. She planned to use the break in the cold to give the house a thorough cleaning, and she all but shooed them out the door with her broom.

Her glad to have them gone, them glad to go, and now not one of them might see each other ever again.

The wind and sand-fine snow were hundreds of tiny knife-edges, flaying the exposed skin between his scarf and the brim of his trusty felt Stetson. The wind would have liked to whisk the hat clean off him, but Paul had snugged the drawstring up under his chin tight as it would go. Felt like a gallows necktie, but it did keep his hat from flying away.

The scarf had its own problems. He wore it up over his nose the way he'd worn a bandanna as a dust-kerchief back in his ranch-hand days, but the trouble this time was not trail dust kicked up by a few hundred head of cattle. The trouble was that moisture from his breath collected on the scarf and there it turned to ice. It got weighted down. When he first tried to pull it loose, he learned the hard way that more ice had frozen the wool to his bushy moustache, and he damn near ripped himself bald-lipped.

His eyes were the purest misery. He tried to wipe away the ice that formed around them and only rubbed his skin raw. The eyes themselves were swollen with runoff like a spring creek, and the more they watered, the more ice formed, the more they swelled, and the more they ran.

Paul would have given just about anything right then for a cheerful campfire. The way it had been on the trail, back when he'd been a young man with no wife and no responsibilities. Cowboys gathered around the fire at night, sitting on logs or just hunkering there on the heels of their boots.

Ahhh... the muddy black coffee that could stand a spoon upright... big bowl full of beans cooked in pork fat and brown sugar... the bright gold campfire and a desert sky wheeling overhead with a million burning stars...

He sang a little, an old trail song, only half-aware that he did so. Then he smiled, and the smile tugged his iced-over moustache, and he stopped singing. What the tarnation was he doing? He needed to be thinking about finding shelter from this storm, not remembering the old days.

Maybe he should've stayed at the Granger place.

While he'd told Hannah he was going over there to help with the chores, the plain truth was there weren't many chores the Grangers needed help with. But Hannah never would have understood his real reasoning.

She'd gone all pious on him in the years since their eldest girl run off and the baby died. She took her comfort in the Bible, and the words of traveling preachers before Reverend Erlich came to settle in town. Hannah was the one who always spoke up as to how they should build a church, they had a schoolhouse and next they needed a church. Come spring, she'd finally get that wish.

No, she wouldn't understand one whit the real reason her husband needed to pay a call on Nelson Granger.

Gambling was a vice he'd picked up back in those trail-days. Not card-playing. Paul Trotter never could get his head around the skill it took to be a good card-player. Dice was his game. Pure chance. Pure luck of the toss.

Those hot, smoky saloons... men all crowded in shoulder to shoulder... sweat and leather and tobacco and whiskey... the rattle of dice, piano music, laughter, arguments... sometimes a fight, knife or broken bottle or gunshot... the smell of gunpowder and blood...

Nelson Granger also loved a good game of dice, and Nelson Granger always had a few dollars he was willing to wager. Some of those dollars had already made their way into Paul's pocket when Nelson's sister-in-law came hollering in that they better come look to the north, they better come look at the storm a'coming.

His numb, leaden foot must have struck up against something, because a jolt went up his leg and the next thing Paul knew, he was face-first in the snow. He came up sputtering, and crawled around until he could grope into the deep whiteness and see what it was he'd tripped on.

It was a big stone. The stone that bordered one end of his west field? Seemed like... seemed familiar... but it couldn't be because that stone was nowhere between his house and the Granger place. No way he'd gotten turned off course that badly.

Sure did seem like the same stone, though.

He got up, rubbed more ice – and torn skin – from around his eyes, and tried to sort himself out. If this was the stone... the house would be...

Damn blizzard. Damn winter. This never would have happened in the desert. The sun shining down so brilliant, baking into a man's flesh all the way to the bone. Metal too hot to touch, the fittings of a bridle, tools, stirrups, spurs. Rocks that could fry eggs on their surfaces. Sagebrush all dusty green and the heat rippling the faraway air like hazy pools...

Paul tugged down the scarf, despite what it did to his moustache. He was finally feeling warm. Almost too warm, not that he was going to complain. He would never complain about the desert sun again.

He loosened the drawstring and let his hat sail away into the wind. He opened his coat, then his collar. Much better. He'd gone all stifling there for a while. Overdressed for the desert.

Hot.

Too hot.

Not sweating, but burning up. It was so hot he could scarcely breathe, and he shucked his coat and popped the buttons off his shirt. It helped some, let him feel like he was taking air into his chest again.

He tripped again.

Same stone?

Couldn't be.

Sure did seem like... but it couldn't be. That would mean he was not only off course but going around in circles, and...

He was too damn tired to get up. Too damn tired to do much of anything except lay here and rest a little. Just a little. He'd set out again soon. Real soon.

Real soon.

SNAP-LIGHTNING

They had been in the middle of a spelling lesson, Miss Emma saying out the words for them to write on their slates, when there'd been a noise that made Kirstie Renneke think of the time she and Johann got an empty barrel and took turns rolling each other in it down Thorpe's Hill. A shaky-loud-rumbling-whoosh.

Everyone looked up from their slates. Miss Emma left off the spelling lesson to go to the window. When she didn't see anything on the east side, she went to the west side. When she still didn't see anything there, but the rolling noise was getting louder, she told them all to stay put and stepped outside.

Then Miss Emma did a kind of gaspy scream or screamy gasp. She ran back in. All the color had run right out of her face so she was the color of a bland cheese.

All the kids sprang out of their seats and tried to run to see what it was, but Miss Emma slammed the door before any of them were past the coatroom.

She started hollering at them to shutter the windows and for Amos to stoke up the fire good and hot.

"A blizzard!" she cried. "A blizzard heading straight for the valley!"

When the wind hit, it hit like a giant flung a spadeful of dirt against the board walls, except the dirt was white and cold. The whole schoolhouse rocked from it, and the icy-sandy-snow whirled in through every single crack and knothole. Everything went dark and eerie.

Some of the girls screamed, Kirstie among them. It was as much at being plunged into the cloudy white gloom as anything, and then they started to cry. The boys acted mostly excited at first, a blizzard being far more interesting than a spelling lesson.

Miss Emma sent those who'd worn their coats to get them and put them on, though most of them hadn't even bothered.

Oma Hildie had made Kirstie bring hers. Had argued about it with Kirstie's mother, who'd finally given in with an air of humoring her so they could have some peace in the house.

Now, in the warm coat, Kirstie wondered if Oma Hildie had known.

They all gathered close around the woodstove, but as big as the fire was, it still hardly held the chill at bay.

Sarah, Maggie and Polly Jordan wanted to go home. Their pa, they said, had gone to his smithy and stable to ready the wagons to help the men making the trip to Juniper. Their ma, who'd been poorly what with the baby on the way, was all alone and would be worried. Sarah was a big girl, almost as big as Miss Emma, a strong and stubborn farm girl.

That was when the arguments happened among the rest of them. They should all stay at the school. They should each try and get home on his or her own. They should go together to the nearest house. They should wait for someone to come for them. They should send one person for help while the rest waited.

Finally, when Miss Emma couldn't talk Sarah out of it, she said all right, since the Jordan place was close anyway, they could chance it. So long as they stuck close together and came back if it got too bad.

The rest of them, Miss Emma declared, would stay put and sit tight for now. Maybe the storm would blow itself out. Maybe it'd let up soon.

So, the Jordan girls left, holding hands all in a line, with Sarah in the lead, little Polly in the middle, and Maggie bringing up the rear. Maggie glanced back once before the snow swallowed them up from sight. Her eyes were wide and oh-so-frightened, but, when Sarah led, she followed.

Amos mentioned that they didn't have a lot of firewood, but Peter said they could bust up and burn the desks if they had to.

Then Cora wanted to know would they starve, and Miss Emma had them collect the lunch-pails to see how much food there was. Not much. Bread with jam, bread with butter, bread with honey, some dried fruit, a chunk of sausage, a slice of ham, a chunk of cake.

At first, it seemed like Miss Emma's decision to stay put was right. They had firewood and fuel, not a lot but enough, and they shouldn't dare risk going out when hardly any of them had worn their winter clothes.

If nobody came to get them and it meant they had to stay all night in the schoolhouse, well, what of it? They could sleep on the floor, and by morning, the worst of the storm would have passed.

The heat from the stove wasn't strong enough to push back the cold that found its way in through every crack. Snow dusted at the corners and edges of the schoolroom. A window-shutter was torn off one hinge and went flap-bang-flap-bang until Amos was able to fix it.

Miss Emma wrapped her own wool cape around Cora and Minnie, who were still crying.

Kirstie wasn't, but she felt like her eyes had a wide-eyed starey look that reminded her of the time Uncle Jorgen caught a rabbit under a trap made from a crate, a stick and a length of string. That rabbit had looked like one more fright would send it straight up to heaven, and Kirstie's eyes felt exactly the same.

When the battering wind had let up some, the arguments in the schoolhouse started again. All the air inside felt crackly, and when Ben went to add more wood, a bright snapping white spark leapt from the stove to his hand. It made him jump and yip like a dog, which would have been funny if it hadn't been so strange.

Elias said he was old enough to go for help on his own and he had to because he was Peter's brother and Peter — who was a bookworm but skinny and clumsy and always seemed to have sniffles or a cough — was getting sick. He was shivering worse than any of them, his nose was flowing like a river, and he said his throat felt sore.

James, the other Thorpe brother, was only six and too little, but he threw a tantrum about wanting to go with Elias. When his sister Mary tried to calm him, he bit her hand and pulled her hair, so Mary slapped his face, and then James commenced howling and blubbering.

In the middle of that, Billy and Tommy Wood exchanged a look and didn't have to say a word to each other.

Their home wasn't far either, they announced. They were older than Elias, and they knew their way. If girls could do it, they said, then so could they. They'd send help, and be heroes.

The others begged them not to, but the prospect of being heroes was more powerful. The prospect of arriving triumphant at their cabin and telling their father how brave they'd been, venturing through the blizzard to fetch help for their schoolmates... that must have been too much for them to resist. Everybody knew how Mr. Wood was a hard man to please, but this would almost have to make him proud. Or maybe they just didn't want to be shown up by girls, when Sarah and Maggie were brave enough to leave.

Even Miss Emma couldn't make them stay.

They'd slipped out quick, barely opening the door, but it was still enough to send freezing winds rushing through the schoolhouse. The whipping white snow swallowed them up almost instantly.

"Billy! Tommy!" Miss Emma shouted after them. "This is crazy, come back! Don't risk it!"

But they didn't come back. They risked it.

Amos busted up desks into a pile of wood and kindling. The little stove in the center of the schoolroom blazed red-hot enough to hold back some of the chill, though beyond that yard-or-so circle of warmth was another matter.

But someone had to keep adding the fuel to the fire, and the air was so cold-dry-electric that every time one of them approached the stove, loud white sparks snapped from the metal to bite their hands. They smarted, those sparks, and they scared the dickens out of everybody.

Minnie Granger got too skittish to sit near the stove, preferring the colder reaches of the room. "What if it strikes us dead like lightning?" she'd asked, and none of them could reassure her because none of them — not even Miss Emma — were feeling very sure themselves.

Soon the fear of those snapping sparks was such that they all flinched and cringed and hid their eyes whenever someone had to add more wood. Only Amos could do it, but not without wincing in anticipation, and not without a greater and greater reluctance each time.

So... they had fire, and wood enough to last all night if it came to that. It gave them heat enough to ward off the deadly cold. It gave them light enough to see by, even for Miss Emma to read to them by, in the white-shadow gloom of the blizzard's depths.

RAISING THE ROOF

rieda Bauhaus sat in the fireplace corner, half-wishing she was as deaf as her daughter and son-in-law thought her to be.

Lord, how they bickered!

His drinking, her cooking... his smoking, her gossiping... his indifference at keeping up with the chores, her always wanting finer shoes or a fancier bonnet... his reluctance to start a family, her insistence on caretaking for her doddering old mother... his lack of ambition, her nagging... if it wasn't one thing, it was another.

And the house was small. Not much more than a shack, really. A plank and tarpaper box, with tin shutters and a tin chimney, and a hung curtain partitioning off the side of the room where Trudy and Russ kept their bed — yet another reason Frieda sometimes had occasion to wish herself deaf.

The subject of the current bickering was as to whether or not Russ should stick tight at the home place now that their few animals had been seen to, or whether he should go lend a good Christian hand to their neighbors.

"Since when have the likes of them done a damn thing for us?" Russ demanded. "You see any of them come to lend us a good Christian hand?"

"Which maybe they might if you weren't so surly to everyone whose path you cross!"

"I ain't surly! I just don't fall down on my knees to kiss William Thorpe's backside, the way the rest of them do!"

"Which as if anybody ought to, you should!" Trudy shot back. "The man is our landlord and your boss!"

"The hell he's my boss!"

"We work his land!"

"And we pay rent for it!"

"But we still work for him!"

"We're tenant farmers, not sharecroppers."

"As if there's a difference?" Trudy braced her hands on her hips. She was a diminutive woman, like her mother, but feisty like her father had been.

"Damn right there's a difference! Being a sharecropper ain't but a step removed from being a slave. I'm my own man. Soon's we save up enough to buy this parcel outright—"

"Which I reckon as you blame me for!" said Trudy, eyes flashing.

"You are the one as had to have that new dress!"

"For Sundays! For Sundays when they've got the reverend's church built and there's sermons to go to! You say how we're tenant farmers and all, but it'd suit you just as well if your own wife wore patchwork and rags to Sunday sermon?"

They'd been pent up in the single-room shack most of the winter, with nothing but that curtain for a pretense of privacy. When this morning had dawned so warm and fair despite the ominous sun-dogs of the day prior, they'd taken it for the blessing it seemed to be.

A short-lived blessing indeed, as it happened.

Now, the tarpaper shack shuddered and groaned in the wind. Sleet pellets tinged on the tin chimney and pinged on the tin shutters like spates of birdshot. The cold whistled in through every crack.

"You want me to go out in that?" Russ waved at the door. "It's a true jeezer of a blizzard out there! I was lucky to get back from the cow-shed without being blown clear across the territory!"

"Which is as to what I'm saying!" Trudy said. "Must've been a lot of folks out when it hit, out in their fields, out tending their livestock, fetching firewood or hay—"

"Suppose as there was? What do you expect me to do about it?"

"They could need help, is all."

"Then let Thorpe do it; it's his damn town. Or your precious reverend, if it's that Christian kindness you're talking about."

"Probably as they are, and they can use whatever strong hands as they can! How would it look if they got a bunch of men together to do something and you weren't one of them?"

"None of my concern."

"But, Russ, what if there's kids as was sent to school this morning? They could be trapped in that schoolhouse."

"Not like any of them are ours."

"That's a right awful thing to say!"

"True, though."

"Only because you—"

Russ flung his arms in the air. "All right! All right, already, I'll go, whatever you say, as long as it means I don't have to listen to you go on about having babies again!"

He hauled on his coat, stomped his feet into his boots, wound a long woolen scarf around his neck, donned his gloves and grabbed his hat. The whole while, he threw Trudy looks of mingled challenge, expectation and reproach, as if waiting for her to suddenly ask if he was crazy, thinking to go out in this, and convince him to stay after all. When she didn't, his look went decidedly sullen.

Snow, fine-grained as salt, whirled across the floorboards as Russ opened the door. The fire guttered in the icy draft. The chill leaped in like a living white beast. Russ, his hat almost tossed from his head by a vicious gust, glanced back with his eyebrows raised.

Last chance to talk him out of it, those eyebrows said.

"Do you want us to freeze?" Trudy cried impatiently, hugging herself.

Glowering at her, he stepped out and shut the door behind him.

"Jackass," she muttered.

Frieda, adding wood and stirring some life back into the flames, made as though she didn't hear.

"Ma?" Trudy came over and touched Frieda's shoulder, raising her voice to that deaf-as-a-stump loudness she customarily used when she wanted to get her attention. "How're you doing, Ma? Warm enough?"

She looked up at her, nodding. "Where's Russ off to?"

"Checking in on the neighbors, see if they need any help," Trudy said in the loud voice. She then added, in the mutter, "...or just gone back to the cow-shed, like he thinks I don't know he hides a bottle under the feed bin... he'll have a nip and a nap, then come back hours later making as if he's worked himself back-broken, the lazy—"

"What's that?" Frieda asked.

"Nothing, Ma! Worried about Russ, is all. Let's build up that fire. Lordy, what a storm!"

Lordy, what a storm indeed!

So they built up the fire, and they chatted at the tops of their lungs about winters past. Christmases when Trudy had been a young girl... the worst blizzards Frieda had heard of... the year her brother, on a dare, pressed his tongue to a pump-handle and it stuck there...

It got colder by the minute. The wind hooted and howled in every crack. Even with the fire built high, the snow that had come in through the door and the gaps between the planks soon stopped melting. It began piling at the edges. Frost crept in pale lattices up the walls.

Talking became too much effort.

They sat side by side, as close as they could get to the fire although the flames seemed to be all light and no warmth. Trudy pulled down the hanging curtain between the bed and the rest of the room, wrapping it around their shoulders as they shivered together.

"Ma?" she said through her clattering teeth. "Ma, I'm frightened. And so cold."

Then, with a great flapping noise like the wings of some enormous bat, the wind tore off the tarpaper roof in tattered sheets.

COUNTING

"**D**o you..." Billy Wood faltered and couldn't finish the question. He kept his head down and his gaze straight at the ground. Didn't look at his brother. Went on counting his steps.

...forty-seven, forty-eight, forty-nine...

Tommy finished it for him anyway. "... think we made a mistake?"

Billy nodded. *...fifty-three, fifty-four...*

There was a long pause while Tommy considered, a pause that took Billy's silent count to seventy. Then Tommy said, "Maybe."

"We were dumb," Billy said.

...seventy-five, seventy-six, seventy-seven...

"Uh-huh."

"We should've listened to Miss Emma."

"Uh-huh."

"We should've stayed at the school."

"Uh-huh."

"Could we make it back if we turned around now?"

The pause again. Billy kept counting. *...ninety-nine, one hundred, one hundred and one, one hundred and two...*

"I dunno," Tommy finally said. "How far are we?"

"A hundred and four steps since the creek bridge."

"Well, how far is that?"

"However far a hundred and four steps is, how should I know?"

"How far is a step?"

"As far as it is," Billy said. "A foot?"

"So a hundred and four feet?"

"More than that now."

"How much more?"

"Um..."

"You lost count?"

"You made me lose count!"

"Wait," Tommy said.

He stopped, which meant that Billy had to stop too because they'd been going along with their arms linked tight, Billy's left to Tommy's right. They'd done that when the storm picked up again, so that the wind couldn't force them apart and the snow couldn't make it impossible for them to see each other.

Billy was glad to stop, but he also didn't want to stop. Glad because he was already tired, the muscles in his legs feeling like big wobbly Christmas puddings. Didn't want to because he was already cold, and got even colder when he wasn't moving.

"If it's even a hundred and twenty feet to the creek," Tommy said, "then we're still closer to the school than we are to home, closer by a long way."

"So we should go back," Billy said, his teeth chattering and making the words come out in snippets and mouse-nibbles.

"But if we go back," Tommy went on, "we'll have to say we were wrong."

"Oh."

They leaned together, forehead to forehead, arms still linked. Billy knew he would never need a fancy glass mirror, because if he wanted to know what he looked like, all he had to do was look at Tommy. They even had the same freckles in the same places, and the same crooked front teeth.

"Ben will say how he told us so," Tommy said. "He'll go on about the sun-dogs and his grandpa and the Injuns and how he knew this would happen."

"He already did that," Billy said.

"He'll do it more."

"Oh."

"And we'll be sissies because Sarah and her sisters could do it, them only girls, when we couldn't."

"Oh," said Tommy again.

They trudged on a while further.

"Wish we'd listened to Miss Emma," Billy said. He couldn't hardly feel his feet any more. "I don't care what Ben Adams says. Let's go back."

"All right. Which way is it?"

"It's..." He glanced around and winced as ice whipped into his face. "I dunno. Can we follow our tracks?"

"They're all covered up."

"Tommy, I'm freezing," Billy said.

"Me too."

"We have to walk."

"Where?"

"Anywhere. We just have to walk."

They walked.

Billy hadn't ever cared for school, seeing it as a waste of time. Reading and mathematics were for citified folk, lawyers and bankers and the like. He was going to be a railroad engineer, and take his train back and forth from one ocean to another, seeing the whole country from way up high in his steam-chugging locomotive, and he would blow the whistle whenever he wanted.

So, yes, he hadn't ever seen much use for school, but he would have been overjoyed to suddenly find the schoolhouse in front of them. They'd go back in, where the fire was, and their friends were waiting all anxious and glad to see them safe.

And if Ben did gloat how he told them so? Let him. Ben could gloat all he wanted. It didn't matter. Billy would be so happy just to not be out in this storm any more than he might even break his gingersnap into pieces and share some with everybody. Even with Ben.

"Do you see anything? A house? A barn? Anything?" Tommy asked.

"Nuh-unh. Do you?"

"Nuh-unh. The snow hurts my eyes."

"Mine too."

"We have to be close to somewhere," Billy said.

"How many steps now?"

"I dunno... I wasn't counting."

"You were supposed to be counting!"

"You didn't tell me that!"

"Maybe we should go another way."

"Billy?"

"Huh?"

"Are you... are you scared?"

"Scared?" He tried to laugh, then quit. "Uh-huh. Are you?"

"A little," Tommy said.

"Know what I want?" Billy said. At least, he thought he said it out loud; sometimes it was as if he and Tommy didn't have to speak with their mouths. Which was good, because the snow and wind were making it impossible to talk or to hear.

"Fried chicken all crispy and hot?" Tommy said wistfully. "With biscuits and gravy and all the fixins?"

Billy almost fell over from the wave of longing that rushed through him at Tommy's words, and the image they conjured. "Besides that."

"What?"

He thought. "I forget."

"Oh."

They'd gotten from the schoolhouse door across Thorpe's Meadow to the plank bridge across the creek before the icy wind almost knocked them flat. That was when Billy had started counting his steps. Hadn't he and Tommy raced from the creek to their house, or from their house to the creek, enough times that he should have known how far it was?

"Billy?"

"Huh?"

"Are we going to..." This time it was Tommy who faltered and couldn't finish the question.

Not that he had to.

"Die?" Billy asked.

"Uh-huh."

And it was Billy's turn to pause. Dying was something that happened, sure enough... it happened to old people, and babies, and skinny kids like Peter Thorpe who always had a runny nose. It happened to animals all the time.

It wasn't supposed to happen to them, though. Not him and Tommy.

"Maybe," he said after the pause.

"Think there'll be angels?"

"Sure," Billy said, and it seemed he could almost see the angels, glorious and golden, smiling and singing, the light of Heaven beaming all around them and shining from their eyes.

"Should we pray?" Tommy asked.

"Uh-huh," Billy said, and together they sank down onto their knees in the posture their mother had taught them, the way they said their prayers before they went to bed each night.

THE BRIDE

Lettie ached all over.

The parts of her she could feel, anyway.

By now, there weren't so many of those parts left.

But the ones she could feel, oh, they ached plenty. They ached enough to make up for all the parts that had gone so numb they might not even have been there at all.

What she wanted most right then, most in the world, was to lie down and rest.

Just that.

Just to stop, lie down, curl up, and rest.

More than she wanted anything else, more than she'd ever wanted anything else in her whole life. More than she wanted a fine house of her own, or silk dresses, or rides in a fancy carriage and dinners at a fancy restaurant in the city.

More than she wanted Sam Thorpe's kisses. Even more than she wanted to be his wife.

To rest.

To stop forcing her exhausted legs to move.

It had taken on the sense of some horrible dream, the kind where she ran and ran but moved slower than a bug in molasses. Getting nowhere no matter how she tried. Getting nowhere, while behind her, a monster came steadily closing in.

The monster was real. The monster was Mr. Thorpe.

She had seen how he murdered his wife, she had seen what he'd done to Sam, and for that, he wanted to kill her. It was unlikely that people would believe the word of a simple hired girl over that of a wealthy man like William Thorpe, but that didn't seem to matter to him.

At first, leaving the house, Lettie had crossed her arms over her face and ran. Soon she'd fumbled her apron up – she couldn't see anyway, and the apron at least helped to protect her eyes – and ran that way. Ran as best she could through the snow, praying she didn't fall and break her neck, praying she didn't blunder onto a frozen creek and crash through the ice into a deep spot, praying she reached safety before Mr. Thorpe found her.

A barn would be good. Another house would be better. A house where there were lots of men, and lots of guns, and they wouldn't stand by and let Mr. Thorpe wrap his hands around her neck and choke the life from her, too. Her neck might not be as slim and graceful as Mrs. Thorpe's, but Lettie was sure she'd throttle near as easily.

She went with the wind at her back, not caring where it took her so long as it took her there at a faster pace. Helped that the wind also, for now at least, seemed to be taking her downhill. Sooner or later she was bound to come to something. A fence she could follow, a tree she could crouch behind to catch her breath... something.

What if she did reach a house, and there were men with guns, but they decided that they'd sooner have Mr. Thorpe's goodwill than intervene on behalf of the likes of her? Half the people in town were beholden to him one way or another.

Beholden enough to stand by and let an innocent girl be killed?

The ground dipped, and Lettie cried out as she pinwheeled her arms. She kept herself from going head over heels by taking three clumsy leaping steps.

One foot struck what she guessed was a rock, in what she guessed was a glancing blow because it didn't hurt much. Of course, she supposed, she might have broken all those toes like twigs but hadn't felt it on account of how numbed her feet had gotten.

Her poor toes slammed into rocks again and again. Then her foot came down on ice swept bare by the wind. Her leg shot sideways. Again, she pinwheeled her arms and cried out, but this time she did not keep from falling. She landed on her stomach and slid, knocked breathless. Her chin bounced on ice. She bit her tongue and tasted blood, felt it startlingly hot on her cold lips.

Lettie came to a stop, still sprawled belly-down with her arms and legs splayed. Beneath her was flat smoothness. The frozen surface of a creek or someone's cowpond. She imagined she could hear the ice creaking under her, imagined the cracks spreading out like hairlines at first and then widening, until the sheet broke into a thousand fragments and she fell into deep water and drowned.

Creak. Crack. She tried to hold still but she couldn't, she was shivering so. Her eyes didn't seem able to open. The lids or the lashes were stuck together. Trying to open them sent pangs darting through her entire head.

She cupped her hands — or the stiff things that she thought must be her hands, as they were at the ends of her arms — in front of her face. She blew into them, thinking that this would warm her hands and also help thaw the crust of tears.

Her eyelids, not without another quick flash of pain, peeled open. Lettie blinked. The eyes themselves hurt, they felt as if they'd been rolled in coarse-ground cornmeal and then poked back into their sockets still covered in grit. But she could see.

She couldn't see much... but she could see.

The stiff things at the ends of her arms were indeed her hands, though she had never seen them that particular color before. A bloodless fish-pale color, tinged with blue. She could see the icy surface of the pool, broken here and there by rocks or the jutting fingers of half-submerged sticks.

Moving with slow care, Lettie tried to push herself up on hands and knees. She crawled, wincing at each crack and creak, toward the edge.

"Lettie," a voice called from behind her.

Her head had been hanging, her tangled snow-frosted hair in her eyes, as she hauled herself across the ice. Now she shuffled around in a clumsy turn, raised her head, and peered through the frozen hair-snarls with her aching eyes.

"Sam?"

It was.

She could hardly believe it, but it was!

Sam Thorpe, standing on the far shore of the pond! He wasn't dead, like she'd feared. He wasn't injured at all. He was wearing a fine new suit... his hair combed smooth and his face clean shaven. Smiling at her, smiling in a way that made something light up inside her. As if she had swallowed a coal that didn't burn but only filled her with a wonderful warm glow.

The snow spun and blew around Sam without touching him. His feet didn't even sink into it. If he felt the cold at all, it didn't show.

Lettie knew there was something peculiar about that, but she couldn't quite think of why. All she could think of was Sam there, her Sam, smiling at her. In his fine new suit, looking more handsome than ever.

"Lettie," he said again, and held out his hand.

Her own hand came up, stretched toward him. She saw that it wasn't the stiff and bloodless bunch of hooked sticks after all... it was a delicate lady's hand, soft as butter, with a lacy wristlet glove.

"Everyone's waiting," Sam said.

And beyond him now, not in the snow — *what snow?* — but in a beautiful summery meadow with grass just as green as green could be and the sun shining down, she saw rows of people. Everyone she knew. All of them dressed in their Sunday best, all of them beaming with joy and approval. They flanked an aisle marked by swags of ribbon, leading toward a bower of roses.

That wasn't a snarled skein of her own ice-clotted hair she was peering through. It was a veil, a veil just as gossamer as cobwebs. She was head to foot in satin and lace. She held a spray of flowers and their sweet perfume wafted over her.

Sobbing with happiness, Lettie moved toward her Sam. This was their day, their wedding day, the perfect day she'd always dreamed of.

Then the ice cracked to pieces under her feet, and she plunged through into a wet and freezing darkness.

A FEAST

"**L**ord have mercy," Zelda Adams said. "Lord have mercy on us all, one and all, Jesus' sake amen." She was in her rocker by the stove, going back and forth, a scuffed old family Bible hugged to her bosom.

"Amen," Jonas Adams said. He bent, kissed his wife's wrinkled cheek, and then picked his way carefully over and around the dogs at her feet to return to his big chair at the head of the table. "More coffee, Henry?"

"I'd not say no," Henry Greeley said.

The Adams clan — Jonas and Zelda, five of their six grown sons, two of their daughters, a son-in-law, three daughters-in-law, the one widowed daughter-in-law with nowhere else to go, and assorted grandchildren — occupied what Henry was sure had to be the largest farmhouse from here to Missouri. They'd built it at the place where all their homestead parcels met up, and filled the good meadowland for acres around with flocks and flocks of sheep.

Jonas nodded to one of his daughters or daughters-in-law, and she bustled over with the speckleware coffee pot to refill their mugs.

The main room of the farmhouse was kitchen at one end and cluster of spinning wheels at the other, with the long table and benches down the middle. At the moment, the benches were full of Adamses. They'd seen the cloudbank coming in time to secure their flocks in the long low sheepfold, and had been wondering ever since whether or not they could risk trying to get to the school. Only nine-year-old Ben had gone that morning, eager to escape his chores for part of the day despite his grandfather's misgivings. The rest were too young to have walked so far in the snow even on such an unseasonably nice day.

"Had a sense it was going to be bad," Jonas said. "Saw sun-dogs the other day, and the Injuns say that's a sure way to know a bitter cold is coming."

"The teacher will keep them in the schoolhouse," one of the Adams women said. Ben's mother, Henry supposed, and in a way that said she was trying to convince herself as much as anyone else.

"She's a sensible girl, that Emma Curtis," agreed another Adams woman.

"That she is," said a third. That one was the widowed sister-in-law, the one with the snub nose and the big brown eyes, though courting was about the furthest it had ever been from Henry's mind.

"Schoolhouse isn't much, though," one of the Adams men replied. "Thorpe has it knocked together out of planks not much thicker than a newspaper. Even with a fire, if this wind keeps up they're bound to freeze."

Yet another Adams woman, this one likely the wife of the man who'd spoken, gave him an elbow nudge and a hold-your-tongue look as she leaned past him to put a platter of mutton on the table. It wasn't freshly butchered and roasted meat, had been salted and stored in the fall and then soaked before being stewed with corn and cut-up vegetables, but it was hot and drenched in gravy, and they dug in with a right good will.

"Pass the bread?" someone asked, and Henry did so. There was bread, some butter but not much, dark molasses, and the last jar of orange marmalade.

It might as well have been a Thanksgiving feast as far as Henry was concerned. He'd been fairly certain for a while there that his last meal, the oatmeal he'd had for breakfast, would be his last meal of all time.

His dogs had saved his life. If not for Chief and Queenie dragging him those last few feet, if not for Buttons and Bows leaping at the farmhouse door barking fit to split, he would have lain out there in the snow until he froze to death.

As it was, one of the Adams men had heard the barking and scratching, and come to see what was going on. He'd opened the door and there was Henry. They'd hustled him indoors, gotten him into dry clothes, and had him by the fire with a slug of whiskey warming his gullet and a mug of hot coffee in his hands before he was sure he was still all-the-way alive.

Now he and the dogs were safe, warm, dry and fed. Poor ol' Nugget had managed to totter across the room to flop down by the stove at Zelda Adams' feet, and there he'd stayed ever since. He hadn't even bestirred himself when the Adams youngsters fed out some scraps and the stewbones.

"Where's your dog at?" Henry asked, finally noticing that his five were the only dogs in sight. "Shadow, isn't that what you called him?"

"Dead," one of the Adams sons said. Flat. Matter-of-fact.

"Dead," Henry echoed. "The storm?"

"Naw," a different Adams son said. "Few days ago. Latch broke and some of the flock got out. Wolfpack found them in the night, we figure. Killed three ewes and a ram. Hell of a scene. Blood, meat and wool everywhere."

"Walt!" The woman beside him gave him the little pitchers have big ears look, and tilted her head sideways at the children, who were listening all agog.

"They need to know," he said. "Facts of life and such."

"Looked like the pack dragged off at least one of the carcasses," said an Adams son with a great shock of bushy black beard. "Shadow went after. When he got the scent... lordy, I've never seen a dog carry on like that."

"Baying?" Henry asked. "Wild out of his skull?"

"That's about the size of it. Took off like a split streak and wouldn't mind us no matter how we hollered. Straight into the woods."

"I don't know as this is fitting conversation for the supper table," another Adams woman said. "Can I get anyone more to eat?"

"Then we heard a hell of a ruckus," Walt Adams said, ignoring her. "Yowling and I don't know what-all. Shadow let out this yelp... this hurt yelp... and come staggering back out from the trees with blood running out of his neck like a river and his guts half trailing in the snow."

"Walt!" the little pitchers woman said again, and matched her sharp tone with a sharp elbow to the ribs. This time he looked properly chastened.

"He got partway back to us and fell over dead," Jonas said. None of his daughters or daughters-in-law dared give him a look, a sharp tone or an elbow. "We couldn't bury him, not with the ground froze solid, but we put an oilcloth over him and weighed it down good with stones. Soon as there's a thaw..."

"You sure it was wolves?" Henry asked.

The Adams men shared around a glance. Finally the one with the bushy black beard said, "Might've been a bear, I reckon." He spoke with reluctance, and as soon as the words were out, crammed a hunk of bread into his mouth.

"Didn't sound like a bear," Walt said.

"Didn't sound like wolves, neither," another man said. This one, Henry thought, was married to an Adams daughter. "Not entirely. Sounded almost like a catamount."

"Sounded like the shrieks of Satan's own devils," Zelda Adams said from her rocker, hugging that Bible to her bony chest.

"Or some evil Injun spirit," Jonas said. "And the way Shadow was, baying like that, wild out of his skull as you said there, Henry... how'd you know, by the way?"

He told them, in a cautious way to be mindful of those little pitchers, what he had seen out in the woods. The sheep carcass lodged high in the fork of a tree, and the way all of his dogs had gone into a frenzy over whatever they smelled in that pile of droppings.

"But I didn't see any tracks that looked like bear or wolf," he finished. "Didn't see much in the way of tracks at all, come to think, aside from what the dogs made."

THE BELL

"Please, Lester, please!" Rufus pulled on his brother's arm. "Lester, get up!"

Lester didn't get up. Lester didn't say a word. Lester just lay there.

"Mumma be mad at you something fierce," Rufus said. "Don't pretend at me!"

Lester wasn't pretending.

Lester was...

"No," Rufus said, emphasizing it by shaking his head so hard he made himself dizzy. "He ain't. Lester ain't. Lester can't be."

But Lester wasn't moving. Lester wasn't talking. The arm Rufus held was cold and stiff.

"You quit fooling now." Rufus tried to sound like Dadda when Dadda had just about had enough. When Dadda, normally a mild-tempered man, sounded that way, they knew they better listen or Dadda would get out his paddle and there'd be sore backsides when they were sent to bed that night. Sent to bed without their supper, even.

It didn't work on Lester. Lester still just lay there.

They'd been out playing when some of the Kradenmeyer kids came along on their way to school, and stopped to join in a while, what with no grown-ups around to look all disapproving. They'd got a good snowball war going, then sledded, then the others decided they wanted to skate on what they called Willow Pond. Or, since they didn't have proper skates, slide around on the ice in their shoes.

Lester, though, had decided he wanted one more last good sled run down Thorpe's Hill first. Rufus had agreed with him. So up they climbed, Rufus with a burlap sack slung over his arms, Lester toting a splintered old crate they'd taken from behind the henhouse.

All the way to the top of the hill.

That was where they'd heard the terrible train-rushing wind, and seen the storm coming. Rufus wanted to run but Lester said they'd get there faster if they both squeezed into the crate and slid to the bottom of the hill, then ran for it.

Except the crate had hit a rock or a bump or something halfway, and flipped them like flapjacks into the snow as the wood broke all to pieces. Except the storm was coming even faster than they'd thought, and was almost on them by the time they'd righted themselves and started running after all.

When it hit, Lester grabbed Rufus by the hand so they wouldn't get lost from each other. He also made Rufus stop, and put his own jacket on Rufus, then wrapped the burlap sacks around Rufus like a pair of rough musty-scratchy old blankets. He'd told Rufus to keep his face covered and hold on and keep walking.

Rufus had done exactly that. Shivering, teeth chattering, but trusting that Lester knew what he was doing.

Lester would get them home. Mumma would have hot bowls of hoppin' john, their favorite meal, waiting for them. Dadda would build up the fire nice and high, maybe give them each a sip of strong whiskey to unfreeze their bones. All their brothers and sisters would gather 'round. Later they'd have a story to tell about their adventure, yes indeed they would. He just had to follow Lester, and do what Lester said.

Until Lester stopped again, and sat down for a rest. He sat there for a long time, while Rufus hopped in place from foot to foot, trying to keep warm in the burlap and Lester's too-big-for-Rufus jacket.

When he went to shake Lester's shoulder, Lester fell over onto his side, and that was where he stayed.

Rufus pulled again on his arm. "Lester, you gotta get up!"

Lester didn't answer. Lester didn't move.

"Don't make me go by myself," Rufus said.

He didn't want to leave Lester. He didn't know which way to go, or what to do. He didn't know where he was.

"Lester?"

Rufus crouched down to see if Lester was awake. He had to brush snow off of Lester's face, and he saw how Lester's skin looked more grey than brown.

Lester's eyes were open... but Lester wasn't awake. He didn't blink. He didn't look at Rufus. His eyes had snow in them. They were empty eyes, empty, but full of snow.

Something all drained right out of Rufus then. He stared at Lester for a long time, so long that he hardly even noticed when he stopped shivering. He thought he might sit himself down, just plop down in the snow beside Lester, and stay there. It would be better than being alone.

He couldn't see Lester's face any more. The snow had covered it up again. But he imagined he could still see Lester, and that Lester was looking at him. Looking at him and talking to him. Telling him he best not dare give up, he best keep going.

"By myself?"

Had to be by himself. There wasn't anybody else.

Rufus discovered that he must've sat down after all, though he sure couldn't remember doing so. He had to force himself to stand, leaning into the wind when it tried to swat him flat over.

Seemed like he should say something more to Lester, but he didn't know what. He held the burlap sacks around his shoulders and head, and began shuffling. After a while he turned around, but there was nothing to see except flurrying white. No Lester. Lester was gone.

"Lester!" he shouted.

Only the wind answered, with a piercing shrill hoot like the laugh of a mean old woman.

He turned around again and kept shuffling. Every now and then, imaginings tried to form in his head, warm and cozy imaginings. The whole family around a fire, singing lively songs while Dadda popped corn in the long-handled popper.

Uncle Cyrus taking all the boys frog-catching on a hot summer day. The wooden tub where they took their baths in turn, full to the brim with steaming water.

But every time those imaginings started taking shape, Lester's blank white snow-filled eyes would appear, and Lester's cold voice would be telling him that those things weren't real.

Then he imagined he was hearing a bell, a bell like the iron one that hung by their door, the one Mumma clanged with her metal cook-spoon to call them all in for dinner. Baked beans and biscuits, ham and red-eye gravy.

The bell...

The bell wasn't Mumma's dinner bell.

The bell wasn't an imagining, neither.

He could only hear it in snips and snatches through the wind, a small clinking-clunking sound and not the mighty iron clang. But he was hearing it. Hearing it for real.

Rufus shuffled faster, following the sound as best he could. At last he noticed that the snow was shallower on the ground and not so thick in the air. The wind was suddenly less. The bell clinked and clunked very nearby.

He uncovered his face, the ice-mask on the burlap breaking away in shards like a piece of glass. He blinked his sore, stinging eyes again and again, in disbelief as much as anything else.

Looming tree trunks, the steep-sided rocky tumbles of a ravine. The little creek down its middle, frozen solid.

The boulder... and by the boulder... in the opening to the cave behind it, a shape. A person-shape.

He staggered closer, sure that his poor eyes were playing tricks on him, and saw that it was a person-shape. It was his sister, Tessa, ringing that dented old cowbell for all she was worth.

DETERMINATION

William Thorpe wouldn't let the blizzard stop him. The snow was no match for his purpose. The relentless wind-blown grains of ice and the bone-deep bitter chill didn't hamper him in the slightest.

"I'll find you," Mr. Thorpe said.

He had taken the time before pursuing the girl into the blizzard to seize his hat, coat and scarf. The hat was long gone, snatched away by the wind before he'd made five steps. But the coat was a long buffalo-hide overcoat, and the scarf was thick. He was well-bundled against the cold, and further warmed by his ire.

Bundled or not, he had still taken his share of the weather's harsh punishment.

The skin and flesh of his cheekbones and all around his eyes was rubbed raw, and what remained was so blanched it felt like a bare skull with bulging red-veined orbs set into it. Frost clung glittering in his hair, from his sideburns and moustache. He was caked with snow, blue-grey with frostbite, and his hands were like the hooked talons of a frozen rooster inside his leather gloves.

But he kept going.

Was it pure luck? Was it willpower? Grit and tenacity?

Didn't matter. He would find her, find the foolish slut, and then he was going to take care of her once and for all.

The practical side of his mind spoke up and told him that this was probably unnecessary. Lettie had fled out the door and into the storm with just her house-clothes. No shawl, no boots, not even a bonnet. It would be impossible for her to survive in conditions like this.

A reasonable certainty, but Thorpe wasn't about to take that chance.

He was confident he could overcome even this disastrous storm. If it turned out he couldn't, if it turned out that despite all his efforts at coaxing and persuasion, some people still wanted to pack up and leave... well, he would have to accept that. It wouldn't mean the absolute end of his plans and dreams. They wouldn't all leave. Some would stay. They'd recover and rebuild. He might yet have the town of his own.

What he couldn't overcome was having his own hired girl bleating like a sheep to anybody who'd listen about how William Thorpe, a respected and respectable man, had murdered his wife.

Lettie had to be silenced.

Oh, he knew all about her goings-on with his son. Nothing took place under his own roof without his knowledge. If she thought she could use that to plead for clemency, if she thought he would spare her because she let the boy pound a fuck into her every chance they got...

No, the girl had to die. That was it, plain and simple. He wouldn't trust any promise that he might extract from her, and he certainly wouldn't buy her silence by allowing Samuel to marry her, for God's sake.

Samuel might squawk some, but ultimately he would understand. He'd see the need to keep quiet about what had happened. He'd agree that it was in the best interests of the entire family.

Assuming Samuel was even still alive.

If he was, he was. Thorpe knew that he could, given enough time, convince the boy that he'd only done what he'd had to do. His son had much to learn about women... deceitful, manipulative, underhanded witches that they were... and the time to do that learning had evidently come.

And if Samuel wasn't alive? If he had cracked his fool skull open when he'd gone headfirst into the corner of that chest?

Well...

If he wasn't, he wasn't. Served him right for interfering in his father's business. Thorpe hadn't intended to clout him aside so hard, had never intended for Samuel to get hurt, but the boy shouldn't have been meddling with what didn't concern him.

Squinting through eyes that were hard slits in his hard face still did not let him see the fence before he walked into it. The unseen barrier's topmost rail caught him across the midsection. A grunt — *whurf!* — burst through his clenched jaws.

He stopped for a moment, and grasped the fence, thinking. He could follow it, use it as his guide through this blinding white hell. And if Lettie had come this way, foolish though she might have been, she'd have done the same thing.

THE WAY HOME

Klaus Renneke knew that no one would fault him if he stayed in the barn.

He'd gotten the cows to safety, and a right chore it had been. Too dumb to go in out of the cold, they were. Glad enough to be there, once he'd driven them, but too dumb to seek it on their own.

Left to themselves they would have planted their feet to wait it out, and like as not smothered on the ice that'd form from the steam of their breath. Or they'd have trudged along the path of least resistance, letting the wind push them where it would, and dropped from exhaustion miles from home.

But he'd done it, he'd guided and driven them all to shelter. A fight to be sure, a real struggle against their stubborn inclinations. What choice had he had? None. The herd was their livelihood.

Once the cows were seen to, though, he'd been faced with the problem of what to do next. Stay where he was, keep himself safe and alive... or face the storm again in hopes of reaching the house.

The barn was sturdy, it was warm, it was dry. He had grain, and plenty of milk. Could go half the winter in here if need be.

But his family...

Had Jorgen and Johann made it back? What of Kirstie, off to school with the teacher? Was his mother alone and frantic with worry? Where was Johanna, was she out in the blizzard, or with the Rutgers?

Going out there again seemed like madness.

Staying here would drive him just as mad.

If they weren't at the house, if they were lost out in the snow, there would be no earthly way to even begin a search until the storm had passed. How could he hope to find someone else when he had barely been able to see his hand in front of his nose?

The cows in their pens stood placidly, contented. They munched hay and chewed cud, idly swishing their tails. Large brown eyes blinked at him as he passed by.

His brother... his mother... his wife... his children.

It hurt his heart to be safe and warm without knowing whether they were the same or not.

Before opening the barn's side door, he spared a moment to concentrate, trying to fix his location in his mind. He did not want to veer off.

He remembered the lengthy discussions they'd had, discussions that almost became arguments, over where to build the house and barn in relation to each other. The one too close to the other meant nearness to manure-smells and flies during the summer... the one too far from the other meant extra distances to walk back and forth on the daily rounds of chores. The balance of comfort and convenience. He'd never reconsidered until today.

The wind whirling around him as he wedged himself through the gap and re-closed the door felt twice as cold as he remembered. The granules of ice stung twice as hard, flew twice as thick. Returning to the blizzard after the warm reprieve in the barn no longer just seemed like madness... it was madness.

Klaus drove himself now, as he'd driven the cows before. Onward, step after step, keeping to the path he had plotted in his mind, not letting the wind coax his direction. He bent his head to help keep his hat on. He pulled his collar up over his nose and ears.

From time to time, the wicked gales dropped enough to let visibility return in teasing, tantalizing snippets. He hoped for a glimpse of the house, or the line of young trees they'd planted partly as windbreak and partly for fruits and nuts.

Why hadn't he stayed?

The barn, he would have been warm in the barn, warm among the cows, could have weathered this storm there until it blew itself out.

But, once the cows were safe, he had to see to his family. Had to know if Jorgen and Johann were all right, if Mutti was all right, if Kirstie and Johanna had made it home.

If they hadn't, then, decisions must be made. To go to the school? To make for the Rutgers' place?

Something caught at his feet, ensnared his lower legs. Numbed to the knees, Klaus couldn't tell what it was, couldn't kick or shake loose of it. He lost his balance and let out a yell of mingled frustration and surprise as he went over backwards.

Then he heard, or thought he heard, someone calling out. "Hello? Hello! Is someone there? Klaus? Klaus, is that you?" It was his mother's voice.

"Here!" he shouted.

"Da?" And that, that was his son, his Johann. "It is! It's Da! Da, where are you?"

He thrashed his way to a sitting position and saw what tangled his feet. It was a heavy quilt, in a multicolored starburst pattern, that Johanna had hung out on the clothesline that very morning.

Moments later, a large and hulking shape pushed through the sheeting snow. Thick arms swathed in wool blankets reached out for him. Gloved hands hauled Klaus upright. With sore, swollen eyes, he squinted up into Jorgen's ice-blasted face as his brother helped him the last few steps to the door.

LUNCH-PAILS

The storm showed no signs of letting up, and Emma knew their plight in the schoolhouse was only going to keep worsening and worsening.

Though she could see their pale, drawn faces all around her, she stirred every so often to call the roll. Amos Trotter. Ben Adams. Minnie Granger. Mary Thorpe, Elias Thorpe, Cora Thorpe, Peter Thorpe, James Thorpe. Kirstie Renneke.

Once, Ben wondered aloud about Billy and Tommy. Whether they'd reached safety yet, and how long it would take for the help they were sure to send to arrive. Or the Jordan sisters, who'd left even earlier.

Emma only pressed her lips tight together. No one else answered. No one made accusations, though Emma was sure that sooner or later, the accusations would come.

She should have stopped them. She shouldn't have let any of them venture into the storm. She'd suspected the lull wouldn't last long, and when the winds resumed they would do so with even more power than before.

If they hadn't made it through... if they were lost out there, if they were found frozen dead in a snowbank... it'd be her fault.

"I'm hungry," James said.

And that was another concern. The food, or lack thereof. The lunch-pails hadn't held much to begin with. In an effort to lift their spirits, Emma had already portioned out the piece of cake Mrs. Trotter had sent to school with her son. It had been a generous piece, but divided amongst so many mouths, they'd gotten what seemed like mere crumbs.

Hours ago, it had been.

"We're all hungry, James," Mary said.

"And I'm tired and cold. I want to go home."

"We're all tired and cold. We all want to go home."

"I want Mother." James drew a hitched, sniffling breath.

"Wouldn't you hush?" Elias said with sudden harshness. He kicked at James. "Quit being such a baby!"

"I'm not a baby!" James kicked back. "Grace is the baby! Not me! Not me!"

"You are so! You're being a baby!"

"Stop it!" Mary cried. "Elias, James, stop!"

"He's being a baby, a baby-baby-baby!"

"That's enough," Emma said. She whacked her stick on the floor and Elias jumped. "Enough."

The younger girls — Cora, Minnie and Kirstie — huddled together in a listless, doleful-eyed bunch. Ben had his head down, scribbling on his slate. Amos shuffled his big feet and looked uncomfortable. They seemed to be doing their best to ignore the squabbling that had just gone on.

Peter Thorpe wasn't paying attention to it either, but that was because Peter was a concern of his own. He lay wracked with feeble shivers and painful wet-sounding coughs. His cheeks were bright with fever, his lips dry and chapped, his forehead burning almost as hot as the stove. If it kept up, Emma thought, they could gather around Peter instead and be warmer.

"Should we maybe have something to eat?" Amos asked.

Emma glanced at him. He wasn't going to say he was hungry. He wasn't going to complain. That he'd say as much as he just did was a sign in itself. Amos was a husky farmboy, used to hard labor and hearty meals. Amos had been breaking apart the furniture and keeping the fire stoked, while the rest of them for the most part sat and did nothing. He had to be feeling it more than they were. He had to be starving.

"Must be near to suppertime by now," he added, seeing her glance.

"There isn't enough food for everyone," Minnie said.

"But I'm hungry," whined James.

"Let's take a look," Emma said. Her legs were stiff from sitting, and her backside felt like it had gone to sleep. She got up, groaning and thinking that this was what it'd be like when she was an old woman.

She'd collected the lunch-pails onto her desk, and just like the stove she got snapped at with a spark when she went to touch one. She inspected the contents. Although she knew for a fact no one had been eating any of it, there somehow seemed to be much less now than there had been before. A few pieces of bread, some wrinkled bits of dried fruit, the chunk of sausage and the slice of ham.

Right then, Emma felt like she could wolf down every speck by herself, and still have her stomach growling for more.

"Could we eat snow?" Elias asked.

"Don't be stupid," Ben said.

"You're stupid!"

They started punching each other, and Amos seized them with fistfuls of shirt-backs. He pulled them apart and held them up so that the toes of their shoes could only paddle at the floorboards without going anywhere.

"Miss Emma?" Mary primly raised her hand, just as if this were any other school day.

"Yes, Mary?"

"We could use snow. We could scoop some into one of the lunch-buckets, and melt it on the stove. If we chopped up the sausage and ham into it, it'd make a soup, wouldn't it? And be more to go around?"

"Worth a try, I reckon," Emma said. "Good idea, Mary. Will you help me?"

They chopped up the meat, and chopped up the dried fruit as well – apples and apricots, and a handful of raisins. Amos braved the weather long enough to scoop two pails of snow from the heaping drifts outside, one for this makeshift soup, and one to melt so they could have something to drink.

The activity roused the children, all but Peter. Soon they were all poking about the schoolroom in search of anything edible that could be added to the pail. Kirstie found a little bag of nuts she'd been using to help her practice her sums, and in they went. So did the half-dozen dried peas Elias had been saving for his peashooter.

"I wished and wished my Da would come," Kirstie said. "But he isn't. Why isn't he? Why isn't anybody coming to get us?"

"Someone will," Emma said.

The simmering mixture sent up heavenly cooking-smells. Most of the students had at one time or another brought old cups to school, tin ones or wooden ones, and Minnie Granger fetched them now. Mary cut them each a small slice of bread, saving the rest back so they would have something left to eat if they were here long enough to need it. Which, they all knew but didn't say, was seeming more and more like it'd be the case. Emma poured out the soup, and they all sat as close to the stove as they dared, cradling the cups in their hands for the welcome warmth, sipping it eagerly.

"What about Peter?" Cora asked.

"Try and drink some soup, Peter," Emma said.

He coughed until she worried his throat would split, and pushed the cup away.

"He's really sick," Mary said.

Emma nodded. He was, and being in this drafty schoolhouse where the snow found its way in through every crack wasn't helping. He needed a proper bed, quilts, a doctor, medicine.

"I could go," Amos said, in a way that suggested he'd been thinking about it for some time. "Couldn't take him, not when he's so sick, but I could try and get to help, bring someone back. With provisions and a sled, or..." He trailed off, and shifted his broad shoulders in a shrug. "... the like."

"Our house isn't that far," Elias said.

"Mine is closer," Kirstie said.

"Yours is across the creek."

"There's a bridge."

"Can't find the bridge if you can't see where you're going."

"Amos can't go," Minnie said. "If Amos goes, who'll see to the fire?"

"I'll go," Elias said.

"I'm oldest," Amos said.

"I'm plenty old enough, and Peter's my brother."

"I'm bigger and stronger."

Elias puffed his chest and stuck out his chin. "I can do it!"

"None of you are going out in the storm," Emma said.

"But Peter—" began Cora.

Emma gestured her to silence. "I'm going." Then she had to gesture them all to silence as they made with outcries. "I'm the oldest, older than Amos. I'm the teacher. You're all my responsibility. So I'll go."

"Miss Emma, no, you can't," Amos said. "You're... well... you're a... girl. Oughta be me that goes."

"You're needed here, Amos," Emma said. "Look after things, keep the fire burning, make more desks into firewood if you have to." She finished her soup, aware of it warming her insides.

"What if you get lost in the snow, Miss Emma?" Cora asked. She looked very young, and tearful. "Who will take care of us then?"

"Your sister Mary will, until someone comes. And someone will come, Cora. You'll see."

She didn't need long to make ready to leave. Since she'd brought no boots or mittens, and Kirstie's wouldn't fit, she slashed her short cape into wide strips and wrapped them securely around her hands and feet to help protect them from frostbite. She borrowed Mary's shawl and Cora's scarf. Amos, who'd walked a long way from the Trotter place, had worn a good wool coat and he insisted that she take it.

"All right," she said to her students, who gathered at the stove watching her with the sad dread of people who were sure they'd never set eyes on her again, not unless it was at her funeral. The only one who seemed oblivious was Peter, who had lapsed into a thin sleep. "I'll be back or send someone as soon as I can, I promise."

Amos accompanied her through the little vestibule and past the empty coatroom. He wrestled the schoolhouse door open for her, fighting with it against the wind and piled snow. They both looked out. Amos whistled low.

"You sure about this, Miss Emma?"

"No choice, is there?"

"Wish we had a rope, ball of twine," he said.

"Rope wouldn't be long enough, twine would break." She took a deep breath and regretted it instantly because the air was a freezing dryness that sucked every bit of heat and moisture from her nose, throat, lungs and body. "Take good care of them, Amos."

"I will. This is awful brave of you, Miss Emma." Then he just about startled the life out of her by leaning over and planting a kiss on her cheek. "Awful brave."

She was speechless, though there was nothing to say. And embarrassed, though it was far too cold to muster any sort of a blush. Instead, Emma clutched Cora's scarf over her face, and headed out into the snow.

NOT HIS PLACE

What had made him go and waste the time to search it out and pick it up, he didn't exactly know.

The storm had already been building itself up, getting its second wind as it were, and he hadn't had much time to spare.

But he'd done it anyway, and Brody O'Connor was glad.

He had proof. Proof that the thing he'd seen wasn't some conjuring out of an Irishman's jug. People aplenty would be quick to say so, until he showed them the broken tooth he had plucked from the snow.

Tooth?

More of a fang, a right proper fang. Or a tusk, not the kind they said elephants had in far-off Africa, but more the kind they said walruses had in the far-off Arctic.

All he knew was that he'd never seen the like. He could hardly wait to show it to someone, see what they said.

He'd crossed the pasture, following the fence with his trusty walking stick held up at the ready in case the white beast came back. It hadn't, and Brody got to the house, let himself in by way of the back door that led into a sort of mudroom behind the kitchen, and there the blessed warmth of being indoors hit him better than a good knock of the finest whiskey.

There in the mudroom, he stripped off his sodden outer clothes — coat, boots, socks, hat, scarf. His inner clothes were damp with sweat or melted snow or both, but those he left on. Didn't care to startle the lady of the house by having her walk in unexpected on the undressed hired man.

His next stop was the kitchen, though he got quite a jolt when he touched the iron door handle and it cracked a flashing spark into his hand. The air felt strange and charged, as if the hairs on his arms were prickling to stand upright.

The kitchen was empty. Half-finished chores done. Unwashed breakfast dishes piled in a tub. Pantry door wide open. The makings of a pie crust were on the counter. A big pot bubbled on the stove. Beef, by the smell. And overcooked, also by the smell. Not burnt to ruin, but only because the stove was down to embers.

"Lettie?" Brody said.

Wasn't like her to shirk her duties this way. Mr. Thorpe would not be happy if he got a look at this mess.

Brody frowned as he picked up the coffee pot, and frowned more when he only poured out a thick brown dribble into his cup. He set it aside, and moved the pot of boiled beef to the counter before tossing more sticks from the woodbox into the stove. He set about making more coffee, and wondered where the dickens Lettie had gotten to.

Off with Sam Thorpe again?

Wouldn't stop her being in a spot of trouble over leaving chores half-done and the beef to burn.

"Anyone home?" he called, a bit more loudly. "Lettie? Mr. Thorpe? Mrs. Thorpe?"

No answer... though he could hear the youngest start crying upstairs. Brody winced. Went and woke the baby, he had, and that wouldn't put him in anyone's good books.

While the coffee heated, he helped himself to a slice of bread and slathered it with jam, then opened a tin of oysters he found in the pantry and gulped them down. He was next door to starvation.

No one came in while he was eating. No one answered when he called again. The baby was bawling like hell, with no one up there shushing or comforting her.

It all finally struck him as too odd, so he set down his cup on the table, beside his walking stick and the broken tooth, and pushed through the kitchen door.

Colder out in the hall, and Brody right away saw why. The front door wasn't all the way closed. Snow had blown in to powder the hallway rug.

"Anybody here?"

Just the baby, screaming her lungs out by now.

He hesitated. He was welcome in the kitchen but didn't have the run of the entire house, wasn't supposed to set foot in the sitting room unless invited and wasn't to set foot upstairs at all.

"Mr. Thorpe?"

Still no answer, but for the screams and howls of Baby Grace.

Brody went to the sitting room doorway and poked his head around the jamb. "'Scuse me? It's just me, Brody O'—"

His gaze darted around the room the way a bird caught indoors will batter itself from wall to window to ceiling to corner. Chair and table overturned, busted lamp and crockery on the floor, torn magazine.

And the bodies.

"Mrs. Thorpe?" Brody asked in a voice that was hardly his own.

She was crumpled in a heap of fine dress and petticoats, her head lolling against her shoulder. Face purple, eyes open and staring but sightless. Deep angry welts, finger-marks blossoming on her neck. One of her shoes had come off, and somehow it was that small stocking-clad foot his gaze kept returning to.

Sam Thorpe was nearby, sprawled facedown beside a fancy chest with intricate carvings in its wood and a needlepoint cushion padding its top. There was a sticky dark puddle around Sam's head, which was turned toward Brody. It looked like molasses or tar in the room's shadows, but Brody guessed it was neither of those. The boy's mouth was split, his lips puffy and crusted, as if he'd been pummeled.

He forgot all about being invited into the sitting room. He ran in, knelt beside them, paused only briefly, and then reached out to touch Mrs. Thorpe. His hand shook worse when he did that than it had the entire time he'd been outside in the blizzard. He almost couldn't bear to put his fingertips against her poor throat, which was so swollen and abused, but he did, and pressed gingerly.

No throb of a pulse. No breath. Her skin was cool, going to cold.

Brody wasn't much given to piety, and never would have thought he still remembered any of the lilting prayers he'd learned at his mother's knee, so it was a surprise to him to hear the words come whispering out. He prayed for Josephine Thorpe, who had been such a dear lady, so gentle, so pretty.

What kind of a brute would do something this terrible to such a sweet lady?

When he moved to Sam, he saw the matted wound on the boy's scalp, and the dark smear and strands of hair stuck to the corner of that carved wooden chest. He set his fingertips to Sam's neck as well, expecting the same. Expecting death. Finding the faint beat and warmth of life.

"Sam? Samuel Thorpe, can you hear me? It's Brody, the hired man. Can you hear me?"

The boy moaned. His eyelids twitched.

"What happened here, Sam? Who did this?"

One eye fluttered partway open and Sam Thorpe looked up at Brody. "It was him," he said in a slurred, mumbling voice. "He did it... choked her... hit me... it was him. My father."

MILKSOP

The white cub went into a panic as soon as the dazed look halfway cleared from its open, pale eyes. It went into more of a one when it tried to hiss at Claire and found itself muzzled by the strip of cloth.

Uttering stifled yowls, fur bristling and tail puffed, it scrambled around in a desperate but clumsy effort to escape. It tripped over its own big paws and tumbled. It swiped at the cloth, shook its head, backed up in a rapid scurry, and bumped rump-first into the wall.

Finally, it crouched in a corner, trembling and making piteous mewling noises.

"You really are just a baby, aren't you?" Claire said.

It arched its back and flattened those furry triangular ears.

"There, now. I'm not going to hurt you. Poor lost little thing." She kept her voice soothing. "You must miss your mother. You must be hungry."

Which led again to the questions of where and how big its mother was, what it was, how many of them there were, why she'd never heard tell of anything like this before... but for the time being, Claire knew there weren't going to be any ready answers.

"Well, if you were in the goat shed looking for milk..."

She went into the kitchen and poured some from that morning's milking into a shallow bowl. The cub did not move from its spot in the corner. It hunched up again as she came back into the room, but its nose twitched like a rabbit's and she knew it had caught the scent.

Claire sat cross-legged on the rug, barely aware anymore of the blizzard battering against the house. She set the bowl between herself and the cub. It eyed her, then eyed the bowl. It mewled again, plaintive, through its muzzled jaws.

"I'll take that off," she said, reaching.

It cringed and pressed into the corner.

"It's all right."

The softness of its fur again amazed her as her fingers brushed the white pelt. The cub quivered at her touch. Carefully, she unwound the cloth, ready to snatch back her hands at any sign of biting or clawing. It spit a tiny, feeble hiss that was more frightened than frightening.

"There, now," Claire said again. "Isn't that better? Want some milk?"

She nudged the bowl. The rich, creamy liquid sloshed. The cub, nose still twitching, crept forward but then shied away.

"Let's try this." She dunked the end of the cloth strip into the milk and dangled it enticingly close.

A tentative flick of a greyish-pink tongue... and the next she knew the cub had latched onto the cloth, sucking with half-starved eagerness. Moments later, it seemed to have forgotten all fear of her, its side pressing against her leg, hooking a paw over her wrist. Its mewls became greedy slurping grunts.

"Someone is hungry!" she said.

Soon, the bowl was licked-clean empty and every drop had been wrung from the sop-cloth. The cub heaved a sated sigh. It crawled into Claire's lap. A huge yawn showed that impressive mouthful of curved frost-white teeth.

It still didn't feel as warm as something of that size should. Yet it wasn't shivering, didn't seem to be cold or uncomfortable in any way. It dozed, content, not purring but... sort of... thrumming... a sensation she could feel more than hear.

Even when she picked up the cub and moved to a chair, it just stretched, yawned again, and settled on its back with its luxurious tail draped over her arm and its fuzzy, full, round tummy exposed.

WHAT TO DO

The closest to a doctor that Far Enough had was Albert Marlowe, called "Doc" by all those who knew him.

This despite his lack of any sort of college education, professional license or formal training. But, as his neighbors said, in an emergency, any doctor was better than none.

He'd learned his trade during the War Between the States, when his mother converted their home to a hospital for injured soldiers. Union or Confederate, Yank or Reb, Eliza Marlowe hadn't cared which. She and her children helped out with the nursing, and even gone to the battlefields to assist the surgeons.

Young Albert became a deft hand at cautery and amputation. The bonesaw suited him better than the stethoscope. He was much better at applying maggots to an infected wound than leeches to balance the humors.

Twenty years later, a man of his qualifications could find little work in the citified East, but the wild untamed West was another story. Out here, there were hazards aplenty. It was a violent place, dangerous and unforgiving.

This severe winter even more than most.

And this blizzard?

The worst he'd ever seen.

A real jeezer.

Shortly after it struck, four men came by, bundled up against the snow. Bart Jordan from the smithy, a couple of the Grangers, and tough old Zeke Rogers.

They were, they said, getting an effort together. There would be, they said, a lot of folks caught out in it unawares.

Homesteaders with their livestock. Women hanging their washing. Kids off to the school.

"Dean Hadden set off for his daughter-in-law's on foot," Bart Jordan had said. "I don't know if he had time to make it there or not before this hit."

"Then there's them as what went with Lars Rutger and John Arlen," said Zeke Rogers. "Somewheres between here and Juniper by now and God knows what they'll do."

"You can't mean to go after them," Marlowe had protested.

"No, can't, they're on their own," Michael Granger said. "But we've got to be organized. I'm thinking we go 'round, checking in, seeing who's all right and who's needing help. Head upstreet for Thorpe's, maybe. Set up there, and you know he'd want to be involved."

"Want to take charge, more'n likely," Rogers muttered.

"Let him," said the other Granger, Lewis, Michael's uncle. "Who gives a damn? People could die in this."

"They will," Marlowe said, having treated his share of frostbite and exposure.

"There's that heavy sledge-wagon out back of my smithy," Jordan said. "We're thinking, load it up with as many spare coats and blankets, as much gear as we can..."

"Just, nothin' handy to pull it," Rogers said. "Less'n we use your Perch."

Marlowe owned two horses, a light and swift gelding for when he had to be somewhere in a hurry, and Bump. Bump was a crossbred Percheron mare, a stout and sturdy plodder who made up for in stamina and uncomplaining nature what she lacked in speed, grace or beauty.

"Of course," he'd said at once. "I'll grab my bag."

With Bump pulling the sledge-wagon, they made their way up the lane. It was a slow, painful, punishing trek. Snow sheeted sideways on the wind. None of them could see more than a few yards in any given direction at any given time. The cold had viciously sharp needle teeth and a knack for finding the weaknesses in their bulky winter garments.

Ned Allan and Russ Corvill, their own homes and families secured, joined them. Bart Jordan left to go look in on his wife, pregnant and alone with the girls having headed to school that morning.

They did reach the Thorpe place.

Only to find the lady of the house dead, her husband missing, the oldest boy hurt, the baby in a state, and the hired man with no idea what to do.

MISTAKEN

She had to keep moving. Whatever else, she had to keep moving.

To stop was to die.

To keep moving might also be to die, but moving at least offered the chance that she'd come to a house. Stopping offered no such chance.

Emma Curtis tried to keep her wits sharp by silently saying lessons to herself as she walked. She listed the presidents, and the states. She spelled difficult words. She recited the dates of famous historic battles... Civil War generals ... Indian chiefs. She did sums and multiplications.

Sometimes the panic tried to seize her. She would get lost. She would freeze. She would fall off a cliff — there were no cliffs anywhere nearby, but this hardly mattered. She would be eaten by wolves.

When those thoughts came, Emma clenched her fists in the scraps of her cut-up cape that served as mittens, and kept going. The children, her students, were depending on her. For their sake, she had to find help. Peter needed medicine, they all needed food and warm clothes. Their parents needed to know they were safe.

What about the Jordan girls? The Wood twins? Were they safe?

If they had gotten home, why hadn't anyone else come to the schoolhouse to fetch the others?

What would she do if she found them, if she quite literally stumbled over their bodies, out here in the snow?

Dread cramped her heart at the prospect, but she didn't stop moving.

Amos' coat weighed her down. Her wool skirt flapped until it was too snow-caked and heavy, and then it dragged, slowing her even further. The cloth she'd tied around her left foot was unraveling. The leather shoe beneath might have been made of paper for all the good it did.

She came to a fence. Almost walked right into it.

Emma could scarcely believe her eyes.

A fence... the closest fence she knew of to the schoolhouse was the one bordering Mr. Thorpe's pasture. If this was that same fence — and it didn't seem possible it could be any other — then she had been headed in a much more westerly direction than she'd thought.

But she wasn't about to quibble with this stroke of good fortune. She could follow the fence, and it was bound to lead her eventually to the house or the barn.

On she went.

The cloth around her left shoe came all the way off. She considered going back to retrieve it, trying to re-wrap her foot. Too much effort. She kept going.

She had Cora's scarf over her face, trying to shield her eyes from the wind and the cruel pelting of the icy, gritty snow. It wasn't as if she could see, anyway. She had a hand on the fence so she couldn't stray from it, and—

Bumped into someone.

"There you are, you stupid slut," a hoarse voice growled. "Knew I'd find you! Thought you could hide from me?"

A man seized her by the shoulders and shook her. Emma's head snapped back and forth on her neck. Then he flung her to the ground. The toe of his boot drove into her hip, sending a sudden hot pain racing through her.

Emma clawed at the scarf, and winced at the scouring frost that sought to peel the skin from her face. She peered up into the howling storm as best she could and made out the shape of the man looming over her. Tall, in a warm buffalo-hide overcoat.

It was Mr. Thorpe. He kicked her again, this time on her thigh so that her entire leg first felt turned to stone, then set afire.

"Mr. Thorpe," she said, but it came out more a desperate cough than sensible words.

"I won't be ruined by the likes of you!"

Another kick. Emma tried to roll away, but it caught her square in the small of the back. Her scream was smothered by a faceful of snow as the kick flipped her onto her belly. Snow was in her mouth and up her nose, suffocating her.

"You won't be telling anyone what you saw!"

He stomped on her, setting the sole of his boot between her shoulderblades. He held her down, face buried in the snow. Emma flailed her limbs. She couldn't breathe. The frost burned against her cheeks, in her throat.

Mr. Thorpe was still ranting, but between the wind roaring all around and the snow clogging her ears, Emma couldn't catch but bits of what he said. It struck her that he thought she was someone else. He thought she was someone else, and he meant to kill her.

Bright specks and motes flickered crazily in front of her eyes. Her chest ached from the need to draw a breath. The cold was not just seeping into her body, it was flooding in, taking her over.

The boot lifted. Emma heaved partway up out of the snow, coughing, pawing it from her face, spitting, gasping for air. Then the boot slammed into her side, her ribs. She felt something crunch, felt a flare of pain that laced her body like a whalebone corset cinched unbearably tight.

"— with my own son under my own roof —"

She yanked at the scarf and the shawl over her head, hoping that if she pulled them loose and showed him who she was, he'd realize he was making a terrible mistake. He'd stop kicking her, stop killing her.

Again, the boot. Lower on her side, digging into the softer flesh at her waist. She managed to roll with the blow, roll away from him, though not without sending more jabs of pain through her ribs. Mr. Thorpe snarled and rushed after her, hauling back his leg for another kick.

"No," Emma said, but the word was weak and lost, didn't carry.

He was going to kill her.

Somehow, she got her arms up as he launched the next kick. The boot met her hands instead of her face, and Emma shoved with all her might.

Mr. Thorpe pitched backward, uttering a rough bark of astonishment. His arms wheeled. His coat came open and fanned out like buffalo-hide wings. He landed on his back, vanishing from her sight in a billow of dusty snow.

Emma lay where she was for a moment, trying to regain her breath. Every shiver and gasp made her ribs seem to stab inward, as if she was a pincushion. She had never been so cold, never. Cold, numb, exhausted.

"You miserable bitch," Mr. Thorpe said. He got up, brushing at his coat.

She had a glimpse of his expression through an eddy of white flakes that blew past, and it chilled her so that she thought her skin had turned to ice.

Then something moved in the churning whiteness behind Mr. Thorpe. Something large and indistinct, and closing in. Emma saw only a rushing blur. She heard a shriek that made her feel even colder, and the something was upon him.

He sensed it at the last moment and started to turn, only to have his legs swatted out from under him. He dropped. It sprang. Mr. Thorpe screamed.

Emma would have screamed as well, but she was too frozen, too frozen in every sense.

White fur and a heavy, muscular body. Huge paws that pinned and held. A head that rose up, jaws that gaped, teeth that slashed down like the fangs of a striking snake. She saw that one of those teeth was broken off into a jagged stub, and then couldn't see them at all because they sank into flesh.

The white creature tore through Mr. Thorpe's neck in a shower of blood. Some splattered over Emma. Hot. Scalding. Like being splashed with boiling soup. His head flopped back, connected only by strips of purplish meat and the knobby bone-cord of his spine.

He fell again, knees unbuckling, borne to earth by the weight of the beast that hunched over him. Emma heard cloth shredding, then a thick wet ripping noise followed by ravenous smacks and chomps.

It was eating him. Feeding on him. Devouring him as his blood fumed hot into the snow. Organs bulged out, glistening and steaming. There was a reek of guts and shit and blood and slaughter.

Her gorge lurched and rose, but Emma fought to keep from vomiting. She tried to inch away in a fast but stealthy manner, and only scrambled, clumsy as a crippled grasshopper.

The big head came up. Frost-pale eyes fixed on Emma. The white fur was streaked with red, the jaws and teeth dripping. It growled at her, setting a paw atop the savaged corpse.

She raised her shivering hands, palms out.

The pale eyes kept watching her as the head lowered again for another bite. The creature resumed its grisly meal, making a low and satisfied grunting rumble.

WILLOW POND

The girls and little Freddie Kradenmeyer were too cold, too tired, and too scared to try and make for the house.

"Dadda will come fetch us," Nancy Burdock had said.

"How's he gonna know where we're at?"

"Rufus and Lester will tell him we came here to skate."

"What if Rufus and Lester ain't got home yet either?"

At that, Liza Kradenmeyer piped up. "What about Nell?"

"She wasn't going home though," said Roy. "She was going to school."

"Could she even get to school in this?" Jolene Burdock asked, jumping up and down in place. "How far is it? Far, isn't it?"

Freddie puffed himself up. "Pretty far, yeah, but we can walk it easy."

"Most days," Liza said. "Not like today."

"No day's ever been like today," Isaac said.

There was no argument, not that there would be. None of them had seen a storm like this in all their lives. None of them had imagined there could be a storm like this.

The Burdock kids had been out playing, sledding down Thorpe's Hill on scraps of wood, burlap sacks, and Sondra in a dented old tin pan Momma said she could use, when they'd seen four of the Kradenmeyers making in the direction of the schoolhouse. It got sometimes frowned upon by their parents — Momma held that the white folks wouldn't want their children making friends with nigrahs, and the way Mr. Kradenmeyer always looked like he'd just bit into something sour suggested he agreed – but with both their big families out here nearest neighbors, the temptation often was too much.

So, that morning, Roy, Liza and Freddie chose to skip school after all in favor of joining in the fun. Nell, anxious about getting in trouble with their father, went on without them, marching off like a good little soldier in check gingham. The rest of them sledded, chose up sides for a snowball war, and shared a mess of oat-cakes smeared with walnut butter that Momma had packed for their snack.

Then Jolene took a snowball to the face, which made her cry, and Nancy said they should go skating on the pond instead. Which sounded grand to the rest of them –

"We don't have any skates," Liza had admitted, looking downcast.

"We didn't bring any either," said Sondra, "but we can still slide in our shoes."

— and it was decided. Well, decided except for Lester and Rufus, who wanted one more sled-run down the hill. They'd stayed while the others went on ahead toward Willow Pond.

They called it that on account of how it was half surrounded by a stand of willows that bent their long branches down to the water, branches that were flowery in the springtime and leafy in the summer but just skinny barren sticks since autumn. Skinny, barren sticks with their ends stuck in the thick ice.

But, they'd no sooner started skating than the storm bore down, and now here they were taking what pitiful shelter they could underneath one of those frozen willows. The down-hanging branches, ice-covered, almost made a sort of a bird-cage that got more and more closed in as the spaces between the branches became packed with snow. That helped to block the wind, but didn't do much against the cold.

The longer they'd stood there, the colder they got. Even crowded in a tight, shivering clump, and never mind white folks or nigrahs when in this weird snow-dark they were all grey anyway.

It was like whatever warmth there was in them went draining down through their feet into the very ground, even where that ground wasn't shin-deep in snow.

"We can't stay out here," Isaac said again.

Roy Kradenmeyer nodded. "We'll freeze to death for sure."

"Don't say that!" his sister scolded. "You'll scare Freddie!"

"Will not!" Freddie protested. "It's girls who get scared!"

"I'm not scared," said Sondra.

"I am." Jolene jumped up and down again. "But I'm more colder than I'm scareder."

Just like that, everyone fell to complaining.

"I'm cold, too."

"I'm tired."

"—thirsty—"

"—need to—"

One of the girls began to cry. Then another. Then Freddie started sniveling.

"That's it!" Roy stamped an angry foot. "Let's go!"

"Can't go out there in that!" said Nancy. "Can't hardly see!"

"Wind would blow us away," Liza said.

"Not if we hold hands all in a line."

They'd fussed, whined and complained more.

"I'll go," Isaac said. "I'll get Dadda with the cart, or if the storm's too bad for that, a rope."

"And coats and boots?" Nancy asked.

"And coats and boots."

"And warm milk with honey and cinnamon?" asked Jolene.

"And flapjacks!" added Sondra with a ravenous moan.

Several stomachs rumbled loud enough to be heard through the wind. It made them laugh despite everything else.

"I'll make sure Mumma has some waiting," Isaac promised.

"I'll go with you," said Roy. "We're the biggest and the oldest."

Finally, it was settled. Isaac and Roy struck off in the direction of Burdock place and were almost instantly lost to sight. The rest of them, the four girls and Freddie, pressed as all-close-together in a clustered circle as they could, sitting turned inward with their backs to the outside.

At first, they talked and told stories. As time went on and the cold seeped in, talk became more desultory. Nancy tried singing to keep their spirits up, but her voice soon trailed off into silence. One by one, they retreated into themselves, falling quiet, letting their minds go away from their shivering bodies.

None of them knew how long they sat there. Only that it seemed like forever.

Like forever and forever.

GUIDED BY FAITH

All her life, since being taught at her mother's knee, Hannah Trotter knew that Hell was a very real thing ... fire and brimstone, lakes of boiling excrement, searing smoke, burning sulfur.

Now, she wondered.

Not about the existence of Hell or the reality of it, goodness no.

But about the heat of it. And whether, truly, Hell could be cold.

If Hell could be cold, this would be a foretaste of it. A frozen, terrible Hell on earth. A place of driving wind and bitter ice, blinding whiteouts, deep drifts that mired and dragged ... numbing chills and stinging frost-nettles of pain ...

She kept up a steady murmur as she walked, repeating the 23rd Psalm over and over.

The Devil's winter demon had prowled all around the house, clawing at the door, snuffling at every crack. Seeking weakness. Trying to frighten her. Perhaps hoping to lure her outside, in surrender or confrontation.

Hannah had not weakened. She'd knelt in prayer, steadfast, and finally the demon left her door. It gave up. It went away.

A trick?

No. No trick.

The certainty had come to her, sure as anything, that the white devil was gone.

Then another certainty, equally sure, came to her.

It came in the form of an angel.

Her own sweet little Charlotte, called to Heaven... a vision of Charlotte, serene and beautiful...

Paul was in trouble.

He needed her.

Amos?

She didn't know. Amos had gone to school; he must have stayed there at the schoolhouse or else he would have been home by now. Of course he'd stayed. Stayed to help the teacher, and comfort the younger children. He wouldn't have left them on their own, and he hadn't brought them here, so he must have stayed at the schoolhouse. Amos would look after his fellow students. Amos would be their guardian.

Paul, though...

Paul had gone to the Grangers' place that morning to help with the chores, and he hadn't come back yet. Even if he'd waited at first, she knew her Paul, how he could be. It'd gall him something fierce to stick snug and wait, while not knowing how matters stood at his own house.

As the storm got worse, so would have his need to get home.

Or, one of those lulls might have done for him what lulls were said to do and lulled him, lulled him into thinking the worst was past and he could make it, only to have it rise up again.

Her Paul was out there, caught in the blizzard, and he needed her.

The Devil's beast?

It wouldn't harm her. Couldn't harm her. God would see to that.

God, by way of Charlotte, their gentle and innocent little lamb, their angel, would see to that.

So, she'd dressed herself as warmly as she could. Long johns under her heaviest skirt, one of Paul's flannel shirts over her blouse and a coat over that, boots, gloves, a beaver hat, a long scarf. She finished by taking down the black and white cow hide Paul had tacked up to the wall and wrapping it around herself like a big leather cloak.

And out into the blizzard she'd gone.

Almost at once, she'd regretted it, but steeled herself because this was her test.

Hours, it seemed, she broke a trail through the deep snow, a trail that the wind gusted full again behind her almost as soon as she'd moved on. She lost all sense of direction. The cold was like a living thing trying to devour her.

She paused, exhausted, partially sheltered from the wind in the lee of a big stone. It struck her how restful it'd be to just sit down for a while, set a spell, as they said. Only for a moment, or a moment or two... just to catch her breath, ease her aching legs, work some feeling back into her fingers... then get up and go on.

"No, Mama, no," said a voice like golden bells.

Hannah lifted her head and saw Charlotte. Not as a vision, but saw her, a right proper angel... gowned and haloed, with wings softer and purer than the best goosedown... with God's light beaming all around her and shining in her eyes ...

"You have to get up, Mama," the golden voice said. "Papa needs you."

"Oh, my baby, my dear Charlotte," Hannah sobbed.

"Get up, Mama, get up. You're almost there."

"My precious girl..."

The wind did not ripple Charlotte's gown, did not stir her hair or the feathers of those angelic wings. Her perfect pink-toed little bare feet did not stand in the snow or even atop it but floated above it. She beckoned. She held out a tiny, delicate hand.

"Yes, all right, Mama's coming." Hannah heaved herself up.

"This way, Mama."

The angel drifted untouched through the storm. Hannah struggled after.

Something dark stuck out of the whiteness. It looked familiar, and when she bent to examine it Hannah discovered it was the empty sleeve a coat. A man's coat. Paul's coat, the one he'd worn that morning when he left the house.

Two steps on, snagged in a dead branch, she found the faded bandanna he liked to wear, in memory of his cowboy days.

Another step further, and she found Paul, or found his boots and denim-clad legs protruding from a snowy heap that had drifted over the rest of him where he lay. Hannah dropped to her knees, using both hands to sweep away the cold covering.

He was grey as a ghost, face frosted with icy stubble, lips the same color as his denims, eyes hidden behind grainy lumps of congealed tears and blood. Yet he'd shed his coat and thrown aside his bandanna, and as she looked at him she saw that he'd also yanked his collar and shirtfront wide open. As if he'd been suffocating, desperate for a lungful of air.

"Paul!"

She shouted, and shook him, but Paul did not stir. Hannah took hold of him under the armpits, straining to budge his weight. She couldn't lift him, couldn't carry him. More harsh sobs wracked her throat.

"Please, God! Please help me!"

"Pull him, Mama," Charlotte said.

Pull...?

Hannah unwound the cowhide, spread it, and somehow hauled Paul onto it. When she pulled, though it was not easy, the cowhide did slide over the packed snow. She could drag him. Slowly, with effort, but she could drag him.

"That's my girl, that's my dearest angel, such a good girl, such a good idea."

She covered him with his discarded coat.

Which way was the house?

For that matter, where even where they?

The big stone, that was on their land, wasn't it?

"Mama, over here."

Again, Hannah lifted her head, peering through the blowing sleet and snow. There was the light, God's glorious light, beaming from all around Charlotte like rays of sunshine.

"Over here, Mama."

Reciting the Lord's Prayer silently to herself, Hannah let her angel daughter guide them toward home.

DISBELIEF

She found the fence the same way she'd found it the first time, by almost colliding with it. Not at a shuffling walk this time but at as much of a run as Emma could manage.

Fence... up... over... her ice-heavy skirt snagging... falling...

Pain clenched at her chest and side. Her ribs felt like the slats of a flimsy crate, or a tumbleweed crunched beneath a wagon wheel. Broken? Cracked? Stabbing her innards? She didn't know.

Mr. Thorpe had tried to kill her.

Would have done, if not for that... that... thing... that thing emerging from the blizzard, tearing at him.

It would come for her next. Finish what Mr. Thorpe had begun.

A desperate look back showed her nothing but snow. Not blowing or coming down as heavily as it had been, but, still, snow as far as her bleary eyes could see.

Snow, and a dark smudge that might have been Mr. Thorpe's coat, or might have been a bush, a shadow, a trick of her eyes, or nothing at all.

No sign of the creature, or the blood.

Emma got up again.

The fence.

It had to be the one around the Thorpes' cow pasture.

If she followed it, therefore, it had to lead her to their house or barn.

Unless the creature—

She banished that thought unfinished and set out along the fence, hoping she'd kept her bearings enough to be taking the shorter route instead of tracing the long way around the entire pasture.

Feet numbed to deadness.

Legs like jelly stuffed with knitting needles.

Body aching.

Ribs throbbing sharply with each step.

Back and shoulders feeling knotted, gnarled.

Chunks of frozen meat for hands.

Face flayed by swarms of tiny, stinging, icy wasps.

Ears and nose? Might as well have been cut off, for all she could feel of them.

Eyes? Peering almost uselessly through swollen, gritty, painful slits of blood, ice, and tears.

Moving hunched and bent nearly double, with head bowed, she found the side of the house the hard way. It didn't hurt — she was too cold — but the jarring knock drove her teeth together and made bright spots dance in her vision.

She reeled, recovered, and groped along the wall until she found something that felt like a door.

Which would be locked, a sour voice in her heart said. Locked, because Mr. Thorpe had wanted to kill her, he hadn't even known who she was but he'd wanted to kill her, so of course the door would be locked and she'd die this close to salvation after all.

It wasn't locked.

It opened, spilling Emma and a gout of wind-blown snow into a room that, for all it might have been cool, was so much warmer than outside that the heat hit her like an enveloping slap.

She somehow pushed the door shut again behind her, then sank to the floor with a tired moan she'd intended to be a loud cry for help.

Someone heard anyway, or had heard the door open and felt the draft, because a rush of footsteps and querying voices flocked around her.

"Blessed Mary, mother of God!"

"—a woman—"

"—who is she?"

"—get here in this?"

"—must be freezing to death—"

"—careful there—"

Meanwhile, she felt hands grasp under her arms and around her waist. She was lifted, carried into another room even warmer than the first, and set down in a chair. Pinpricks began tingling all over her skin.

"—the schoolteacher—"

"Curtis, her name is, Emma Curtis, I think—"

"Emma, that's right, she roomed with us—"

"—doing here? What about the—"

She thought she recognized some of the voices ... the one who'd said she'd roomed with them might have been Michael Granger, and the Irish lilt could only belong to the Thorpes' hired man ... she still could see nothing, her watering eyes making runny, bloody melt-trickles down her cheeks.

"Back off now, all of you back off and give the poor girl a chance to breathe."

The babble retreated a bit.

"—out of those wet clothes before—"

"—some sense of decency, man!"

"—to look outside, see if—"

"—good idea, God forbid—"

Someone touched her shoulder. The voice that had told the others to back off now addressed her directly. "Miss Curtis, it's Albert Marlowe, do you remember me?"

Emma managed a nod. "Doc," she said.

He chuckled a little. "Well, so they call me, and it seems I'm the closest we've got for now. Know where you are?"

"Thorpe ... place?"

"Yes, ma'am. Now, this might hurt some—"

A blissfully soft, warm, wet cloth — it still felt like a wire scrubber — pressed to her face. She winced as Doc Marlowe gently laved her eyes clear, then began chafing life back into her hands.

"—no one else out there—"

Emma blinked and squinted, and finally saw as if through a film of egg whites that she was in a spacious kitchen, with brick floors and rows of copper cookware, and a large iron stove. The smell of boiled beef and coffee made her stomach growl like a hungry dog.

A half-dozen men stood around her, looking concerned. She was surprised to not see Samuel Thorpe among them; he hadn't accompanied his younger siblings that day, and this was his house. Nor did she see Mrs. Thorpe, or indeed any women... the Thorpes had a hired girl, too, or so she'd thought.

But it was their hired man — O'Connell? O'Connor? — who seemed to have more or less taken charge. He brought Emma a steaming enamelware cup, which she held between her palms when her fingers did not want to bend.

She sipped. The coffee, liberally dosed with whiskey, coursed like liquid fire down her throat and deliciously heated her insides. The pained throb in her ribs seemed to dwindle down to a dull soreness.

And wasn't it just as well none of the Thorpes themselves were here? When they heard what had happened, what she had to say?

"The school," she said in a hoarse whisper.

"The children?" asked Michael Granger. "Minnie? My sister? Is she all right?"

As Doc Marlowe removed her shoes to tend her feet, Emma falteringly told her story around more sips of whiskey-laced coffee. How the storm had struck during lessons, how so many of the students had come that day without coats, how the Jordan sisters and the Wood twins decided to try for home while the others resolved to sit tight and wait for rescue, but then the weather continued to worsen.

When she mentioned the loud snapping and sparks of cold electricity leaping from the metal, several men nodded knowingly. She described how they'd had plenty of firewood once Amos broke up some of the desks... and some food, not a lot, but some.

"Peter, though, Peter Thorpe, Peter kept getting sicker... and the younger ones were scared... well, we all were... and when no one came, I knew someone had to go for help."

"Brave girl," someone said. "In a freezing gale like that?"

Emma shuddered, and drank more coffee before she could spill it. "I ... then, in the storm, I... Mr. Thorpe was there."

She expected disbelief from them then, accusations of hysteria or imagination, as she described how the town's very founder seemed to have gone murderously mad. But then they told her about Mrs. Thorpe, and Samuel.

"Lettie's gone," the hired man said. "If she'd witnessed it, and he went after her, he might have mistaken you for her."

Their grim, sober expressions only went skeptical when she reached the part of the tale that seemed impossible even to her.

"A great white beast?"

"The snow, playing tricks on her eyes—"

"No," said the Thorpes' hired man. "No, the lassie speaks truth. I've seen it too."

"You, O'Connor?" A wooly-bearded man scoffed, hooking his thumbs in his suspenders. "As if you're any kind of a reliable—"

"And I more than saw it," O'Connor interrupted. He put a rag-wrapped object on the table and flipped back the edges to reveal the long, pointed tooth concealed within. "Cracked this right out of the devil's head, so I did."

They examined it, with a grudging and unwilling belief.

"How big was it?"

"Huge," said O'Connor, and Emma nodded.

"Attacked Thorpe, you said?"

"Killed him, I think." Emma shifted her gaze from one man to the next. Most of them had trouble meeting her eyes, and she supposed they were horrid red harridan's eyes, lunatic's eyes. "And it's still out there, whatever it is. But we have to go save the children."

MASKS OF ICE

Andrew Kradenmeyer crawled through the snow on numb hands and knees. His lower legs were also numb. His feet, dragging along behind him, might not even have been there at all for all he could feel of them.

How long had he been out here?

Where were the others?

Where was Dora-Lee?

Was she safe? Had she made it back to the house?

It seemed simultaneously the least he could hope for and the most he could ask.

He crawled, crawled.

Head down. Hair hanging like icicles in his face. Nostrils stoppered with plugs of frozen snot. His cheeks felt glazed, felt coated thick in a shell that also crusted around his lips and in his sparse young-man's beard.

His eyelids were sealed shut, sealed in a rime of tears that left him blinded.

At first, he'd rubbed them, trying to clear them, but only irritating them afresh so that they watered and stung. The more he did it, the more it hurt, and the more aggravated his eyes and the flesh around them became. Finally, the scraped-raw skin bled. Even the blood turned to ice, which only scoured and abraded deeper the more he rubbed at that.

He made himself stop trying to wipe at his eyes and concentrated on keeping moving. On crawling, on following this furrow so that he did not veer off or go in circles.

Andrew, at almost twenty-one years, remembered a time before Far Enough. He remembered his father, an able-bodied father with full use of both legs, taking him ice fishing with his uncles and cousins on some Wisconsin lake.

They'd auger a hole in the ice to drop their lines through. One of his uncles, who'd been a whaler when he was no older than Andrew was now, used to tell stories of the northernmost seas... how, there, the seals and narwhals would poke their heads up through holes in the ice to get a breath of air. How, if the hole closed up, they might drown.

That was Andrew's mouth, his breathing hole in the ice-mask forming over his face. If it closed, he would suffocate.

He remembered the fish they'd pull up, how the fish would flop on the lake's icy surface, gaping and gasping their wide-open mouths.

That was him, too.

Gaping and gasping. Gulping for breath.

He crawled. Snow lashed against him in wind-driven relentlessness.

When the deadly white wall of the blizzard loomed in the north, the five of them had been ranged out across the fields, armed with spades and hoes and digging sticks, searching for stragglers. Some barley, a beanstalk, a few carrots or onions still buried in the cold dirt... anything at all would have helped.

Thom saw it first, that rolling mass of clouds bearing down. He'd yelled and run to his mother. But when Berta hollered for the rest of them to make for the house, Andrew, Jamie and Dora-Lee had stood staring as if spellbound.

The speed of it, the terrible rushing speed!

The sound it made, that hollow turbulent roar!

The way twisters of snow seemed to whisk upward from the earth into the storm's black, churning maw!

The sputter and dance of eerie lightning!

Hills and trees vanishing, blotted out, just erased by solid white... their house looking an incredible distance away, then suddenly swallowed whole...

Andrew had heard Dora-Lee call out his name, had seen her rushing toward him, skirt hiked, brown ringlets bouncing beneath the brim of her bonnet. He'd started toward her, tripped on his spade, and gone sprawling. He'd gotten up again and gone on.

They'd been four, maybe five furrows apart before it engulfed them.

"Dora-Lee!" he'd shouted.

If she'd answered, it was lost in the wind.

Only four or five furrows... he should have been able to reach her with ease. He'd raised an arm to protect his face and made for where he was sure she'd been, but couldn't find her. Had they missed each other, passed each other, unable to see? Had they gotten turned around?

He wasn't sure where his brother Jamie was, either. Or his stepmother, and stepbrother Thom. For all he knew, the five of them could have been blundering around inches apart.

The chill was a white-hot silvery freezing burn.

It sapped his strength. It burrowed into his bones like woodlice.

It crisped and crackled inside his nose. It made his eyeballs throb and contract into what felt like small jellied stones.

Andrew had continued trying to walk, until he'd been forced to admit to himself that he was wandering aimlessly with no real sense of direction. He'd found it harder and harder to stay on his feet, eventually sinking to his knees. The blizzard's fury blew less harshly nearer the ground.

He'd decided to crawl the length of the furrow in a straight line. At the end, he'd reach either the wall of piled stones bordering the edge of the field nearest the house, or the plowed and turned earth giving way to the rockier land sloping off toward the ravine between their property and the Burdocks' hog farm. If the former, he'd make his way to the house. If the latter, he'd reverse course until he did find the wall, and then make his way to the house.

And, hopefully, there he'd find Dora-Lee waiting, safe and sound.

They should have left, like they'd talked about, like they'd wanted to and planned.

They were going to anyway, this coming spring as soon as the weather got good enough to travel.

Before anyone found out she was pregnant again.

They'd take little Travis with them. They'd leave Far Enough and go someplace else, from Far Enough to far away. Where nobody knew them. Where they could be married, live as husband and wife with their children, where it wouldn't be known and it wouldn't matter that she was his stepsister.

Wasn't as if they were blood-kin, after all. Wasn't as if they were related. Andrew had been a little boy when his father married Berta, introducing him and Jamie to Thom and Dora-Lee, telling them they were all now as brothers and sister. They'd grown up that way, but they'd known, always known —

As he crawled, his numb hands encountered an obstacle. A large snowy lump taking up his path in the furrow... something half-buried and with a drift building up on its windward side.

Andrew raised his numb hands and used the heels of them — his fingers would not bend, and were useless — to try and uncover his eyes.

The ice clung, hurting when he pawed at it. He almost thought he felt his eyelashes, or the lids themselves, wanting to peel away. Something tugged at his cheek, then ripped like a seam. Wet warmth welled up suddenly underneath his left eye, then congealed in a slushy wad.

He blinked as best as he could, squinting his eyelid slitted until some of his vision returned. He looked at the ice stuck to his glove, the bloodied ice, with scraps of strange greyish stuff frozen into it.

The strange greyish stuff was part of his face, plucked loose like a scab but not a scab, a dead-cold chunk of spongy frostbitten flesh that must have exposed him down to the bare cheekbone. His gorge lurched. Bile squirted into his mouth. He choked it back and peered at the lump in the furrow.

It was Jamie. His brother. Jamie, curled on his side, knees tucked to his chest, white-faced and blue-lipped, features distorted beneath a masklike layer of ice. Jamie, unmoving even when Andrew nudged and shook him.

A brief lull in the wind let the snow part enough to tease him with a glimpse of the next furrow over. He saw a leather shoe poking out of the snow, a leather shoe and a bit of striped woolen stocking.

Clumsily, Andrew crawled past Jamie's body, into the next furrow, to where Dora-Lee lay in a similar knee-tucked position. Frost whitened her brown ringlets and powdered her dress. She'd tied her bonnet like a kerchief over her mouth and nose, the cloth frozen solid from the moisture of her breath. Above it, ice-waterfalls of tears had formed around her swollen, glued-shut eyes.

She had her arms folded against her waist, as if to protect their tiny unborn baby. Andrew burrowed himself into the snow next to Dora-Lee, wrapped his own arms around her, and let the cold take them.

WITH THE DEAD

"**I**s it still out there?" Ruby Erlich whispered, clutching Edgar's arm.

"I don't know."

"Did it go away?"

"Ruby, I don't know."

"What should we do?"

"Wait," he said. "Wait, and pray, and have faith in the Lord."

She nodded, which she knew he couldn't see in the utter darkness, but would feel in the motion of her head against his shoulder.

How long had they been here?

What in heaven was going on?

First the creature, so white and strange, unlike anything she had seen in all her born days... most certainly no deer or elk, white or otherwise... no wolf, no bear, no mountain lion...

It had come after them more in the manner of a cat than anything else, she reckoned. Its paws, when she got a glimpse, were huge and splayed, wide furry pads that served as snowshoes... while she and Edgar had gone floundering along, boots plunging through that icy crust into deep drifts, it moved with grace and ease, hardly appearing to sink into the snow at all.

She'd seen how it paced them, its gait almost lazy, tail swishing, ears perked, mouth ajar in a way that might have been natural for something with such... such teeth... dear God such teeth!... but reminded her of a grin.

It had been stalking them. Playing with them like a cat after a pair of elderly mice.

Though, for elderly mice, they had made a good show of themselves. Crossing the creek, scrambling over the fence — she had lost one of her knit gloves to the barbed wire — and running as if their very lives had depended on it...

Which, Ruby knew, they had. Playing or not, nothing with that kind of a jawful of fangs would have been content to let its prey go.

So, run they had, weaving a clumsy course through the wooden crosses dotting the slope of the graveyard hill. They'd run and the sky above them had gone some unearthly color, a sheen like ivory satin gone yellow with age.

They'd stood no chance of reaching town from the far side of the hill. Even had they gotten within sight, nobody could have come in time to help them.

And something else was wrong, a terrible noise like a runaway train bearing down from the north...

She'd thrown a quick glance that way and seen the end of the world. As if God had held true on his promise not to destroy them by rain, but decided a scouring of wind and snow would do instead. A lightning-shot storm front, a raging death-blizzard ... with Far Enough right smack in its path.

With a yank that near pulled her arm off, Edgar had made a sudden veer to the right. A log frame of sorts jutted out from a steeper part of the hill there, the entrance to a dugout where undertaker's tools were kept.

Undertaker's tools, and...

...in the winter...

...until the thaw...

...when the ground was frozen too solid to dig...

A stout wooden door fit into the opening, secured from the outside by a latch and bolt but not a lock. Had it been locked, they'd have been done for. But Edgar smashed through a rime of ice to throw the bolt and lift the latch, then dragged the door open against a resisting layer of snow.

The pursuing creature must have known then that its game had gone on too long, the prey about to slip from its grasp. It had yowled at them, jaws gaping, giving Ruby an all-too-good view of a pallid bloodless greyish-blue maw lined with long frost-colored curves of teeth... teeth like something out of a nightmare.

She'd stared, unable to wrest her gaze away, until Edgar swept an arm around her waist and bundled her into the dugout. Like any root-cellar, it had a low earthen ceiling and a hard-packed dirt floor. Shovels and spades leaned against the walls.

Set in the center...

A glimpse of the coffins was all she got before Edgar dragged the door shut again. In that endeavor, the lunging white beast helped him when the weight of its furry mass struck against the planks.

It yowled again, a soul-blanching screech of cheated fury. Claws like sickle blades raked at the wood. But it held.

Hardly any light came through the cracks; the door was well-made. She and Edgar hugged each other. Both of them shivered from head to toe, partly from the cold and partly from the fright. In Edgar's case, he was even the worse off because his splash through the creek had left him half soaked.

The door had continued to hold, so they'd retreated a few steps and sat down on the largest coffin. Disrespectful of the dead, perhaps, but Ruby didn't imagine old Tom Jordan would mind. She nonetheless made a silent promise to herself, to God, and to Tom that if she and Edgar made it through this alive, they'd do him the best burial service Montana had ever seen.

The furious clawing kept on a moment, then ceased. A silence as utter as the darkness descended. Even that terrible train-roaring of the wind sounded muffled.

The dugout, where the winter-dead were kept until their graves could be dug, was not as cold as an icehouse... but neither was it warm. When that storm front reached the hill, the temperature plunged further.

But they were inside, sheltered from the brunt of the blizzard as well as from the creature that had chased them. They just had to wait.

In the dark. The utter, absolute, entombed dark. With the dead.

The waiting was very, very hard.

Ruby and Edgar huddled close, sharing what body heat they had.

"Will Claire be all right?" Ruby asked.

"She's a good, smart girl," Edgar said. "I'm sure she's buttoned up safe indoors."

The air smelled earthy, tinged with just the merest hint of decay because the chill kept the corpses from rotting, like sides of beef, hams, or legs of mutton kept in an icehouse.

"Did you see its teeth?" she asked.

"Couldn't miss them," Edgar said.

"It walked on top of the snow. I don't think it left tracks. Edgar, was it real?"

"As real as we are."

"But what was it?"

Talking helped the time to go by. Concern for their neighbors, for the state of the town... for their own home, their niece, their goats...

And speculation, endless speculation.

If not for the beast chasing them, they would have been caught out in the storm. So, in a sense, it had saved them. But why them? Why like that?

Eventually, they'd even dozed, overcome by weariness. The light doze became a deeper sleep, leaning tilted against each other with Edgar's head resting on Ruby's as hers rested on his shoulder.

RESCUE PARTY

"**W**e?"

More than one of the men had asked it, but, the schoolmarm wouldn't be dissuaded.

She was going with them. Cold or no cold, storm or no storm, frostbite or no frostbite, devil take her cracked ribs... those students were her responsibility and she was going with them.

Doc Marlowe might not have agreed with her decision, but he had to admire her grit. When she could have stayed here, waited in the warm kitchen —

With poor strangled Mrs. Thorpe laid out dead on the parlor settee where they'd moved her, covering her with a lace-trimmed tablecloth for a shroud?

Lewis Granger stayed instead, to look after the injured Sam Thorpe and his baby sister. The youth hadn't been told yet about his father; Marlowe had bandaged his head and instructed him to try not to move around much, as, if he was concussed it could lead to a bad spell of vomiting.

The rest of them gathered as many coats, quilts and blankets as they could find.

They armed themselves as well.

Marlowe wasn't sure how convinced the others had been by what O'Connor and the schoolmarm told them, but the tooth was undeniable evidence that something strange — even stranger than the blizzard and William Thorpe attacking his own wife and son! – must be going on. The tooth was not from any wolf, bear, catamount or other animal any of them had ever seen.

"Escaped from a circus or Wild West show?" was one theory he heard put forth as the men readied rifles and shotguns.

"Something from up the high country, the mountains," Zeke Rogers said. "Like that shaggy beast-man giant they talk about over Oregon way."

Marlowe himself thought of the bones that got dug up out in the badlands, bones of a size such that staggered the imagination.

Meanwhile, Miss Curtis bundled up better and borrowed a pair of Sam Thorpe's boots. They were too large, but she pulled on a few pairs of wool socks over the greyish-blotched flesh of her feet. She took the pot of boiled beef from the stove, bracing it in the back of the wagon so it wouldn't tip and spill.

The distance from the Thorpe house to the school would have been, on a normal day, a matter of minutes.

In this blinding bone-chill, with night coming on, it seemed more distant than the banks of the mighty Mississippi.

Bump plodded along at a steady pace, head low, dragging the sledge-wagon behind her. Then she stopped in her tracks, halfway across the snow-covered meadow, stood obstinate, and refused to budge no matter how Michael Granger snapped the reins.

The wind eased again, in that mocking way it had. Like a girl giving a fellow the come-hither smile, only to turn him the cold shoulder, cutting him dead, once he'd mustered the nerve to approach.

The air had not felt right all that long day, not since they'd wakened to that unseasonable thaw. Now, as fat flakes fell wet and heavy from the tarnished-pewter sky, it felt even less right than before.

"Think I see the schoolhouse," Zeke Rogers said. He pointed away at an angle toward a shadowy blotch that seemed made of lines and squared edges. "Off there, and how's that when we should have been making straight for it?"

"Damnable weather," someone else said.

Bump snorted and stamped a forehoof, as if she agreed.

"Jesus homespun Christ!" hissed another man. "Look yonder!"

The others all turned to follow his wide-eyed stare.

The creature that the schoolmarm and O'Connor had described blended so well into the white-and-silver day that it was hard to discern its true size or make out details. All Marlowe could say for a certain was that, yes, it was huge... huge and furred, long-bodied, wolflike in shape but bearlike in bulk and catlike in posture... and that it stood atop the snow in the way someone wearing snowshoes might do... and that as they looked at it, it looked back at them.

Ned Allan swung a borrowed rifle to his shoulder and squeezed off a shot that cracked like a bullwhip. Snow puffed up about three feet shy and wide of the white beast.

Everyone jumped. Several men swore, Ned among them albeit for different reasons. The white beast's pale eyes narrowed into shining glitters. It started toward them.

"The hell'd you go and do that for?" cried Russ Corvill.

"To kill the damn thing!"

"All's you did is miss, and piss it off!"

Bump tossed her head, breath pluming from flared nostrils, and lurched into a trot that almost unseated Michael Granger. The rest grabbed for handholds, but the jolt caught Ned still standing and he went over the side with a surprised yell, dropping the rifle.

The beast gave chase, loping at first, almost at its leisure, pacing them, tufted ears laid low and wary.

Brody O'Connor jumped down to help Ned, wallowing in a drifts. Michael fought with the reins, trying to bring Bump under control. The snowflakes began falling more densely again, spinning to earth in white veils.

"It's coming!" said the schoolmarm, who clung to the pot of boiled beef as if not sure whether it would make a better lifeline or weapon.

Zeke Rogers fired his Colt and missed by a mile. Russ Corvill got to one knee, bracing himself, taking aim with a shotgun from Thorpe's gun cabinet. Marlowe picked up the rifle.

The shotgun barked. The pursuing white beast's right foreleg exploded into shredded meat, bone and fur. Its agonized screech drilled into their ears. It stumbled and fell in a flurry of red-splattered snow.

"Get it!" Zeke yelled, vaulting from the wagon with his Colt waving in his fist. "Get the sumbitch!"

Russ was hot on his heels, and Marlowe right behind them. More maroon flowers burst on its white pelt as they fired. The screeching rose to a horrendous fever-pitch. It swiped with a paw. Claws whickered like blades, shearing through Zeke's thigh. He fell, rolling back and forth, clutching at his leg, adding his screams to the din. The stink of blood and gunsmoke wafted thick and hot.

Then it was over. A final bullet to the side of its head finished it off. They stood around it, those men of them that still could stand, gazing in amazement at the dead beast.

Doc Marlowe ran to Zeke. Here was something he knew, a battlefield wound, and in a mad way it cleared his mind to be confronted with a familiar problem. He'd been of an impressionable age when he'd seen men with their limbs blown off by cannonfire or slashed to the bone by sabers; this mauling was little different.

Zeke was already blanched from shock. The severe cold might even have been helping slow the spurt of the artery. He passed out before Doc cinched his belt as a tourniquet.

"We killed the damn bastard!" Russ Covill shook the shotgun in the air and whooped like an Indian brave doing a war dance.

"What about the school?" Emma Curtis asked, from where she still sat in the bed of the sledge-wagon. "The wind's gathering again!"

And, by the shouts coming from that direction, the gunshots and commotion hadn't gone unnoticed by her pupils. A dim rectangle of light filled with mostly-small silhouettes suggested that the children had opened the door to try and peer out.

The wind, as she'd said, was gathering again, regaining its strength. Hailstones and ice pellets spat down amid the snowflakes.

"Load him in," Marlowe said. "I'll tend him on the go; won't be the first time."

Michael Granger, who had calmed Bump, moved to obey.

But Brody lingered by the carcass, frowning. "I sure and do hate to be the bearer of bad tidings," he said, "but we might have ourselves a bit more of a problem."

"What do you mean?" Russ kicked the animal's leg. "We got it, we'll be famous, what a story we'll have, and wait until Trudy hears about this!" He laughed.

Brody didn't. "Remember what I showed you, back to the house? How I'd bashed one of the white devil's teeth smack out of its head?"

"Yeah..." said Russ, his laughter trailing away.

Squatting, Brody lifted the great shaggy head from the snow. The beast's pallid grey-pink mouth gaped. Its teeth, including both front fangs, curved in fierce, unbroken perfection.

"There's more than one of them," Emma said in a horrified hush. "There's more than one."

RAMSHACKLE

The wretched piece of work that was the old Goss place somehow still held together as the storm began to settle and night began to come on.

They could all thank their lucky stars for that, Cyrus Freedman knew. He'd been right that they'd be thankful for having the horses in there with them; what Lucifer and Gunpowder cost them in elbow room, they made up for in body heat.

In patience, as well. A goodly example. While Cy himself, Franklin Wood, the Rutger boy and the little Arlens might have fretted and worried, or been tempted by the lull in the storm to try again for town, the horses just stood patient. They stood heads-down, sometimes shifting their hooves or flicking their tails, but were otherwise prepared to just wait it out.

What else was there to do?

Going back out would be insanity, not to mention suicide.

Cyrus had seen that for himself already. Just what short taste of the blizzard he'd gotten when searching for Franklin, who'd gone after Missus Arlen, had convinced him.

Better and quicker to shoot himself with his own gun, if it came to that.

The cold... the cold was wicked. Sinister. Downright evil.

The wind laughed and the snow cackled.

Time and again they'd each looked toward the gap of their miserable makeshift door, hoping against hope that another of their party would come in, stamping and ice-covered but at least alive.

That Missus Arlen would have come to her senses and found her way back.

That Lars Rutger and the other men would have been able somehow to follow.

No one did.

No one came.

The Arlen kids only stopped their caterwauling when they'd exhausted themselves into a state more like unconsciousness than sleep.

He and Franklin, they did what they could for the kids, kept them to the center so as to benefit them most from what warmth as there was. With Franklin himself already in a bad way, Cyrus took the spot nearest the door where the chill was the strongest.

Each wind gust threatened to bring the whole shack down atop them. At first, snow had blown in through every crack and hole, but defeated itself by plugging the smaller openings.

Stefan Rutger, slim and blond, pretty as a girl, sat with his arms around the younger children. He'd tried to sing to them for a while, as they'd wailed for their mother. Now, though he looked awake, upright and with wide eyes occasionally blinking, something in his face told Cyrus that his mind had taken itself someplace far away.

Cy hardly blamed him. His own mind sought refuge in frequent wanderings, thinking of Sissa and Aaron and how things might be faring back home. Then he'd remember Sissa letting the kids out to play... telling them how they might as well make the best of the nice weather while it lasted... his nephews and nieces whooping with glee as they ran outside... shouting plans back and forth...

Ran outside without coats, just as he'd ridden off without his.

Would they have realized the danger as that storm front bore down? Or would they have gone right on sledding and playing until it was too late?

No, when his mind wandered there, it was not a comforting refuge. He did not want to imagine their dark faces whitening with frost. He did not want to imagine Sissa's agonized grief.

Thoughts of Rose were more pleasant. True, the same blizzard would have hit Juniper first, but even if Rose had been out and about that morning, she would have gone no further than the milliner's, the dressmaker's or the general store... all of which were right in a row along Juniper's Main Street... she would have had her choice of shelter.

If they got through this...

She'd never marry him.

Keeping company, that was one matter, one they'd both already faced their fair share of troubles over and more. He'd been warned away by plenty in Juniper who didn't think the likes of him ought to be sniffing after a white woman. The War might be over and the slaves might be freed, but a nigrah still was and always would be a nigrah.

He'd heard similar from his own sister, Sissa saying how he should find a girl of their own kind. Aaron had cousins by the dozen, she'd say, many of whom had expressed admiration in him and might be willing to make the trek West.

Rose swore up and down how she didn't care two shakes what folks thought. Rose had once shot a fellow for taking his hand to her in an attempt to cure her willful ways, announcing that she would spend her time with whoever she chose, and anyone who didn't like it could discuss it with her derringer.

But, that said and despite all...

No, she'd never marry him.

And if by some miracle she would, was there a preacher who'd do the honors?

Not in Juniper, there wasn't... the preacher there, when Cy was in town of a Sunday, scowled like thunder if Cy so much as entered his church.

Reverend Erlich?

He seemed a friendly and fair-minded man so far, but there was a difference between sermons and even welcoming nigrahs into his house when business brought them there — Cy grinned at the recollection of how his niece Tessa's eyes about popped when she got a gander at the reverend's book-lined study — and conducting a wedding.

Still, if by some other miracle, he would...

Lucifer, who'd been standing placid and puffing breath, suddenly tossed his head and let out a whinny of alarm. Gunpowder did the same, rearing up, striking out with his forelegs.

Franklin glanced up as if not knowing quite where he was. Cyrus moved to try and calm the horses.

Before he could take more than a step, Gunpowder's front hooves kicked against the shack's rickety wall. A plank splintered. Snow whirled in through the crack and dumped down on their heads from the precarious ceiling.

Something outside snarled. The very sound of it reached right down deep into Cyrus, caught up his nerves like a bundle of strings, and yanked. The horses did not care for it, either.

Shaking off his daze, Franklin started to get up. He looked as if he didn't half know where, or even who, he was.

The snarl grew into a roaring howl, or a howling roar, as if a grizzly and a timberwolf were trying to outdo each other.

Both horses went into a frenzy of terror, rearing, kicking, stomping and bucking.

The Rutger boy yelped, paddling backward with his heels, arms still hooked around the Arlen kids to drag them out from under the flailing hooves. Franklin, less quick or less lucky, took a blow to the temple and dropped like a sledgehammered pig.

A wall gave way. The roof tilted further, dumping more snow onto them.

Cy grabbed for Lucifer's bridle and missed as the horse charged from the disintegrating shack. Lucifer's shoulder knocked him spinning aside. Cy's ankle twisted with a grinding snap. He crashed into one of the other walls, into it and through it, taking more of the shabby structure with him.

It collapsed in a jackstraw jumble with Gunpowder still caught underneath. The dapple-grey stallion heaved with all his might, bursting out of the wreckage, shedding scraps and debris in all directions.

Cyrus had to do a sideways rolling dive to avoid being trampled. Freezing snow caked his face and corked up his nostrils and spilled down his collar. He choked on a mouthful.

The roaring howl rent his eardrums, practically on top of him.

An immense white blur crossed his vision.

Gunpowder screamed like a woman.

Blood flew, froze in mid-air, and hit Cy like a fistful of red hail.

Another white blur had leaped upon Lucifer, grappling him with claws and biting for the neck with teeth the size of cavalry sabers. Lucifer's own square teeth ripped out a hank of white fur. He bucked and kicked like crazy. The white thing catapulted off, and Lucifer's powerful hind legs slammed a double hoofprint into its ribs with a thudding, meaty crunch.

Lucifer galloped full speed one way while Gunpowder, raining blood, took off at a limping but strong pace in the other.

Cy's chest hurt with a burning, stabbing ache. He couldn't remember being kicked or if he'd been bitten... then he realized it was the frigid blast of sucking in huge gasps of breath.

He also realized he couldn't see anything of Franklin or the kids under the ruined pile of sticks, planks and snow that had been the Goss place.

And that, at some point in the confusing proceedings, he'd drawn his piece, the Smith & Wesson double-action he'd worn at his hip for six years and never fired on anything more dangerous than a row of target bottles and old cans.

A white beast, bigger than a bear but shaped more like a mountain lion, lay on its side a few yards away, ribs staved in from Lucifer's kick, legs scrabbling fitfully as it tried to get up.

The second one, paws stained and pelt speckled with Gunpowder's blood, padded toward Cyrus with a deadly, menacing hiss.

It leaped, and he fired, at the exact same time.

TERRIBLE DECISION

Warm!

Finally, oh, finally, she was warm!

Stella Hadden smiled sleepily.

First time since winter really got itself a foothold that she'd felt altogether warm and comfortable.

Almost too warm, if such a thing were possible.

She nudged the quilt from where it had been bunched in the hollow of her shoulder and neck. She rolled from her side onto her back, letting both arms flop loose atop the covers.

Warm as toast!

"Ah," she sighed. Then she stretched, yawning in a full, deep, smoky breath.

She coughed.

Smoky?

The air thick with it, hot with it, stinking with it.

Wide awake now, she sat upright into a cloudy layer of dense smoke hanging above the bed. She coughed again, harder, lungs protesting, and dropped back down, wiping at her watering eyes.

The fire —

A sullen red-orange glow filled the cabin.

Yellow flames tumbled and wrestled across the braided rag rug like playful kittens. More crawled, spiderlike, up the legs of the wooden chairs and raced in sizzling lines of fire along the chinking in the log walls.

She knew at once what must have happened. She'd stoked the woodstove and fireplace, built them both to blazing in an attempt to ward off the blizzard's insistent, pervasive chill. Then, as she and Danny slept, some embers had jumped free and —

Danny!

Wild terror seized her.

But he was there, still nestled in the quilts, sound asleep with his thumb in his mouth.

"Danny! Danny, wake up!" She shook him.

He made a drowsy, irritated mutter.

Stella scrambled out of bed, coughing as she sucked more of the smoke into her lungs. She seized the pitcher from the washstand and flung its contents, eliciting nothing more than a feeble splash and rush of steam. She seized the quilt next, flailing at the flames, beating at them, succeeding only in fanning them about and catching the quilt itself on fire.

Her eyes burned and watered so she could barely see. The smoke, the smoke invaded her nose and mouth... the more she coughed, the dizzier she felt, head swimming.

"Danny!" she cried again.

From too cold to this, to roasting alive in their own home?

He woke with a rattling cough. "Momma?"

She dropped the smoldering quilt, swept him into her arms still partially entangled in a plaid wool blanket, and ran for the door.

"Momma, there's fire!"

The storm... the snow...

They'd have to risk it!

She wrenched the door open.

Freezing air swirled past her in a rushing gust.

The flames leaped high and fierce, no longer playful kittens but vengeful tigers. A blast of roiling heat seemed to explode behind Stella, shoving her forward like the swat of a huge fiery hand.

She lost her balance and they went headlong. Danny somersaulted into a drift and began to wail. Stella, sputtering, pawed snow from her face. The cold shock cleared her head. The frigid air rasped in her lungs more painfully than the smoke.

The cabin was engulfed, its gaping doorway the entrance to an inferno. Stella grabbed Danny again and backed away from it, trying to catch her breath.

They'd both still been dressed when they laid down, there was that. She had a pair of Dan's flannels on under her skirt. But, even if the wind seemed to have lessened from its earlier full-force icy howl, they'd be done for if they had to stay out here in this.

Where else to go? She couldn't expect any rescue. Her father-in-law would have arrived earlier if he was coming at all... anybody within sight of the fire wouldn't see anything in this, and her nearest neighbors would all be buttoned up safe in their own houses against the storm anyway...

Stella wrapped Danny more snugly in the blanket. They'd need to walk, to try and reach shelter. If she cut through the woods to the field, wouldn't that bring her right to the Grangers' place?

"Momma?"

"Hush now, Danny, just hush now," she said. "Put your arms around my neck and hold on tight, there's a good boy."

He did so, sniffling and shivering.

She started walking. Her feet sank into the snow. It soon soaked through leather shoes and woolen socks. She found herself fighting harder for each step. The thought of breaking her toes on an unseen rock or plunging into some unseen hole terrified her.

From too cold to too hot, and now too cold again.

Shivers steadily wracked their way up her spine. Her breath shuddered, blowing ghostly white plumes.

Ice clung to her skirt, crackling as she moved. It clung to the blanket around Danny, and to the long disheveled mess of Stella's hair.

Her eyes, which had been watering from the smoke, now watered from the wind, her eyelashes sticky with frost, nearly glued shut.

The woods offered some relief from the wind, and under the evergreens the snow was more thin. Stella paused to lean against a tree.

When had Danny gotten so heavy?

Her arms felt like lead, her shoulders like knots of rusty chain.

The Grangers' place couldn't be much further now, could it?

Oh, but she was so tired...

A bough snapped with a sound like a gunshot. Stella twitched her head up, aware that she'd been halfway asleep where she stood.

Danny had fallen asleep, his face buried against her collar, his clasped hands loose around her neck.

The wind had eased further. The snow, hard though it was to tell with the tree cover, seemed to be falling more gently. Although it had been gloomy already from the clouds, some change in the quality of the shadows made her think that it might be almost dusk. Which meant nightfall wouldn't be far behind.

Another bough snapped, closer. From the storm, Stella supposed.

She rubbed at her eyes. The tender skin around them was chafed, abraded by sand-fine granules of ice. Her fingertips came away touched with bloodstains from the raw, weeping flesh.

Hefting Danny's sleeping weight higher on her hip, Stella began walking again.

A low, strange warbling hiss made her heart skip a beat.

More boughs and branches snapped, shedding snow. White shapes moved among the trees.

The warbling hiss was repeated, and answered from several sides.

Despite her sore, bloodied eyes, Stella saw them clearly.

As frightened as she'd been of what wildlife might roam the Montana territory... as frightened of bears, wolves, and savage Indians... nothing in her fears or imaginings equaled this.

If her cabin had been consumed by vengeful tigers of fire, then here were their icy counterparts.

Her bladder let go. The sudden hot gush, and the acrid yellow smell, broke Stella out of her stunned shock.

She ran.

Fast, very fast.

It surprised the white beasts; she sensed them recoil before giving chase. A mere moment's delay, but she'd take it, she'd take whatever delay – whatever inch, whatever second! — she could get.

Danny, jarred awake, saw what pursued them and screamed.

Stella burst from the treeline. To her amazement, she saw the open field spread before her. Clouds streamed in layers across the sky and snow fell in tattered sheets, but, she saw the field... could even see a wink of light that had to be the Grangers' house on the far side.

But, in the field, the snow was knee-deep or deeper.

She threw a panicked glance over her shoulder as she plowed ahead, hoping it was hindering them at least as much as—

It wasn't.

They loped on top of the snow, paws barely disturbing the crust. Their strides were long and graceful, easy, even lazy, as if they now knew they had her. Knew she was trapped, and could not get away.

In her arms, Danny screamed and screamed.

Why did he have to be so heavy?

If he wasn't so heavy... if she didn't have to carry him...

The Granger house, that wink of light in a window, looked tantalizingly close and mockingly far away.

If Danny could run on his own...

They'd still overtake him, he was too little, the snow would be up to his waist, they'd be on him in a flash...

They'd be on him in a flash.

Oh, but—

She yanked his arms from her neck.

"Momma!?!"

"Danny, I'm so sorry!"

She dropped him, blanket and all, into the snow.

"Mommmmmmmaaaaaaaaah!" he shrieked.

His eyes, oh, the look in his eyes, utter disbelief and betrayal—

"Momma! Momma! Don't leave me!"

The white beasts converged.

Stella ran.

HARD LESSONS

"**P**eter's going to die, isn't he?"

Mary Thorpe spoke quietly, as if in hopes none of the others would as to overhear, but with the wind finally having dropped and all of them clustered so close around the stove, Amos Trotter reckoned at least some of them did.

Not that any of them reacted, even the other Thorpe kids.

The littler girls — Cora Thorpe, Minnie Granger and Kirstie Renneke — huddled together like three baby chicks. They had a listless, staring-eyed look to them that left Amos powerful worried, but with no idea what to do.

Take good care of them, Miss Emma had said.

He'd tried, Lord knew.

He'd kept the fire going, despite those awful sparks that had snapped so hard, scaring the boys as much as the girls.

Scaring Amos, too, though he'd tried hard not to let it show.

How they'd smarted, too! Like how he imagined a right jolt from an electric wire would feel. One had flashed so bright blue-white and cracked so loud that everybody but Peter screamed. That one left a scorch mark on Amos's hand, and a taste in his mouth as if he'd bit on a shiny new penny.

Through it all, he wouldn't let it make him go chicken. They were not going to freeze, not on his watch. He'd do all he could, if it meant busting up every single stick of furniture in the schoolhouse.

Trouble was, that was about all he could do.

No amount of busting up desks and chairs would fetch them anything more to eat. It wouldn't get any medicine for Peter Thorpe. It wouldn't help if the roof lifted off, the way it seemed it might when the wind was highest – heck, for a time there, Amos feared the entire building would be blown to matchsticks.

And then there was the matter of whatever it was they'd heard howling a while ago...

"Just the wind," Amos had said.

Had lied.

Lied.

In a good cause, for which he hoped his mother and Jesus would forgive him, but it still hadn't done any good. Not a one of the kids, having heard that wavering shrill cry, believed it was 'just the wind,' no sir.

He looked into Mary's serious eyes and chewed the inside of his cheek, not wanting to have to lie again. True, he was no doctor, but just the same...

Peter's brothers, James and Elias, were watching, Amos caught at the edge of his vision. Watching and listening intently, waiting for him to answer their sister's question.

The gunshots saved him having to.

Gunshots, shouts, a terrible inhuman shrieking, and a much-more-terrible all-too-human screaming.

Then a hush fell, leaving the bunch of them staring at each other.

"What's that?" Ben Adams sprang up.

"Someone's out there!"

"Is it our father?"

"They came to get us!"

"Hold your horses," Amos said. "Don't go rushing out. Let me have a look-see first."

The three little girls obeyed. James stayed by Peter. But Mary, Elias and Ben crowded up behind Amos as he opened the door a couple inches.

Cold though it had been in the schoolhouse, it was indeed still much warmer than the air that dashed against his face like a well-thrown snowball.

Thick clouds still covered the sky, and the waning daylight made it all the darker. The snow slanted down, nuggets of hail and slushy ice-wads mixing with it as the wind began to regain its strength.

The fresh white layers of snowfall on the ground allowed Amos a view stretching down the slight hill to the meadow, where lanterns hung on wagon hook-poles and illuminated a strange scene.

He recognized the horse at once; Doc Marlowe's Percheron, Bump. Amos liked the Perch because it reminded him of himself... not the cleverest of God's creatures, but solid, hardworking and reliable.

"It's Miss Emma!" said Mary, clutching excitedly at Amos' arm with one hand while pointing with the other.

At that, the rest of the children raised up a ruckus, hollering and waving. Amos felt his knees want to sag in relief. Help was on the way.

Help was on the way, and, soon after, help was there.

Minnie Granger burst into thankful tears at the sight of her brother, who swept her into his arms and hugged her until it seemed her brains might go out her ears. Mary, Elias and James all talked at once to the Thorpes' hired man, who drew them aside to give them some almighty bad news. It soon got broke to the rest of them, as Elias started in yelling and Mary burst into tears.

Mr. and Mrs. Thorpe, both of them dead? Sam Thorpe so hurt he couldn't come along on this rescue party but had to stay behind with one of the Grangers to look after his baby sister?

It seemed too unreal.

Then again, didn't everything that had happened that day?

Such as Amos himself having gone and kissed Miss Emma. On the cheek, only a simple buss on the cheek no more than what he might have given an auntie or cousin, but ...

She'd done an all-fired brave thing, she had, going for help like that.

And when he'd done it, she'd went blush-pink, he remembered.

Miss Emma went blush-pink again now as she came over to him, having finished checking on and comforting the other students. The effect was spoiled some, given how roughshod the weather had done on her... where her face wasn't blotched, it was greyish and chapped... and Miss Emma wasn't much in the way of pretty to start with, but...

Lordy, what was he thinking?

Well, so she wasn't, so what of it? Not like he was any prize-winner, big dumb oaf that he was.

She'd done right by them, then done it one better. When she could have sent the men while she stayed someplace warm after winning her way through the blizzard, she hadn't.

"Thank you, Amos," she said.

As for him, he went more than blush-pink; he went beet-red. He scuffed a foot and mumbled.

The men had brought coats and blankets. Miss Emma carried a big pot of boiled beef, which she doled out into the tin cups they'd used much earlier to drink the thin broth they'd made from the contents of their lunch-pails. Luke-warm though it was, Amos had scarce tasted anything better, and gulped down five cups full until his belly felt pleasantly warm, sloshy and full.

Everyone else seemed to have forgotten the earlier gunshots and screams, but Amos noticed how Mr. Corvill held a shotgun at the ready, and how Doc Marlowe wore sleeves and a waistcoat of blood. When the men ushered the bundled-up children to the wagon-sledge and loaded them in, there lay old Zeke Rogers with what looked like his leg half torn off.

If not for that, and for Peter being so sick, it might have turned the whole mood much more festive, the thrill of having a wagon-sledge need to come and fetch them home from school.

Until, that was, the men told them about the white beast, like an ice-wolf or a monster out of some nursery tale. How they'd shot it, needing as many bullets to take it down as might have been needed to drop a grizzly. How, in the process, it'd attacked old Zeke and nearly killed him.

And how they had cause to believe it wasn't the only one of its kind.

The wind-blown sleet made it hard to see much as they rode past the spot, but something was there, right enough. Something furry and bloody that the snow hadn't yet fully covered.

NIGHTFALL

Tended, fed, cuddled and rested, the white cub wanted to play. It frisked about her feet, pushed its head against her shin, then crouched its front end down and waggled its fuzzy rump in the air, long tail swishing.

When she rolled one of Aunt Ruby's yarn balls across the rug, the cub bounded straight up, pounced, skittered, batted, snatched the ball up in its jaws, dropped it again, swatted it, gave chase, tripped over its own big paws, rolled, and sat up with a blink and a yawn as if it had meant to do that. By then, the yarn was strung everywhere in loops and tangles, and Claire laughed.

A wavering, silvery cry arose outside.

The cub stopped short mid-frolic, tufted ears twitching. It wheeled around in a circle, gaze seeking. It uttered a high, yipping call.

The cry sounded again. The cub yipped louder. It turned to look at Claire, head tilted, then yipped a third time.

Bleating and rustling came from the shed, the goats more agitated than ever.

The next cry was longer, a drawn-out ululation of rising and falling tones. The cub plopped down on its haunches, lifted its muzzle toward the roof, and let out a quick, barking series of yips in reply.

Claire slowly got to her feet and went to the window by the front door. She moved aside the curtain to peek through the shutter-slats.

She'd heard the wind lessen a while ago. Now, through the frosted windowpane, she saw that the snow had ceased falling. The blizzard appeared to be over. Night had fallen, the sky diamond-specked black above a world of crystal and white.

And something —

Her breath fogged the glass, obscuring her view. She wiped it clear with her sleeve and peered out again.

She saw the washing she'd hung to dry what seemed a lifetime ago, frozen stiff at strange windblown angles, jutting out from a clothesline bearded in icicles. Of the wash-basket, there was no sign.

The rest of the yard was heaped with drifts but otherwise the same as —

No, not the same as ever.

What she had initially taken for a snow-covered clump of bushes moved, suddenly resolving into a very un-bush-like form. It blended so well with its wintery surroundings she could discern no details, but its outline was that of a large, sleek-bodied creature.

White, richly furred, muscular and powerful.

She knew what it was, of course. Had known in her heart and gut since she heard that first cry. Had been wondering, expecting this, in the back of her mind all along.

Someone had come searching for this little lost baby.

It padded a few more steps across the snow and sang out another of those eerie cries. Its mouthful of teeth glinted.

The cub uttered a yip that trailed into a warbling, plaintive howl.

At that, the adult sprang forward with a strong speed and lithe grace far different than the young one's endearing clumsiness. Before Claire could drop the curtain and step back from the window, it was at the door. It snuffled and chuffed. Its claws scratched on the wood.

Mewing anxiously, the cub scampered to the door and began scrabbling at it.

Tears trickled down Claire's cheeks.

All those years she'd waited for her parents to come back for her...

All those years and they never had.

She opened the door. Icy night air, crisp and intense, swirled around her. If anything, it seemed even colder than the blizzard itself had been.

The adult retreated with a hiss, ears laid flat, tail twitching. The cub, startled, ducked behind a chair and gave an uncertain whimper.

"Your baby's here," Claire said. "Your baby's fine."

It hissed again, baring its teeth. She saw that the sharp, icy rows were uneven... one of the curving fangs was broken off to a stub.

"See?" She nudged the cub into view.

The hiss melded into a rumbling, throaty kind of croon. The cub rushed through the door, making eager, happy noises. They nuzzled. The parent, still eyeing Claire with suspicion, gripped the loose folds of skin and fur at the cub's scruff in its jaws.

It slunk sideways and backward without shifting its eyes from her. The cub squirmed once, then went docile and hung there with its big forepaws tucked to its chest and its tail tucked up under its belly.

Others emerged from the woods, half a dozen or so. A pack. They treaded lightly atop the snow without sinking in, without breaking the crust or leaving tracks.

The largest was fully the height of a draft horse, with a great shaggy silver ruff and fangs like scythe blades. The smallest were a pair of cubs of an age with the one she'd found in the goat shed. They came tumbling and gamboling to meet their wayward sibling.

All of their pale gazes fixed upon Claire as she stood in the doorway. She shivered, but was too transfixed by the sight of them to move. Their beauty and majesty held her spellbound.

Even once they'd gone, vanishing into the snowy night like silent white wraiths, she stayed where she was, staring after them until the cold finally drove her back inside.

PART FOUR:

AFTERMATH

CHILLED BLOOD

Lars Rutger had hated to turn his team loose to fend for themselves, but what else was there to be done? No shelter within reach. No way he could help them. On their own, one or both of them might stand a chance.

So, he'd unhitched the horses from his wagon. They did not immediately bolt in a panic as the Howe brothers' mule had done. Neither did they plant their hooves and stolidly brace against the storm, like John Arlen's oxen. What they did was rear and roll their eyes northward, then gallop off together to the west.

He'd wished them well.

And wished well to the others — Franklin Wood and Cyrus Freedman — who'd taken John Arlen's wife and children, and Lars' own boy Stefan, up onto their stallions to make the desperate race for town.

As for the four of them remaining...

Time was short indeed.

George Howe, his arm broken from when the mule's frenzied bucking destroyed their sled-cart, was in no fit state to do much. He sat dazedly watching them as Virgil rushed over to Lars.

"We're dead men if we don't get under some kind of cover," Virgil said. He hawked back and spat blood from his busted nose.

"My wagon," Lars said.

No easy task, but between them they upended and overturned it, dumping the few sad, sorry sacks of grain they'd been taking to have ground into flour by that greedy bastard in Juniper.

It all went a blur after that. Lars had dim recollections of himself and Virgil hauling George under the wagon, lowering it down over themselves like a wooden turtle shell —

— or the lid of a coffin, which he'd tried not to think.

They'd hollered for John Arlen as the blizzard descended, that wall of snow-twisters, ungodly cold lightning flicking from them like the tongues of vipers. But he'd hunkered down between his oxen and there was no more time for him to reach the other three in the dubious shelter under the wagon. Whatever his shouted reply, it went unheard.

After that, everything went unheard, but for the shriek and howl of the wind, the tack-hammer patter of hail pelting wood, the occasional groaning creak when it seemed the wagon might fly apart like a house of cards.

Time passed.

Lars found some of the sacks and wedged them under his body, aware that the snow and the cold earth would drain the heat from his body faster than the bite of the icy wind itself. He lay on his side, knees drawn to his chest and arms folded around them.

Thoughts of his family occupied his mind.

His tall, proud Anna... beautiful when he'd met and married her... beautiful still, twenty-plus years and three children later... she'd be worried, he knew... worried for him, yes, but worried more for young Stefan... just as Lars worried more for their son than himself.

Anna was strong, Anna had always been strong. If the worst happened, she'd have Hans... she'd have Gretchen, married now with children of her own...

At some point, he must have dozed.

He woke to a dreadful screech splitting through the storm's clamor, followed by deep bellowing and a series of grunts.

Or he dreamed it

More time passed.

Eventually, there'd been silence.

A close, muffled, cotton-stuffed silence.

It was disturbed only once by a flurry of cawing, chirping, rustling and flapping. Then the silence returned.

"Virgil Howe? George?" Lars asked, into the chilly darkness of the space under the wagon.

He sensed a stirring, and heard Virgil's clogged reply. "Lars? We made it?"

"George all right?"

"His arm... I found the jug, there was some applejack left in it, gave it to him for the pain."

"And you?"

"Like I been hoss-kicked in the face," Virgil said. "On the upside, not as if it can hurt my looks. Storm over?"

"Think it must be."

"And can we get out from here?"

About that, Lars had his doubts. The wagon had been heavy to start with, and that with them spurred on by desperation. They'd been fresher then, and well-fed. Now, hours later, stiff-limbed and bone-weary... and how much snow might the blizzard have dumped down atop them?

They had to try just the same, for no knowing how long it might be until someone got out this way. True, Franklin Wood and Cy Freedman knew where they were, but they had Missus Arlen and the kids to see to first, even assuming they'd reached safety before the deadly front overtook them.

He crawled to the corner of the wagon and put his back into lifting. He strained, muscles shaking, groaning through clenched teeth, but with Virgil's help at last raised the edge enough for them to worm their way out into daylight.

The morning air was clear as a crystal bell, the sky palest blue and faintly filmed with the wisps of frosty clouds. An expanse of fresh snowfall glittered and sparkled.

The lone tree alongside the road, which had been crowded with birds packed shoulder to shoulder, stood empty now, bare branches raking at the sky in stark, jagged lines. That flap-rustling flurry of caws and chirps would have been the birds finally taking to wing... those who'd made it. The ground below the tree was littered with small snow-covered heaps, the feathery carcasses of those who hadn't.

"Whuh," said Virgil Howe, or some chuff-sounding noise to that effect. He did a brisk stamping dance, slapping and rubbing his arms. "Cold! Jesus!"

Lars nodded. He looked past the overturned wagon toward the Arlens' oxcart. It lay tipped askew, at an angle with one wheel up and the bed drifted in snow.

Something about the positions of the oxen, and something about the snow around them, didn't look quite right.

"John?" he called. "John Arlen?"

"We'll need to give George a—" Virgil went on, but then his words cut off in an abrupt sort of choke.

"Virgil?" Lars turned toward him.

He'd stopped stamping and slapping his arms. He swayed on his feet. His eyes, ringed with dark raccoon-bruises above his squashed and swollen nose, met Lars' gaze, their expression bewildered.

"Virgil?" Lars said again.

Virgil uttered a wheezing gasp and toppled over.

"Virgil! Virgil Howe!" He ran to the other man, but Virgil Howe was stone dead.

Aside from his nose, he hadn't been hurt... he'd made it through the storm fine... he'd been up and around, lively as could be... then he just dropped dead for no readily apparent reason?

Lars remembered tales he'd heard as a lad, tales from his father, uncles and grandfather, back in Sweden. Tales of men, hunters, who'd spend a long winter night lying in wait to get a shot at a marauding wolf. Holding still, keeping motionless so as not to alert their pre ... and when dawn came, they'd rise, they'd begin moving about again, and the chilled blood from their limbs would flood to their hearts, the shock such as to cause instant death.

Was that what had felled Virgil Howe? Chilled blood?

No mistaking it, the man was dead.

With nothing he could do about it, Lars turned to the oxcart again. There'd been no movements from that direction. He thought of the bad winter eight years ago, when cattle by the thousands lost their lives because of their breath-vapors freezing into masses of ice around their heads, and wondered if that had happened to the oxen.

If so, what about John Arlen, who would've been huddled down between them?

And it just did look wrong somehow...

The snow lacked that clean white sparkle... it was discolored... a blush, a tinge, a faint pinkish stain ...

As he got closer, Lars clearly saw the how and the why of it.

The oxen were dead, but not because they'd suffocated in ice-blocks of their own breath, no sir. They were dead because their throats and guts had been torn wide open. Their hides were shredded, large hunks of meat missing. That blush-pink tinge was the result of a layer of snow fallen onto what must have been a veritable lake of ox blood.

He found John Arlen still huddled down between them after all.

Handsome John Arlen, always so popular with the ladies... handsome John Arlen with frost in his hair and dandy moustache... face drained pale, eyes glazed.

And when handsome John Arlen suddenly shot his hand out to seize Lars by the wrist, Lars screamed as if he'd been pinched by the devil himself.

TWO SISTERS

In her dreaming, it was summer... wonderful, hot, sunny-golden summer. In her dreaming, butterflies danced above the meadowgrass and wildflowers. In her dreaming were picnic baskets filled with all the best things to eat, and jugs of sweet lemonade.

Warm, so warm, as they ran and laughed!

Warm, barefoot and stockingless, skirts hiked above the knees, sleeves pushed to the elbows, bonnets hanging down their backs by the strings.

Laughing and running in the warm, warm sun!

Tossing a ball. Playing hoop-and-stick.

Swinging! A rope swing on the big branch of the old oak, swinging and swinging with legs kicking, with braids flying!

In her dreaming.

Maggie Jordan knew she was dreaming, but did not care.

It was better.

Nicer.

She didn't want to wake up.

Wake up to the snow again. To the cold again.

To being lost.

To Sarah being lost.

She remembered.

How Sarah had just... just vanished... just disappeared... that rushing whiteness went by and snatched her away and she was gone.

Maggie remembered calling for her, calling and calling. She remembered leading Polly onward. Carrying her when Polly simply couldn't go another step.

No idea where she was, or which way was which.

Only... walking.

One foot after another. One slow, heavy, dragging, ice-numbed foot after another.

Walking.

Eyes squeezed to slits, ice on her eyelashes. Nothing to see but snow. Snow and more snow.

Polly's head like a stone on her shoulder.

The wind lashing at them. Swiping at them with sharp, bitter claws. This way. Then that way. Teasing. Cruel.

The dreaming was better. That warm and wonderful summer... the sunshine... the swing...

She woke.

Sarah was still gone.

The hollow...

Maggie remembered that, too. She hadn't felt the ground drop away under her foot. Only falling, and rolling with Polly wrapped in her arms.

Into the hollow.

Out of the wind.

And being tired. So tired. More tired than she'd ever been in her life.

She remembered the snow coming down. Gentler-seeming now. Sifting like flour. Heaping against them as they curled together in a ball.

Her eyes open now, she saw nothing but featureless white.

A thin hiss of air was all that escaped her when she tried to speak.

Everything, or at least every part of her she could feel, hurt with a bone-deep aching stiffness.

The snow had covered them up. Covered them like a blanket, like the layer of sawdust Pa would put over the blocks of ice in the icehouse.

"Polly?" Maggie said, with as much strength as she could muster. It still was barely more than a whisper, sounding muffled and strange from the enclosure of their snowy cocoon.

Her little sister did not answer, just stayed curled up with her head on Maggie's shoulder and one hand clenched tight around a fistful of Maggie's blouse.

When Maggie tried to move, she found that she could, if with a pained and sluggish effort. She brought her own hand up to rub at her face, then flinched when she saw the bluish-grey birdclaw her hand had become. Dark blemishes mottled the third and fourth fingers. Frostbite.

Nonetheless, she used that claw hand to scrape at the snow above her. She dug out two furrows, then a chunk fell on her head and light like cold diamonds poured through the hole.

She somehow burrowed her way to the top, eyes dazzled and half-blinded by the bright glare.

It was... morning?

Had they lain in that hollow, covered with snow, all night long?

Where were they?

She shaded her protesting eyes with her frostbitten hand and peered around. At first, nothing looked familiar. Then the surroundings began to fit into place, the trees, the hills and hummocks.

They were nowhere near home! Home was in almost the complete opposite way! These were the woods north of Thorpe's Meadow, behind the schoolhouse!

But, it did mean that she knew where they were.

She knew which way to go.

Polly still clung to her, supported by Maggie's other arm. Maggie patted her awkwardly on the back.

"Come on, Polly," she murmured. "Ma and Pa must be worried sick."

Her legs did not want to walk, but she made them.

"We'll have oatmeal," she said. "Big piping hot bowls. With butter, and honey, lots of brown sugar, and raisins. How does that sound? Doesn't that sound grand?"

Walking, or lurching, hobbling hunched over like an old granny.

"And a bath," she told Polly. "Ma's copper tub by the stove—"

Somewhere, a dog barked.

Then, closer, it barked again.

Others barked too.

Barking and barking, dogs dashing toward them, bounding through the snow, tails wagging, ears flapping.

And people.

People behind the dogs. Men in thick coats and hats. Men carrying guns. Shotguns, and rifles like the one Pa kept in case of varmints or Indians. One drove a mule harnessed up to a sled. Seeing her, they pointed and hollered, and hurried in her direction.

Maggie floundered to meet them, gasping huge sobs of relief. She recognized one of Ben Adams' uncles, Mr. Greeley with the dogs, Minnie Granger's big brother...

Her numb feet and stiff legs failed her one last time. She collapsed into the snow.

"Here now, girl, we got you," someone said.

She was lifted, turned over, swaddled in a fleecy sheepskin. They took Polly from her arms, about having to pry her sister's grasping fingers loose from Maggie's blouse.

"Ah, dear sweet Jesus," someone else said.

"So young..."

"This will be a sore blow to Bart and May."

A flask tipped to Maggie's mouth. The smell was powerful on its own but the taste! Harsh whiskey! She coughed, swallowed some, and coughed more. A burning tingle spread in her belly and out from the base of her throat.

"What about t'eldest one?" another man asked. "Sally, isn't it?"

"Sarah."

"Sarah, right. Where's she at?"

"Gone," Maggie said. "She was in front... leading the way... and then she was gone."

"See if the dogs have any luck?" Mr. Adams said to Mr. Greeley.

"Polly... needs some..." Maggie pushed weakly at the flask when it was tipped to her mouth again.

"We'll take care of her," Mr. Granger said.

But she saw they'd put Polly in the back of the sled... Polly still with her legs tucked up and her arms bent like they were holding onto a person who was no longer there... she saw them shake what looked like a horse blanket down over her...

"Polly!"

A surge of new strength let her wrench away from the men trying to help her. She ran to the sled and grabbed for the horse blanket.

"Oh, now, don't do that," someone said.

It was too late; she'd pulled it off to expose Polly's face. It was whiter than Ma's best china pitcher, the one saved only for the most special occasions. Whiter, and colder, with that same kind of sheen. Her closed lips and closed eyelids were the color of Ma's periwinkle skirt.

She looked almost peaceful, almost like she was sleeping...

But Polly, poor little Polly...

Maggie buried her face in her half-frozen hands and cried.

SUFFERING

"**M**issus Hadden? Missus Hadden... ma'am? Missus Hadden, can you hear me?"

Stella groaned. She ached from head to toe. Her hands, feet and face most of all stung like fire, stung like she'd scrubbed the skin with nettles.

"Missus Hadden? Stella? Wake up now. Come on. Wake y'self up."

She opened her eyes, then winced them shut again at the lamplit brightness. "Wh... where am I?"

"Our place." The voice belonged to a woman, a husky voice, and half-familiar. "I'm Betty Granger, Nelson's wife."

"What happened?"

"Like for you as to tell us. You turned up here last night, at the tailing of the storm."

"Ask about her boy," another woman said, this one younger-sounding.

"My... boy?" Stella lurched to a sitting position, looking wildly around. "Danny? Danny!"

The room was small but tidy, with knotwood planking, a peaked roof, and a big log bed piled with quilts. A cheery fire burned in a little brick-lined hearth, a shabby old spaniel asleep on a rug in front of it. On the bedside table was a kerosene lamp, hissing faintly, source of that brightness. Beside it were a basin and a cluster of medicine bottles.

The Granger women — Betty, and her sister-in-law Sue, Stella saw — stood by the bed. Beyond them was a doorway through which she could see a larger room with part of a dining table and benches. Other voices, men's voices in conversation, came from out there.

"Danny," she said again.

"Where is he, Missus Hadden?" Betty Granger asked. "Where's your boy? What happened to him?"

"He... he isn't... he isn't here?"

"No, ma'am," Sue Granger said. "Is he with Dean? Mr. Hadden, I mean?"

"Dean? What?" Stella went to rub her eyes, then paused. Her hands were wrapped into bulky mitts of bandages. So too were her feet.

"Frostbite," Betty said, evidently reading her baffled expression. "Ain't bad, but we didn't want as to take a chance. Rubbed them with snow, then put them in warm water a while, then coated them with salve and wrapped them up. Did the same for your face, just not the wrapping."

"Where's Danny?" Stella nearly shrieked. "Where's my boy?"

"Calm down, now. Calm down. That's what we're trying to figure out."

"Was he with you?" Sue asked. "Out there in the storm?"

"What? I... he... what?"

She tried to get out of bed and they urged her back down. Betty gave her a mug of something hot and laced with whiskey.

"You turned up here last night," Betty said again, "at the tailing of the storm, freezing cold and covered with snow, crying, begging for help."

"We brought you in," said Sue, "but couldn't hardly get anything sensible before you swooned dead away. Something about your boy, was all."

"My Nels," added Betty, "took a lantern and tied a rope from the door-post to his waist, and went out far as he could to search, but didn't find any sign of anybody else."

Stella broke into huge, wracking, painful sobs. She covered her sore, tender face with the bandage-swaddled mitts of her hands.

"God have mercy," Betty murmured to Sue. "He was with her, then?"

"Must've been."

"Only they got separated from each other?"

"Lew and Michael said how they could barely see a yard, and couldn't hear each other except by about shouting into their ears."

"Oh, that poor child. He wouldn't stand a chance—"

Stella did shriek then, muffled though it was by her hands over her face. It brought some of the men to the doorway, where there was a hurried exchange in low but anxious tones.

Then Nelson Granger stepped over to the bedside. "Missus Hadden, you're sure you had your boy with you?"

She nodded without lowering her hands, shoulders quaking.

"What about Dean?" asked someone else, possibly Nelson's brother Lewis. "He get there all right?"

"Whu-what?"

"Dean. Dean Hadden, your father-in-law? He didn't get there?"

"Where?"

"Your place, ma'am," said Michael, Nelson and Betty's grown son. "That's where he was going."

"I... I never... we never saw him..." Stella peered around at them, blinking pained and watery eyes. "I fell asleep and... and then there was a... a f-f-f-f-fire and... and we had to run, I had to take Danny and run..."

"A fire?"

"Holy hell and damnation."

"We best have someone ride over there and see—"

The Granger men hustled out, talking rapidly and urgently among themselves. They passed a young girl clutching a rag doll with a chipped china head. Stella found she could not bear the child's solemn, steady gaze and put her bandaged hands back over her face.

She didn't lower them as the women went on to tell her how Dean arrived at their house not long after the blizzard began.

"We expected it must be Paul Trotter, at first," Sue said. "He'd come by that morning to—"

"—help Nels out with some chores," Betty interrupted.

"That's right. To help Nelson out with some chores. Then, when the storm struck, you know, the way it did, of a sudden and out of nowhere, Paul reckoned he best be making for home in case it got worse."

"Which it did," said Sue.

"We thought he'd thought better of it and come back," said Sue. "Wait it out here rather than risk his fool life—"

Betty interrupted again. "Only it wasn't Paul."

"Was Dean. Trying to get to your cabin, only he'd gotten off-course and onto our land. Shivering fit to split, about on his last legs."

"We had him come in and warm himself a spell," Betty said. "Gave him a hot drink, and tried to convince him he ought to stay until the wind let up."

"But he wouldn't do it," Sue said. "Said he had to check in on you and the little one. No matter what."

THE LIVING AND THE DEAD

They converted the Thorpe house into a temporary hospital, there were so many patients needing Doc Marlowe's care in the clear but even fiercer cold spell that followed the deadly blizzard. He more than had his hands full with ailments and injuries ranging from minor to severe.

Frostbite had taken the greediest toll. He found himself forced to amputate many fingers and toes, parts of ears that had gone grey-black, a whole foot here, a nose there. Others endured rigorous treatment, the miserable pain of having their cold flesh rubbed with snow to thaw it slowly. Their skin went fishbelly-pale or sloughed off in weeping suppurations. Gangrene and infection posed lethal risks.

Some had damaged their eyes or abraded the skin around them trying to wipe away the ice of tears. In some cases, the numbed skin tore loose, or even the flesh down to the bare cheekbones.

They would be scarred, sometimes hideously, for the rest of their lives. Crutches and wooden limbs would be a commonplace sight. Some might never be able to do an honest day's work again, crippled or disfigured.

So very many of them were children, that was what most dismayed the heart.

Children who'd gone blithely off to school that morning, or out to play, or to help their parents with the chores... children without boots and warm coats thanks to the treacherous, deceptively mild day... children like Maggie Jordan, who'd carried her little sister so far... children like the ones who surely would have frozen to death under a tree at Willow Pond if Isaac Burdock and Roy Kradenmeyer hadn't made it to the Burdock farm to fetch help...

Worst of all were the children who hadn't survived, their poor bodies found frozen stiff in such contorted positions that it'd be days yet before they could be properly placed into their small coffins... the Wood twins, kneeling together for solace in an attitude of prayer... Lester Burdock, whose selfless act of giving Rufus his coat had saved his brother's life at the cost of his own... Polly Jordan... Nell Kradenmeyer, found curled up in a gully not far from the schoolhouse she'd never reached...

And families, entire families struck with terrible losses.

Russ Covill, whose wife had sent him out to help his neighbors, returned to find that the roof of his own house had blown off. His wife and mother-in-law had not been able to withstand the bitter cold.

Of the other Kradenmeyers, fourteen-year-old Louise lasted another week before succumbing to pneumonia but the rest in the house died with their father, gathered around Leo's chair when they'd run out of wood for the fire ... and the older children, who'd accompanied Berta out to the fields, three died there in the furrows with her; only Dora-Lee, whose stepbrother Andrew did his best to protect her with his own body, survived.

Emma Curtis, the schoolmarm, lost two toes and the rim of one ear, also suffering cracked ribs. But, for all that, she was hailed as a local hero for what she'd done to fetch help for the students in her care. Later on, when word reached Far Enough of the 'Heroines of the Storm' being heralded and praised in the papers, with funds being raised to reward the young women who'd bravely performed their duties above and beyond the call, Doc made sure to send an eloquent letter on Miss Curtis' behalf.

George Howe's broken arm was the least of his worries. He blamed himself with deep recriminations for his brother Virgil's death. Not that there was a single thing George or anyone else could have done about it; the much colder blood rushing from Virgil's extremities to his heart had been a shock that might have felled even the healthiest man. Nonetheless,

George blamed and berated himself for having sought relief from his pain in that bottle of applejack whiskey, so that he'd been passed-out drunk at the time.

Of the men who'd accompanied the Howes on that ill-fated journey for Juniper that day, only the big Swede Lars Rutger had escaped fairly unscathed. He'd lost his team, the corpses of the draft horses eventually located days later and miles away. The same proved true of the Howe's mule.

The same did not prove true of John Arlen's oxen. Arlen himself, found hunkered down in the mess of their remains, seemed to have been driven mad. Even should he recover from that, he would no longer enjoy his status as one of the region's handsomest men.

Franklin Wood and Cyrus Freedman, who'd ridden for safety on their fast stallions with Mrs. Arlen, her two little ones, and Lars Rutger's younger boy, fared somewhat better. Wood suffered frostbite and Freedman a bite of a more savage sort. The children were scared but unharmed, and even the horses, Gunpowder and Lucifer, turned up.

Mrs. Arlen, however, was another matter. Refusing to be dissuaded from seeking her husband, she'd run off into the storm. Her body was not found for nearly a week, when someone spotted a bit of green cloth protruding from a drift.

Dean Hadden, who'd set out with a sack of supplies to check on his daughter-in-law and grandson, would have lived if he'd stayed at the Granger place and not been so hellbent to continue on his way. He might have lived if he'd gotten to the cabin he and his son had built, perhaps in time to prevent it going up in smoke, or dissuade the panicked Stella from fleeing the blaze with her little boy. If nothing else, he could have kept warm by the fire until the storm had passed.

But Dean Hadden hadn't done any of those things. Tough and wise though he was, even he'd gotten disoriented in the blinding, blowing snow. He must have walked for hours, never once losing hold of the sack of supplies. In his weariness, he'd made the same mistake as many others, giving into the direction of the driving wind instead of fighting against it. Searchers discovered his body miles from town, sitting propped against the trunk of a tree as if he'd stopped for a rest and never been able to get up again.

Old Zeke Rogers had lost about as much blood as a man could afford to lose and still cling to life. He vowed that he'd walk again, though Marlowe suspected that remained yet to be seen.

Samuel, the eldest of the Thorpe children and man of the house what with his parents both dead — William Thorpe's body hadn't been found, but neither had he turned up anywhere alive — initially seemed to recover with the speed of any hard-headed young man. The lingering dizzy spells and confusion, however, Marlowe found more than a tad worrisome.

Then there was the younger Thorpe boy, Peter, whose cough and fever worsened until it seemed the poor frail child would drown in his own fluid-filled lungs, and the best Marlowe could hope for was to keep him comfortable until the end. He lasted most of a week before his labored breathing gurgled to a stop.

Paul Trotter, rescued from the storm and dragged home on a cowhide, came down sick and died from his ordeal a few days later, but lived long enough to make his peace with God, and died at home with his wife and son by his side. Hannah swore that an angel had guided her, an angel that was their own daughter Charlotte, and that Charlotte appeared again to welcome her father and lead him to Heaven.

Search parties scoured the land for miles around. Even after all hope of finding more survivors seemed lost, against-all-odds miracles occurred.

Four days after the blizzard, Hans Rutger heard her feeble cries for help coming from inside a haystack. He dug into it and there found Johanna Renneke, who'd sustained herself on the raw eggs in her basket. Her feet had frozen solid, their tissues burst from swelling, and in one of the more gruesome operations of his career, Doc had to amputate both the woman's rotting legs at the knee.

Claire Erlich led a group along the usual routes her aunt and uncle preferred for their strolls. If any of the searchers noticed that she seemed of an even quieter and more thoughtful manner than usual, they chalked it up to worry and said nothing of it. They beat the bushes, poked into deep drifts, and finally gave up. The storm, they said, must have taken the reverend and his wife.

With the road to Juniper still risky, and this disaster having hit there just as hard, there was no good way to fetch enough proper coffins from the carpenter there to make provision for the sorrowful and considerable toll of the dead. The folk of Far Enough knocked the burial-boxes together for their loved ones as best they could from old planks and whatever scrap wood they had handy.

And, of course, there'd be no digging of all the graves that were needed, not until spring. The earth was hard as stone and ice. There was nothing to do but cart them to the dugout on the side of the graveyard hill, where they'd have to be stacked up like split firewood logs —

It was a great and welcome surprise when the dugout's door was shoveled clear and opened, and inside were Reverend Erlich and his wife. Frail, the both of them, half-starved and frail as twin bundles of twigs, but alive.

NEVER TO KNOW

Some of those lost were not found at all. Such as Sarah Jordan, vanished from her sisters without a trace... or tiny Danny Hadden, somehow separated from his mother, who'd gone half mad from grief...

No one knew what had become of the Thorpes' hired girl... had she escaped her murderous employer, fallen victim to him, or died in the storm?

For that matter, what of William Thorpe? They had the schoolmarm's claim he'd been mauled by one of those white beasts, and when his coat was pulled from a snowdrift it was ripped and blood-soaked. But of the man himself, there was no other sign.

Oh, and the beasts, the white beasts, what a source of contention those soon became! Several people swore to have seen them, while several more insisted it must have been storm-fuddled imaginings.

If so, came the counter-argument, how could it be that the descriptions all matched so perfectly? Their shape and coloring, the way it seemed they moved atop the snow without leaving tracks?

What about John Arlen's ox team, gutted and torn to pieces? John, who'd witnessed it, had gone stark raving out of his mind. Or did they think he'd done it himself, driven insane by the cold? One man, unarmed, reducing two sturdy oxen to so much scraps of bone, meat and hide? How, then, to account for what Lars Rutger had heard? The terrible howling, reported also by others?

What of the claw-wound Zeke Rogers had taken? Or Cyrus Freedman, impaled through the shoulder by the bite of the one he'd shot? What of the incidents even before the blizzard, with the Adams' slaughtered sheep?

And what of the proof? The actual, physical proof? What about the ones that had been killed?

Then, said those who did not want to believe in mysterious, inexplicable creatures that no one had ever seen or heard of before, where were the carcasses? Because, when anybody went back to the spots where it had supposedly happened, the most there was to be found was reddish stains in the snow.

The tragedy was bad enough already, people said.

The deadly blizzard had swept across the entire Great Plains. Nebraska and the Dakota Territory had been hardest hit. Hundreds perished, and again, far too many of them children. Trains had been halted on their rails, passengers freezing to death in their seats, mothers with babes-in-arms among them.

The news dominated the papers from New York to California. Easterners wrote smug editorials on the dangers of the prairies, while others fought back by claiming that even with its risks, the freedom and fresh air of the wide-open spaces was better than suffering the stink and miasma of over-crowded cities.

The fate of the West might hang in the balance, if it gained a reputation too deadly. It would do Far Enough no favors if rumors of monsters got out on top of all that.

But there was the tooth, the fang that Brody O'Connor had cracked out of the jaw of one of the beasts —

If the testimony of a drunk Irishman was to have any credit...

Ultimately, it was decided that they would keep those wilder, less believable aspects of their tale to themselves.

This suited Hezekiah Runninghorse quite fine and dandy.

He'd ridden to town on LeCharles' mule during the clear but cold snap that followed the storm. There, he'd seen the activity all around – repairs being made, animals being tended, chores being done, the necessary business of keeping life going even while grieving the dead.

He was none too eager to let on what had happened up in the mountain forest, how his daughter had gazed into the eyes of the *wanageeska* and fallen under its spell, and her man went hunting the beast for the cure but killed it instead... how there had turned out to be more than one, and how their anger had been unleashed in icy, vengeful fury.

LeCharles had killed a *wanageeska*. Two-Bird had shot another, injuring it. All three of them had met the pale gaze of the winter-spirit. They had all felt its frigid breath and heard its shivering cry.

Yet the three of them had survived.

While the people of Far Enough had not been so fortunate.

The people of Far Enough had paid a heavier price.

They would not be pleased to know who'd brought that price down upon them.

As for LeCharles, the frostbite had blistered and blackened his hand, and the blisters wept thick fluid and the dead, decaying skin peeled off like a wet glove... it was an agony to him after he finished off every drop of whiskey they had... but the gangrene did not set in, and between Runninghorse's remedies and his own hardy constitution, he would fully recover.

Two-Bird was better, and that was what mattered most. Runninghorse and LeCharles were in full agreement on that. Two-Bird was better, the cure had worked like the magic it was.

Two-Bird was more than better; she'd make a grandfather of him by the autumn. No other baby's blanket would be so soft or ward off the chill so well as the luxurious white pelt LeCharles had skinned and tanned from his kill.

Far Enough would have a fine spring, a fair summer, and a promising harvest. Some families might leave, but others would come to try their luck.

Bit by bit, the settlement would struggle its way back from the devastating losses of that stark, brutal winter. Even for a place that was no stranger to blizzards, that one would be marked forever in their memories.

The old-timers would tell their children and grand-children about it for decades hence, the kind of storm that comes along but once in a century.

And the *wanageeska*?

Could be they were never to know.

ABOUT THE AUTHOR

Twice married, twice divorced, twice cancer-battler, Christine Morgan relocated to Portland, Oregon a couple of years ago and has been active in the local bizarro and weird fiction scene. She's particularly known for her oddball crafts and bringing goodies to events. An avid reader, she's a regular contributor to *The Horror Fiction Review*. She also occasionally dabbles in editing, being four books into the Fossil Lake anthology series. Her other interests include superheroes, cheesy disaster movies, cooking shows, modifying Barbie dolls, and working toward becoming a crazy cat lady.

There's a monster coming to the small town of Pikeburn. In half an hour, it will begin feeding on the citizens, but no one will call the authorities for help. They are the ones who sent it to Pikeburn. They are the ones who are broadcasting the massacre live to the world. Every year, Red Diamond unleashes a new creation in a different town as a display of savage terror that is part warning and part celebration. Only no one is celebrating in Pikeburn now. No one feels honored or patriotic. They feel like prey.

Local Sheriff Yan Corban refuses to succumb to the fear, paranoia, and violence that suddenly grips his town. Stepping forward to battle this year's lab-grown monster, Sheriff Corban must organize a defense against the impossible. His allies include an old art teacher, a shell-shocked mechanic, a hateful millionaire, a fearless sharpshooter, a local meth kingpin, and a monster groupie. Old grudges, distrust, and terror will be the monster's allies in a game of wits and savagery, ambushes and treachery. As the conflict escalates and the bodies pile up, it becomes clear this creature is unlike anything Red Diamond has unleashed before.

No mercy will be asked for or given in this battle of man vs monster. It's time to run, hide, or fight. It's time for Red Diamond.

Available in paperback or Kindle on Amazon.com

http://bit.ly/OddMANPB

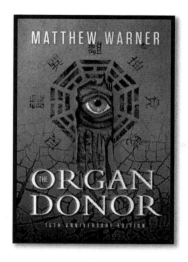

They knew it was wrong to purchase a kidney off the Chinese black market. But what the Taylor brothers didn't realize was that its unwilling donor was an executed prisoner—and an immortal being from Chinese mythology. Pursuing them to Washington, DC, this ancient king will stop at nothing to recover what was once his.

This special 15th anniversary edition of Matthew Warner's acclaimed first horror novel includes nearly 7,000 words of new material, including the author's riveting account of his true-life encounter with China's illegal organ trade.

"A classic of modern horror literature."
— E.C. "Feo Amante" McMullen, Jr.

THE ORGAN DONOR

Available in paperback or Kindle on Amazon.com

http://amzn.to/organ

Psychiatrist Dr. Desmond Carter had always believed that his former patient, author Simon Ryan, was dead.

But, when a bloodstained manuscript penned by Ryan arrives at his office, Desmond begins to doubt everything he thought he had known—not just about the troubled author's past, but his own sanity. Desmond seeks the truth. Instead, he discovers the wellspring of madness.

In Pandemonium, the sequel to his acclaimed 2011 novella The Noctuary, Greg Chapman drags you deeper into the nightmarish reality of the Dark Muses—creatures forged from the very darkness in our own souls.

The words contained within will drive you mad... *and damn you to Hell.*

THE NOCTUARY: PANDEMONIUM

Available in paperback or Kindle on Amazon.com

http://bit.ly/Pandemonium

HOW MUCH DO YOU HATE?

Eddie Brinkburn's doing time for a botched garage job that left Sheraton's brother very badly burned.

HOW MUCH DO YOU HATE?

When Sheraton's gang burn his wife and kids to death, Eddie soon learns the meaning of hate.

HOW MUCH DO YOU HATE?

And that's how the prison psycho transfers his awesome power to Eddie. A power that Eddie reckons he can control. A power that will enable Eddie to put the frighteners on Sheraton...

Available in paperback or Kindle on Amazon.com
ISBN-13: 978-0998067926

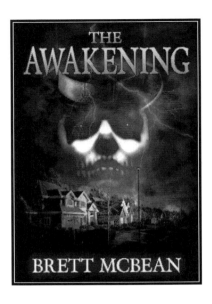

Welcome to the small Midwestern town of Belford, Ohio. It's summer vacation and fourteen-year-old Toby Fairchild is looking forward to spending a lazy, carefree summer playing basketball, staying up late watching monster movies, and camping out in his backyard with his best friend, Frankie. But then tragedy strikes. And out of this tragedy an unlikely friendship develops between Toby and the local bogeyman, a strange old man across the street named Mr. Joseph. Over the course of a tumultuous summer, Toby will be faced with pain and death, the excitement of his first love, and the underlying racism of the townsfolk, all while learning about the value of freedom at the hands of a kind but cursed old man.
Every town has a dark side. And in Belford, the local bogeyman has a story to tell.

Available in paperback or Kindle on Amazon.com

ISBN-13: 978-0692730980

ON THE HORIZON FROM
BLOODSHOT BOOKS

2018*

Stirring the Sheets – Chad Lutzke
Practitioners – Matt Hayward & Patrick Lacey
The Winter Tree – Mark Morris
Bleed Away the Sky – Brian Fatah Steele
Victoria (What Hides Within #2) – Jason Parent
The October Boys – Adam Millard
Tamer Animals – Justin M. Woodward
Dead Branches – Benjamin Langley
The Cryptids – Elana Gomel
What Sleeps Beneath – John Quick
Killer Chronicles – Somer Canon
The Devil Virus – Chris DiLeo
Friends in High Places – Rob Smales
Blood Mother: A Novel of Terror – Pete Kahle

2019-20*

Not Your Average Monster, Volume 3
The Abomination (The Riders Saga #2) – Pete Kahle
The Horsemen (The Riders Saga #3) – Pete Kahle
Not Your Average Monster, Volume 4

* other titles to be added when confirmed

BLOODSHOT
BOOKS

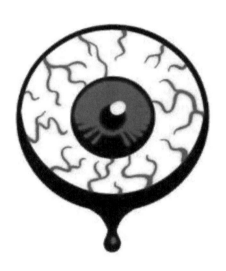

READ UNTIL YOU BLEED

Printed in Great Britain
by Amazon